KEEP IT QUIET

Richard Hull

Dover Publications, Inc., New York

This Dover edition, first published in 1983, is an unabridged and
unaltered republication of the work originally published by Faber &
Faber, Ltd., London, 1935.

Manufactured in the United States of America
Dover Publications, Inc., 180 Varick Street, New York, N.Y.
10014

Library of Congress Cataloging in Publication Data

Hull, Richard, 1896–1973.
  Keep it quiet.

  Reprint. Originally published: London : Faber &
Faber, [1935]
  I. Title.
PR6015.U43K4 1983   823'.912   83-5258
ISBN 0-486-24520-9

CONTENTS

CHAPTER 1

ESSENCE OF VANILLA

*

IN a way it was all Benson's fault; or perhaps it was Mrs Benson's. It might even have been possible for those who must strive to trace things back to their primary origins to have blamed Benson's doctor for prescribing perchloride of mercury for a carbuncle – but that would be going too far.

Mrs Benson had taken the prescription straight round to the nearest chemist, and brought back one of those green bottles of distinctive shape, marked 'Poison' in enormous letters. But that had been her first mistake. She ought to have bought two bottles, one to use at home, and one for her husband to take down to the Club. He could easily have found an interval during which he was not cooking the members' meals, when he could have rubbed on some of it.

But then, when the first application *did* seem to bring some relief, Benson had insisted. Half of it must be put in another bottle for him to take to his work with him, and Mrs Benson had not got another bottle marked 'Poison'. She was not going to risk parting with the beautifully labelled bottle, not with the children about, and so she made her second mistake. She made a feeble little joke; she put it in a bottled labelled 'Essence of Vanilla.'

'Because, Herbert,' she had said, 'though I don't agree with you myself, I know what your opinion of vanilla is. Next door to poison, you call it.'

Herbert Benson had smiled. He was proud of his knowledge of cooking, proud of his job of being chef to the Club. He believed that it was pretty generally recognized that the Whitehall had the best cooking of any club in London. Of course it had no such reputation, but the delusion made life more pleasant, not only for Benson, but, by a process of self-deception, for many of the members.

The smile had broadened into a chuckle.

'Quite right, old girl. To my mind, vanilla really *is* poison. You can spoil the taste of anything with it, even my iced *soufflés*.' A slight frown had crossed his jolly red face. 'And there is to be a *soufflé* to-night – *soufflé glacé praliné* – you know, flavoured with bits of browned almond. Grand it is, really a work of art. All the same, if that old brute Morrison is dining at the Club to-night, it's ten to one he'll send down a message to say he wants vanilla instead.'

'Never mind, dear,' Mrs Benson comforted him, 'he's only one, and I'm sure the others must appreciate all the trouble you take.'

Benson had kissed her and trotted off to the Club to spend a happy but extremely busy day.

It was not till nearly lunch time that the expected annoyance occurred. It was Morrison's habit to arrive at the Whitehall at a quarter past one. How he spent his morning no one quite knew. He had of course retired from business years ago ; so long that even what that business was had been forgotten. He was just a retired nuisance who sat in the Whitehall and grumbled all day about the food, about the members, about the furniture, about the temperature of the rooms and, when all other grievances were absent, about the committee. If by any chance he could find nothing more to say on any of those subjects, he turned his attention to Ford, the secretary. He was very expert at knowing just what criticisms hurt Ford most. It has never been decided whether he excelled most in the devastatingly irritating matter of his complaints, or in the superbly vexatious moments at which he chose to utter them.

From lunch time till late in the evening he was almost sure to be found in the Club, sarcastically abusing every detail, and egging on the other members to complain. Nothing would have induced him to spend his time anywhere else or to belong to any other club. In the Whitehall he knew that he could upset the nerves of every waiter or page-boy in five minutes. There he could manage to be important, not only in his own eyes, simply from being a nuisance. The strange thing was that the other members did not wholly dislike him. They recognized that he did at any rate keep the Club up to the mark for their benefit.

Arriving therefore on this particular day, he screwed his eyeglass in his eye and studied the menu; then with the air of a bored martyr, he beckoned to a passing page.

'Boy! Present Mr Morrison's compliments to the chef and tell him that as – Boy! You're not listening!'

'I'm sorry, sir, but I'm –' The unfortunate youth shifted from one foot to the other.

'Never mind what you're doing. Present –'

A rasping voice cut in.

'I beg your pardon, sir, but that boy was about to take me up in the lift.'

Morrison turned and found himself confronted by his *bête noire*. He was not alone in disliking Pargiter – nearly every member of the Whitehall did – but he had a special reason for his hatred. Pargiter was the only member who in any way equalled him in the art of being a nuisance, and between the two had grown up a deadly rivalry as to which of them should have his idiosyncrasies more carefully fostered. Not, of course, that either of them put it, even to himself, so clumsily as that. Each expressed it by saying of the other that he apparently thought he owned the club.

But between them there was a subtle difference; for while Morrison exerted his influence by baiting the staff, and especially the secretary, Pargiter's strategy was indirect. He irritated the other members, and while always keeping in the right and never allowing anyone to complain of his activities, managed every day to make someone uncomfortable.

With a mutual sigh of joy, therefore, they both saw the unfortunate Ford coming towards them, as innocent a fly as ever walked into a spider's web.

'Isn't it possible –' both of them began in accidental unison.

Mr Pargiter bowed ironically to Mr Morrison. Mr Morrison adjusted his eyeglass and, with a slight shrug of his shoulders, stared through Mr Pargiter. Both waited for the other to begin, and then both once more ejaculated 'Isn't it –' at the same time.

Mr Pargiter gave way. His complaint, he thought, would be more effective if placed second.

'Isn't it possible to send a message by a page-boy without finding he is wanted to work the lift? Can we not afford to keep an approximately adequate staff of at any rate partially trained boys?'

'Whom did you want to send a message to, sir?' Ford asked. He always believed in calling angry members 'sir'.

'Oh, my message, of course, was of no importance. Merely to the chef.'

'Perhaps I could help you by seeing the chef myself, while the boy takes Mr Pargiter up in the lift.'

It was Ford's invariable rule to try to do everything everybody wanted him to do. He hoped it would smooth things over and make life easier. Actually it merely resulted in his having frequently promised two different people contradictory requests, but Ford was an incurable optimist. He even thought that Pargiter would be satisfied if he was merely carried without fuss to whatever floor he wanted to go to.

'Very well, then, I shall leave *you*, sir, to be attended to by the secretary himself. I should like to mention that I was about to ask whether it was not possible to arrange for the lift boy to be allowed to try to carry out his duties without the interference of the members.' Mr Pargiter was at his most suave.

The boy in question rather spoilt the effect by causing the end of the sentence to be delivered to the space in between the ground and first floors.

Once more Ford turned to the impossible task of satisfying Morrison. On the whole he was glad that he had intercepted the message before it reached Benson. The chef was getting just a little touchy, and *soufflé glacé praliné* was a particularly tender spot. If he had received the request, just as it was uttered, that, since the iced *soufflé* had been flavoured with something uneatable consistently for the last six months, on this occasion a small portion might be set aside for Mr Morrison flavoured with vanilla, there was no knowing how he would have taken it – especially as it was vanilla, and especially in the middle of lunch time.

If Ford had tried less hard to do everything that everybody wanted him to do, he would probably have been more efficient, and if he had not attempted to be so tactful, he might have succeeded in satisfying somebody occasionally. As it was, even Benson saw through his attempts to convey Morrison's message diplomatically, and with a savage bang moved the vanilla essence bottle to another part of the shelf. Morrison's special portion of iced *soufflé* should reek of vanilla that evening, even though it did mean a special piece of work for himself.

CHAPTER 2

THE WRONG BOTTLE?

*

To anyone not knowing the object of his existence, Mr Pargiter's conduct that evening, after dinner, must have seemed inexplicable. He had already fallen over a chair twice and kicked a coal-scuttle. As Hughes, the waiter on the library floor of the Club, brought him his coffee he saw him throw four pennies, one after another, with a crash on to the table by his side until they almost spun, then pick up the evening paper and turn the pages over with an exaggerated and almost deliberate rustle. It is quite remarkable how much noise can be made by slapping a paper with the back of the hand.

Hughes, however, was not in the least puzzled. He knew Pargiter's technique perfectly well. There was another member in the room asleep, and that was a thing Pargiter could not bear. The fellow actually seemed to be sleeping soundly and, what was worse, comfortably. Hughes could imagine exactly what would happen next. First the coffee pot, then the milk jug, then the sugar bowl would be raised and put down heavily on the tray, and since the Club used, no one knew why, the most awful metal trays, a good deal of noise would be made.

Then the lid of the coffee pot would be taken up and rattled against the side. You can get quite a large volume of sound out of earthenware without breaking it. If still the member did not wake up, Pargiter would be reduced to (a) dropping the spoon on the tray, (b) crunching the candy sugar. He had once been known to send the tray flying, but since this had involved his paying for a new cup and saucer, Hughes did not believe the performance would be repeated.

He wondered what he had done in the end this time. Whatever it was, he was sure Pargiter must have been furious, especially as Hughes could now see that the sleeping member was Morrison – with whom he had heard that Pargiter had been quarrelling earlier in the day. Anyhow, to whatever tricks Pargiter had been reduced, he had failed. Looking in later, Hughes saw that where there had been two figures in the library, there was now only one. Morrison was still sleeping soundly in an alcove half surrounded by books. So soundly, that his eyeglass had dropped out of his eye. In a short while, Hughes thought, he would wake up and complain that the coffee was always lukewarm nowadays.

He wondered whether he had better risk making so much noise that Morrison would be bound to wake up, but if Pargiter had failed, Hughes thought that he had very little chance of succeeding. At that moment the house telephone bell in his service pantry began to ring violently. Ford's voice sounded agitated.

And indeed it might well be.

Dinner over, Ford had slipped up to the bedroom he had in the Club. Here he could sit in an easy-chair and forget all about the members, all their complaints and worries and all the contradictory promises he had made. To be a secretary of any club, you need a hide impervious to complaints, and an ability to oppose an interminable defence of passive resistance to all those suggestions which are daily offered to you, which sound so logical and right, and which are, in fact, so hopelessly impractical. Poor Ford, pleasant, agreeable, but weak as ditch water, would never be a really good club secretary. He would never be hardened to the necessary degree of callousness. Nature had made him a big, healthy man, but forgotten to supply an adequate backbone.

He pulled gently at his sandy moustache and settled down to read *The Three Musketeers*, in a vain attempt to leave the world of the Whitehall Club. Usually it was easy, but to-day, somehow, everything had gone wrong. Somehow, none of his assistants seemed to be quite up to the mark, and there had been so many small failures at which even less cantankerous people than Morrison might justly cavil.

He found himself vaguely considering the possibility of d'Artagnan taking over his job and in some marvellous way putting everything right and sending all tiresome people about their business. Just as he was regretting the absence from modern life of duelling, there was a knock at the door.

'Come in,' he murmured wearily. Now even his own room was not to be regarded as a sanctuary!

To his surprise he saw Benson in the doorway, his russet face grey with anxiety. But if it was a surprise that Benson should be there at all, his first remark made the secretary gasp.

'Is Mr Morrison all right, sir?'

'*Mr Morrison?*' Now why should anyone in the world, and most of all why should Benson, worry about Morrison?

'Yes, sir.' Even in his agitation, Benson could guess why the secretary was so startled. 'I know, sir, it does seem odd, my worrying about him. But it's like this, sir ...'

Fairly quickly and, on the whole, quite clearly, he explained about his carbuncle, the perchloride of mercury, and the essence of vanilla.

'And then, sir, when you spoke to me about Mr Morrison wanting vanilla specially, it seemed like fate, sir. And so I put the vanilla bottle out carefully, and then, I don't know how it was, sir, but I got a bit confused, I suppose, about it, and – and I don't know, sir, but I think I must have used the wrong bottle. And so, I just want to be sure he is all right, because if he isn't – mind you, sir, I'm not sure it was the wrong bottle.'

With his usual optimism Ford assured him at once that he was quite certain it was the right one.

'Now you just go down and fetch both the bottles and bring them up here. It will make assurance doubly sure.'

In moments of crisis Ford always fell back on proverbs or quotations of dubious relevance.

While Benson went off on the errand, Ford began to use the house telephone. It was typical that he had no idea what part of the club Morrison was in the habit of using after dinner, and that he asked first in all the wrong places. By the time that Benson returned, he had worked himself up into a state of agitation, and had only just found out that Morrison was in the library.

He looked at the two bottles sadly, and murmured something about locking the stable door by way of making Benson really comfortable.

The chef put them down on a table.

'That's the one I used this evening, sir. The one on the left.' He stooped down. 'You can tell which is which because this one, the one I didn't use, has got a bit torn off the corner of the label. Wish I'd noticed that before.'

Ford hardly heard him as he hurried off to the library, leaving Benson to wait anxiously.

CHAPTER 3

THE DOCTOR *EX MACHINA*

*

THE Whitehall Club possessed in fact two libraries. In the larger, smoking was not allowed, and the temperature was kept just above freezing point by one small fire struggling manfully with a series of complicated draughts, largely due to the fact that the windows reached to the floor and led on to a stone balcony surrounded by an old rusty iron railing. It was said that from this balcony one of the finest long-distance views of London could be got. But then who wanted to look for miles over roofs? No amount of distance can lend enchantment to a chimney pot.

Meanwhile throughout the winter it was impossible to sit in the room if any of them were open, while if they were shut the room became at once in some mysterious way both cold and airless. Indeed the problem of ventilation was one which had completely defeated every committee of the Club since its inception.

In the smaller smoking library the problem had been solved. There was no ventilation. Heavy clouds of smoke started to form in it about one forty-five, and continued to get thicker as the day progressed. Into it went all those members who were most afraid of fresh air. Each as he came in looked anxiously but unnecessarily at the windows. The windows never were open. Indeed it had been suggested that, like the bathroom taps, the rooms should be labelled 'Hot' and 'Cold'.

Ford of course chose the wrong library first, but eventually he found Hughes and entered the smaller library. Through the haze of tobacco smoke a large fire could be seen burning furiously, though somewhat impeded by the lack of oxygen. In the background was shelf after shelf of books from floor to ceiling. The curious had often wondered what books had been used to fill the top shelves, but since the only way of finding out was to place an insecure looking ladder on a slippery floor and lean it against a row of books, or at best the shelf on which they stood, curiosity had remained unsatisfied. Judging by the contents of the lower shelves, the question was of little importance.

In the far corner a bookcase had been built at right angles to the wall to provide space for more books. In the alcove thus formed was placed one of the few comfortable chairs in the Club, a chair for the possession of which many petty battles were waged. It was one of Mr Pargiter's self-appointed duties to see, if possible, that no one slept there in comfort for long. It was there that Morrison was sitting, his body completely relaxed, his feet on a footrest, his eyeglass lying on his lap.

With a feeling of increasing horror, Ford called him. There was no reply. He shook him but got no answer.

There was no doubt about it. Benson must have got hold of the wrong bottle after all! Ford stood, quite unable to say or do anything, the sweat breaking out on his forehead. It was very, very sad.

Then he pulled himself together. He ought to give some thought to Morrison, instead of thinking, as he had been, of the consequences, mainly so far as they concerned Benson, but partly as they affected the Club. Perhaps, after all, Morrison was not dead? He looked again. He supposed he ought to feel sorry about it if the man really had been poisoned. It was, had he known it, the nearest approach to sympathy that anyone was to feel, and even that thought faded away into a slight feeling of irritation at the uncertainty. Rather tardily he came to the conclusion that he must get a doctor and find out.

At that moment the door opened, causing Ford and Hughes to jump.

'Ah, talk of the devil,' came automatically to the secretary's lips as a clean-shaven, thin-lipped man came in. 'I was just wanting a doctor.'

The newcomer raised his eyebrows slightly. It was not Dr Anstruther's habit to waste words unnecessarily.

'Somebody ill?' he asked.

'More than ill, I'm afraid.'

Without comment Anstruther looked professionally at the figure in the chair.

'Almost certainly dead,' was the verdict. 'Can we get him into a bedroom where I can examine him properly?'

With the help of Hughes the transference was effected. As chance would have it the passages on the way were empty. In a very short while the doctor straightened up from his examination and nodded.

Ford turned to Hughes who, apparently accidentally, had remained as a spectator.

'Keep quiet about this for the present,' he said. 'We want no fuss here.'

Hughes's assent was readily given. He knew very well that if there was any scandal about this, it would do the Club no good. To his mind it was just like Morrison to be a nuisance even when he was dead. He returned to his service pantry. How it was to be 'kept quiet' for more than an hour or so, he could not imagine. Meanwhile it was hard not to be allowed to tell other people so exciting a piece of news. Even Hughes's really remarkably well developed sense of duty found that difficult.

In the room he had left Anstruther looked at the tall secretary.

'Keep it quiet, eh? Why?'

'How did he die?'

'Can't tell for certain without a post-mortem. Very sudden.'

Ford looked agitated. 'Must there be a post-mortem?'

'Why do you want to avoid it?'

Like most weak people Ford badly wanted someone to share his worries. Barely troubling to ask the doctor to keep the matter to himself, he poured out all the story of the two vanilla bottles.

'What's really worrying me', he went on, 'is what will happen to poor Benson. Of course it was a mistake, an obvious mistake, and no jury will ever think it is anything else. All the same I suppose he will have to be tried for manslaughter?'

Anstruther nodded.

'And he'll be away from the Club while it's going on, and what he will be like when he comes back I tremble to think. He's a nervous little man at the best of times. I don't think he'll ever face cooking here again, and he's the one man on the staff I rely on most, and he's got a wife and family dependent on him, too.

And all because of – well, *de mortuis*, perhaps.' He pulled himself up with a jerk.

'So for the sake of the chef –'

'Yes, and for the sake of the Club too. Whenever any mention of a decent club appears in the press, even a casual remark, it does harm. You know as well as I do that good clubs must never be talked about. Just fancy the publicity there will be if this gets out!' Ford's eyes goggled in horror. 'We shall be known as the club where we poison our members. We shall never live it down.'

Anstruther considered for a moment.

'As it happens,' he said, 'I am the one person who *can* keep it quiet for you.'

Ford leapt towards him. 'My dear fellow –'

'Don't jump to conclusions. I have not yet said that I will.'

'But I'm sure you will. I mean, my dear fellow, think of the Club, think of Benson, think of Benson's children –'

'Don't be theatrical. I know nothing of Benson's children and I care less. I am thinking' – he looked coldly towards the bed – 'of the dead man.'

This was too difficult for Ford. He did not know how to put it, even to himself, but it did not sound, well, quite decent. He gave it up and turned to the question of how the accident of the poisoning was to be hushed up.

'I told you I was the one man who could manage it. That is because Morrison was a patient of mine. Not, I must admit, a very valued patient.' The word 'valued' came out coldly, with a peculiar emphasis contrasting sharply with the normal flatness of his speech and expressionlessness of his face. 'The only way to avoid a post-mortem – and if there is a post-mortem nobody can hush the affair up – is for me to certify three things. First that I have seen him in the last month, secondly that I examined his heart and found something wrong with it, and thirdly that he died of heart failure.'

'And you can?'

For a short while there was silence while Anstruther stood looking at the dead man. Ford would have given very much to have known the doctor's reflexions. Was he debating the degree of risk? Or considering how truthful the certificate would be? Or had he possibly very little difficulty about that, but found his thoughts occupied with some different aspect of the case? Try as he would Ford could not guess. He was never very good at reading other people's minds, and Anstruther's face was too unexpressive to have given anyone much help.

Eventually Anstruther broke the long silence.

'Had he any relations?'

'I believe none. I don't of course absolutely know, but he once gave me to understand that he had no relatives except a nephew with whom he was not on speaking terms. I really think there is no one to make trouble.'

Once more silence fell in the bedroom. Anstruther apparently was making up his mind slowly and with difficulty. It rather hurt Ford's feelings that the doctor was going to come to a decision for himself. He would have liked to have felt that he counted for more; and yet, though the original proposition was his, he was glad that the responsibility for its adoption was not.

At last the silent internal struggle ended.

Anstruther nodded. 'That is my belief also. Very well.'

It was with an immense sense of relief that Ford departed, the slight insult to his pride readily forgotten. First of all he went back to Hughes. Mr Morrison, he told him, had died of heart failure. Fortunately Dr Anstruther, who happened to be his medical adviser, knew all about it and was not in the least surprised. He had known for a long time that his heart was weak. In his anxiety that the right story should be told, Ford rather exaggerated.

'I thought he didn't seem very surprised, sir,' remarked Hughes shrewdly.

'Ah,' said Ford, his attention called to this for the first time, 'you thought so too? At first I put it down just to being, well, professional –'

'Yes, sir, I understand. But of course, sir, Dr Anstruther never does seem to express any emotion at all.'

Ford decided that Hughes, even for an old servant, was getting too confidential.

'Well, anyhow, that's what it was. Heart failure. So fortunately there won't be any fuss.'

'Quite, sir.' The tendency to gossip was too strong. 'I should never have thought, though, sir, that Mr Morrison had a weak heart, or any heart' – he swallowed 'at all', and added 'weakness' lamely.

'Ah, well. It's the unexpected that always happens.' Ford closed the conversation. 'I must go and see Benson.'

He left behind him a puzzled man.

'Why on earth,' said Hughes to himself, 'should he want to see him?'

He gave up the problem and, wrongly leaving the care of the floor to the intermittent attentions of a page-boy, slipped off for a quarter of an hour to spread the news.

On his way back to his bedroom, Ford had time to think things over. He realized that he had left Benson on tenterhooks, and that the feelings of the naturally nervous chef would be given a further shock when he heard what had happened. He tried to concentrate on how best to break the news gently, but he could only think of how very little sympathy any of them had managed to raise for the unfortunate Morrison.

'Another member gone!' he thought. 'That means one less subscription next year. If there are many resignations at Christmas, there will be another proposal to reduce my salary. And times are so hard, you can't expect new members with our entrance fee.'

As a result of letting his thoughts wander, his announcement lacked finesse, to say the least of it.

'Is he all right, sir?'

'No. He's dead.'

Benson fainted.

'My God,' thought Ford, 'now someone else is going to die.'

He poured an unnecessarily large quantity of cold water on the little man, but it was some time before he got him round, and still longer before he got him to understand.

'It was nothing to do with you. Do you understand? Nothing to do with you at all,' he kept repeating. 'It was just an accident. Even in the best regulated families. Nothing to do with the vanilla. Just an acc – a coincidence. Just heart failure. Do you follow me? Heart failure. Natural causes. Dr Anstruther tells me he has been his doctor for a long while, and he's known for years that Mr Morrison has had a bad heart. A coincidence, just a coincidence.' Over and over again he repeated the story, committing himself and the doctor a little further at each repetition.

Gradually the unfortunate chef began to recover.

'Now look here, Benson, you've had a bit of a shock. To-day's Friday. There's very little doing here on Saturday and Sunday; you go home now and stay home for the week-end. Don't come back till Monday.'

Benson was torn in two directions. At one moment he wanted never to cook for the Club again, and at the next he wanted to preserve his record of never being absent from illness for a single day. Besides, the secretary ought to know that the Club could not get on without him! He never took a holiday except when the Club was shut.

Unconsciously Ford blundered on.

'Just for the week-end your assistant will have to manage. Oh, I know. It won't be the same, but still you must.'

With the utmost difficulty, eventually Ford succeeded in persuading him, and having at last seen the chef safely on his way home, with a definite promise that he would not return until Monday, the secretary went off to the smoking-room. He must abandon peace and d'Artagnan to-night. He must see to it that the members knew that Morrison's death was due to natural causes, and to natural causes alone.

It would have been so much better to have lived up to his own suggestion of keeping it quiet.

CHAPTER 4

THE TROUBLES OF A SECRETARY

*

THE following Monday morning was one of those lovely autumn mornings which, to their great disgust, confound those who enjoy reviling the English climate.

Ford sat in his office and looked out over the slates and tried to fall in tune with the pale but intensely bright blue of the sky, and the sparkle of the air. It was not a bit of good. He was worried. It was quite useless to repeat to himself that it was an accident and that 'no one was really to blame'. The fact remained that it *was* an accident and not a coincidence, and that he had no manner of right to have decided to prevent the normal course of events from occurring. In the cold, clear light of morning he could not see how he could have been such a fool as to have suggested keeping the manner of Morrison's death quiet. He even began to wonder if it had been his idea. He would have felt better, he thought, if he could have put the blame on Anstruther.

However, as Ford himself would have put it, it was no good crying over spilt milk, because, by now, he was thoroughly committed, and the secret and the responsibility were not his alone. If it ever came out, there would be just as much trouble for the doctor, if not more, and besides, Benson of course, and even Hughes, he supposed, might be in an awkward position.

He got up and looked at a pigeon walking on a neighbouring roof. No doubt about it. Never a coincidence, no longer an accident. Morrison's death, since the facts had been concealed, was by now a definite crime. There was no comfort anywhere.

'And it isn't as if we were getting rid of our only grumbler. There will still be people here who will complain,' he murmured. 'Pargiter, for instance. There's no gain in it anywhere.'

He turned back to his desk and tried by working to forget the trouble. There was the vexatious business of the Club medium dry sherry to provide a welcome counter-irritant. For some years past the Whitehall club had provided an excellent, sound before-dinner sherry, nothing out of the ordinary, perhaps, but at least it had had the merit of satisfying everybody. But, now that it was almost finished, the problem of finding a successor was proving troublesome.

Ford had started to solve the problem reasonably enough. He had got in samples from the seven or eight wine merchants with whom the Club dealt, and he had obtained the considered opinion of the Wine Committee on them. It would have seemed that to have ordered the one the majority of that body of experts had preferred would have been easy.

But here Ford's fatal habit of trying to satisfy everybody had obtruded. Like all other clubs the Whitehall possessed two members who were, in their own opinion, if not the only connoisseurs of wine as a whole, really well qualified to give an opinion on sherry. To have ordered a new sherry without asking them, would have been to risk a storm of criticism. It seemed best to Ford to let them try the proposed new Oloroso.

Of course it was the worst way. Both of the alleged experts pronounced the new sherry to be disgusting; one on the ground that it was too sweet, the other because it left an unpleasant bitter after-taste. Each insisted on various of their friends being made to sample it. The result was that Ford had concentrated on himself four streams of criticism. Firstly, the too sweet party, secondly, the too bitter party, thirdly the Wine Committee, who rather reasonably wanted to know why the secretary was going behind their backs and trying to upset their decisions – they threatened to resign *en bloc* if the sherry of their choice was not immediately purchased – and fourthly, there was Mr Cardonnel.

Mr Cardonnel was one of the many lawyers in the Club. If there was one thing in which he excelled, it was in finding out minor breaches of regulations and magnifying them into a major difficulty. He had found out – and he had the finest nose in existence for discovering this sort of point – that so many of the sweet and bitter parties had insisted on sampling the proposed sherry free and gratis, that the merchants had mildly suggested that bottles in excess of the first dozen must be charged, and of course Ford had weakly consented. Under what rule, inquired Mr Cardonnel, had either the secretary or the committee any right to purchase sherry at the Club's expense for the benefit of individual members? Mr Cardonnel could find no bye-law which permitted this to happen and, very regretfully of course, he was unable to let the matter drop until he was satisfied on the point. In his small, neat, spidery hand he wrote long letters, all in theory without prejudice in the lay rather than the legal sense of the term, to which no one could find a suitable answer in law – and with common sense Mr Cardonnel was never satisfied. Besides – and this is where the tribe of Cardonnels are always so tiresome – he was perfectly right.

Another party was rapidly being raised by him in the Club which was being recruited from all those who had not yet received a free sample. Ford vaguely wondered if it would not be cheaper in the end to give one to each of them and a dozen bottles to Cardonnel. But that was no good. The lawyer, incorruptible himself, would be screaming 'bribery' to the heavens.

On his desk Ford found yet another addition to the complications. Someone was starting yet another hare.

'Why,' inquired the letter before him, 'is the contract for sherry being removed from the merchants who have so long supplied Oloroso sherry to the complete satisfaction of all, and given to another firm, if rumour is accurate, whose only recent contribution to the Club's cellars was some very indifferent Burgundy?'

Ford looked at the letter despondingly. It would have been quite useless to reply that it was the choice of the Wine Committee, decided without knowing the names of the suppliers; that he liked to give each of the Wine Merchants an order in turn in the vain hope of keeping them all happy; or that the Burgundy in question was excellent and anyhow was nothing to do with it. The truth, as Ford well knew, was that the writer was an old friend of the firm who were in danger of being supplanted, and was writing definitely in that capacity without any regard to the merits of the case. Ford's only hope was to shelter behind the Wine Committee; but then he had offended them very definitely, which in reality is the type of result always achieved by trying to satisfy everyone; but that was a piece of logic that Ford would never assimilate.

He turned to the next letter. A complaint from Pargiter about

Morrison's behaviour. Odd that it should not have been received until the Monday.

'However,' remarked Ford to the pigeon outside, 'thank goodness that complaint has dealt with itself.' He then blushed at his lack of proper feeling, for he still thought that though he could not really feel the smallest regret at the fact of Morrison's death as distinct from its manner, he ought to do so.

He was still suffering from a slightly guilty conscience when the door opened to admit a small birdlike man whose smooth, clean-shaven face looked youthful despite his white hair. Probably the youthfulness of his heart was assisted by the fact that he always managed to pass the responsibility of his every act on to someone else. None of his colleagues in the Home Office were more adept in this, and so far as his daily work was concerned, it seemed to answer, so far as he was personally concerned, at any rate. One of his objections to being Chairman of the Committee of the Whitehall Club, even for one year, was that he occasionally had to make decisions.

He twittered in a birdlike way, rarely finishing his sentence.

'Well, well, so Morrison – very sad.'

'Yes, sir.' Ford wondered if Laming really found it sad. 'Awkward for the Club, too, sir. It would never do for anything to get into the Press.'

'The Press? Why should it? Man dies – heart failure. Why Press?'

Ford shifted the weight of his large body to the other foot and murmured something a trifle incoherent.

'Chef ill too, I hear,' went on the Chairman. 'Saw Cardonnel – tiresome fellow, but often right – seemed to be wondering if there was some connexion. Was saying it was lucky man's doctor was in Club.'

A nasty sensation of prickly heat began to spread all over Ford's body. If Cardonnel started nosing around, there was no knowing what might happen. A good fellow really, Cardonnel, but a sore trial! And in this case, an absolute menace!

Now if Ford had been a wise man, he would have quickly, and without unnecessary emphasis, denied that there was any connexion between the two events. But Wisdom and Ford were barely on speaking terms. In a moment of panic he found himself making a half confession to his chairman. Benson, he said, had got into an absurd panic that he had accidentally confused a bottle containing flavouring with one temporarily used for medicine, which he believed to be poisonous. It had given him a shock naturally, when he had heard that Morrison was dead, but fortunately Anstruther, the dead man's own doctor, had been able to certify that it was a simple case of heart failure. Then, seeing the alarm on Laming's face, Ford had plunged recklessly on.

'As a matter of fact there is no reason to believe that the flavouring in question was used for anything Morrison had eaten.'

'My dear fellow, do stop, do stop. No need to tell me anything. Keep it to yourself. Much better if I heard nothing about it. Why drag me in?'

Horrified at the possibility of being involved in something which might prove unpleasant, the chairman hastily turned the subject to the great sherry question.

'Better approach the old suppliers. Tell them to send a similar wine. Call it the same. No need to tell everyone. Never is any need to tell. Haven't heard what you said just now. No. Good morning.'

He drifted out, masking the wisdom of the serpent beneath the appearance of the dove.

Ford sat down and mopped his brow. Well, there was another accomplice however much he might refuse to listen. Whatever happened they could never own up now!

A polite knock on the door, and Benson came in and shut the door with an air approaching to the mysterious. Then with a triumphant smile of relief, he addressed his fellow conspirator.

'It's all right, sir. It's absolutely all right. My wife's a wonderful woman; she thinks of everything!' He seemed quite surprised about it as well as highly gratified.

'And what did she think of this time?'

'Of marking the bottle. She tore a bit off the label. She says she told me, but I'm not like her, sir; I don't remember her telling me.'

'But what's that got to do with it?'

Benson looked at the secretary with disappointment. He ought to have seen the point long ago.

'Why, sir, don't you remember my saying that the bottle with the piece torn off the label was the one I had *not* used. So you see, sir, I just flavoured that soufflé with pure vanilla – if vanilla ever is pure. I hate the stuff – and Mr Morrison dying was, as you said, sir, just a coincidence – a pure coincidence. Isn't it splendid? Why, what's the matter, sir, you're looking all funny.'

Ford hurriedly pulled himself together and declared that it must have been a trick of the light. He was feeling perfectly well. He even managed to congratulate the chef on the proof that Morrison's death was due to nothing but heart failure, and was in no way connected with vanilla or perchloride of mercury.

'So all's well that ends well,' he added.

Benson hurried back to his work. He hated leaving it for a moment, but he had just had to make Ford comfortable about that business.

CHAPTER 5

DOCTOR'S ORDERS

*

COMFORTABLE was about the last thing that Ford was.

If Morrison had not died as the result of being poisoned with perchloride of mercury, how had he died?

There seemed to be three possibilities. First, the chef might be wrong after all. Ford began to hope that that was so. But, fool that he was, why hadn't it occurred to him to see if perchloride of mercury *tasted*? Was it possible that Morrison, whose taste in food was admittedly difficult, would eat a *soufflé glacé perchloride de vif-argent*, or whatever the French was, without noticing it? Perhaps, though, the stuff was tasteless? Ford made up his mind to find out unobtrusively.

The second possibility was that it really was heart failure. Clearly that was the most desirable thing. It would be very pleasant if he could believe that. But unfortunately he could not be sure. Anstruther's hesitation might have been merely due to his natural caution, to some slight surprise at finding Morrison's heart worse than he had thought, or to the fact that his most recent examination was more than a month old.

On the other hand, was it possible that there had been something to conceal? Something really wrong? If he had thought that it was heart failure, surely he would have said so straight away without all the hesitation he had shown? Ford found it impossible, as usual, to come to any decision, but clearly the only thing to do was to relate the new turn in events to the doctor and see what he advised.

As to the third idea which crossed his mind, it was too horrible to contemplate. Surely Anstruther would not say that he knew that Morrison had in fact been poisoned? Because then – well, how had he been poisoned? *And by whom?*

With the obstinacy of all weak men Ford dismissed the possibility. It could *not* have happened that way.

Braving the draughts in the larger library, the secretary sought the encyclopaedia and hunted round to find out what was the taste of perchloride of mercury. But neither under mercury, nor under corrosive sublimate could he find any reference to the taste of the substance. All that he found was that white of egg was apparently the antidote to it as a poison, and surely there was white of egg in *soufflé*? The more he thought of it, the more he was afraid that Benson's cooking was not responsible. That very thought gave him another idea. Did that particular sweet have to be cooked? And if so, what was the effect of cooking on perchloride of mercury? Ford plunged once more into the encyclopaedia, and emerged as ignorant as ever.

He had not noticed that someone had entered the room as he was reading, but now he suddenly felt stealing over him the sensation that someone was looking over his shoulder, and he turned round quickly to find Cardonnel apparently in difficulty about finding the reference book he wanted.

Shutting up the encyclopaedia with a snap Ford offered to help.

Cardonnel put his finger to his lips and pointed to a notice painted on wood.

'Members are requested to keep silence in this room. By order of the Committee. 1st January, 1880.'

'And of course,' he whispered, with mock sarcasm, 'it's never been broken since.'

Ford managed a sickly smile and pointed to the shelf of books.

'Baedeker's Central Italy,' continued the whisper. 'Of course I've found Northern Italy, Southern Italy, and Italy – but not Central. Ah, here it is.' He picked out a book immediately under his nose. Ford remained looking at the shelf. For the life of him he could see neither Northern nor Southern Italy.

With a feeling of considerably more alarm, the secretary ambled off to seek Dr Anstruther.

There are always some members of a club who are a slight mystery to their fellow members. They use the club house a good deal one way and another; they are known by sight to all those who are there frequently, but though they occasionally exchange such few words as civility may require, they clearly do not wish to be involved in anything of a social nature. They come in, take their meals or sit and smoke behind the barrier of a book or newspaper, and when they leave, their desire for taciturnity has been respected by the most hardened club bore. To them their club is a place for quiet and rest. Unremarked they come, and unnoticed they go, by any but the hall-porter. Of such appeared to be Dr Anstruther.

All through his life he had quietly but efficiently done his job and avoided not only the limelight, but even the majority of normal human contacts. He was believed by those who came across him professionally to be a more than sound general practitioner. There was some surprise that he had not selected some line in which to specialize, but even his fellow doctors could not have said what his particular line was likely to be. In medicine, as in life, he offered a negative front.

Despite the fact that it was his own doing that he had no friends and few acquaintances, there were moods when he rather resented the lack of notice which the world allotted to him. His fellow doctors, in his opinion, should have taken more interest in him, and as to the other members of the Whitehall Club, it was particularly galling that they should ignore him so completely. Considering that they were merely observing what seemed to be his own desire, and that he would have been bitterly opposed to any curiosity on their part, his attitude was weak in logic.

Looking round the smoking-room Ford could just see Anstruther's carefully brushed, slightly greying hair, the rest of his face being concealed behind the *Lancet*. The secretary was just a little shocked that anyone should be so immersed in his work as to be reading about it in what might have been his spare time. Ford could not imagine himself being so energetic.

To his request that he should come up to his office, the doctor assented silently. His thin-lipped mouth showed no expression as he crossed the room, his slight figure of medium height and scrupulous neatness contrasting strongly with Ford's tall and rather corpulent body, and consequent general air of having pushed his clothes out of shape.

To the secretary's disclosure that Benson had now practically proved that Morrison had not died as a result of being poisoned with the ice, Anstruther made no comment. So far as Ford could make out he intended to say nothing at all! The attitude seemed incomprehensible. Ford could never have remained silent himself.

'Well,' he broke in after a long pause. 'What are you going to do about it?'

'Do? Nothing.'

'But supposing – just supposing Morrison died of – look here, what did he die of?'

Anstruther removed his gaze which appeared to have been concentrated on a filing cabinet, and fastened it on the secretary.

'I have already certified heart failure.'

'But – but supposing it wasn't?'

'Why suppose anything of the kind?'

Ford tried more direct methods. This was getting them nowhere.

'Do you think it was heart failure?'

The doctor considered a moment.

'Very possibly,' was his dry answer.

'But supposing it wasn't? Oughtn't we to make certain that it wasn't?'

'And how would you suggest setting about that?'

'Couldn't you do a post-mortem now?'

'Look a bit curious after I had signed the certificate!'

'Well, couldn't you say that Benson had told you afterwards about the perchloride of mercury, and you wanted to satisfy him?'

'After he has, apparently, proved that it was vanilla all the time; and also when he is so happy, so happy that I should imagine anyone would see it. No. Too thin.'

'But surely something ought to be done about it.'

Anstruther got up deliberately and made what was, for him, quite a long speech.

'No. It was you who suggested this idea of keeping it quiet, and now you have got to live up to it. For all you know, Morrison *may* have died of heart failure. Whether he did or not is absolutely immaterial. I see now that I have taken a risk, a stupid risk if you like, in signing that certificate. But the risk is slight, provided that you say absolutely nothing. If you begin talking, you will, at the best, lose your own job and get me struck off the Medical

Register. What further trouble you may cause, I leave you to imagine. You may perhaps reflect on the harm you may cause to the Club and to Benson. You will therefore cease to consider the matter at all, if possible, and you will say nothing to anyone. If you must talk you will talk to me, but to no one else.'

He started to go out, but as he reached the door he turned round once more.

'For your benefit, I tell you once more, Morrison died of heart failure.'

For some minutes after he left Ford crouched back in his chair, hardly able to move. Not for a moment did it enter his mind that it would be possible to disobey Anstruther. In the days that were to come he was often to regret that he had not at that moment taken the affair into his own hands and insisted on the whole thing being properly investigated. He might have made some excuse, that Benson's discovery that the wrong bottle had possibly been used, had only just been made, for instance; that would have allowed him to raise the point again without involving Anstruther.

But even had he done something of that kind at once, it would have sounded thin, and with every hour that passed it would sound thinner. At the moment, however, that Anstruther left his office that Monday, no such idea crossed his brain. Firmly fixed there was the idea that he must do exactly what he was told. He only hoped Laming had forgotten what he had said that morning.

Dancing up and down like a puppet on a string when Fate holds a peep-show, the ungainly Ford weakly took the easiest road – or what seemed the primrose path. He even felt quite cheerful about it. He had to do nothing. Just keep quiet. Not a word to anyone. Morrison had died of heart failure. He resolutely pushed to the back of his mind his doubts as to what the doctor really had meant. He tried to forget the equivocal, the more than equivocal phrases. From his recollection of the interview he expunged 'For all you know', 'For your benefit', and concentrated on the sentences he preferred, such as the last few words that the doctor had spoken.

By dint of his incurable optimism he managed to obtain a certain tranquillity. After all, by keeping quiet, wasn't he helping

Benson? Wasn't he shielding Anstruther? Wasn't he doing his best for the Club? Once more he addressed the pigeon on the roof.

'You can't have murders in decent clubs. It does the place no good – no good at all. Best to let sleeping dogs lie.'

He went to Morrison's funeral quite happily, and returned from it in so cheerful a frame of mind that he even thought he could find a bye-law as to the sherry which would satisfy Cardonnel. A closer examination, however, brought disillusionment.

It was then that he opened the letter.

CHAPTER 6

CURLED OR FILLETED?

*

IT was quite a bulky letter. It was addressed to him by name and marked 'Personal'. Suspecting that it was an advertisement, Ford nearly threw it away, and was only restrained by the thought that 'Personal' letters do not have typewritten envelopes. Glancing, however, at the end, he saw that it was not signed. Slightly puzzled, he turned back to the beginning and saw it began 'Dear Ford'. He decided after all that it was not an advertisement. The opening paragraph was rather strange.

I have for long wanted to be in a position to force you to run the Club properly. It is far too good a club to be allowed to go wrong simply on account of bad management. You have, so far as I can make out, an efficient staff in the main – at least they would be efficient if you kept them up to the mark. It is therefore only with yourself that I shall have to deal.

Ford looked more and more puzzled. The writer seemed very confident, and to be making a large number of assumptions. He puffed his chest out and blew out his cheeks. He wasn't going to be ordered about by anyone! Ford fancied himself a very determined person. He read on:

Of course, I might adopt the simple method of forcing you to resign. That would be useless for two reasons. Firstly, the Committee, led by that pompous fool Laming, would only go and appoint an equally stupid and incompetent man, over whom I should have no control. Which brings me to my second reason. I enjoy power. I shall like watching your ineffective attempts to avoid my grasp. I like watching people squirm and wriggle. It will be amusing to sit quietly in the background, and by a steady pressure, bring you and, through you, the Club, the staff, and the members where opportunity offers, to a state of doing what I require.

Power, let me tell you, is only really attractive if applied anonymously. To your simple mind that may seem to mean that I enjoy it only when it is freed from responsibility. That is not true. From now on I shall be entirely responsible for the real management of the Club, and the joke will be that only you – and perhaps one other – will know that such a person as I exists, and even you will not know who I am. By the way, I hope you will struggle a bit. The only fear I have is that my fun will be spoilt by a too ready acquiescence.

Ford shivered involuntarily. Whoever this man was, and whatever reason he had for thinking he had some hold over him, he must be a madman, the sort of insane person who enjoyed cruelty for its own sake. He had read about such people, but he had always thought that they did not really exist. He turned back to the letter.

But I see I have not yet told you why you are going to do what you are told. The reason is given in one word, and I will give myself the pleasure of typing it in capitals on a sheet all to itself.

With nervous fingers Ford turned over the page. In the middle all by itself was the one word.

MORRISON

Ford sat down heavily. His whole office seemed to be whirling round. It was not until some minutes had elapsed that he was able to get himself a glass of water from a bottle on a side table, and go on reading.

There, now. That *was* fun, wasn't it? I wish I could have been with you when you read that and had seen what you did. If you were standing up, I am sure you sat down quickly. If you were sitting down, you probably jumped up. And then you took a drink of water. You see, I know you quite well. By the way, I think you had better start by taking that water-bottle away. It is quite out of place in an office.

Ford fidgeted uneasily. He hoped he would not have his minor little comforts removed in this way. Soon the fellow would be telling him not to wear his old coat in the office.

But to return. What of the late lamented? (By the way, I think a little more sympathy would not have been out of place.) Of course I know a very great deal of what has been happening. But not, you may be relieved to know, everything. For instance, which of you murdered him? Did you do it yourself? Somehow I don't think – if you will excuse such a vulgar expression – that you have the guts. Still, you had a good deal of provocation, and so did all the rest of the staff. Any of them might have poisoned him, though not, I agree with you, with perchloride of mercury. There are, as I think you are beginning to discover, objections to that. Or was it that quarrelsome, tiresome man,

Pargiter? Did you know he was in the library earlier in the evening? Or that venial doctor?

He, by the way, is the 'one other' to whom I referred just now. It is only fair that he should know. I cannot imagine how you induced him to fall in with your little plan, he seems a sensible fellow. In fact I tell you candidly that I advise you to show this to him, both in fairness and because frankly he will keep you straight.

However, as you see, there are still some details I have to find out. Don't worry. I shall find them. But meanwhile I think I had better receive a message from you which will show that you are going to have the sense to do what you are told, and I think I have hit on rather a happy way for you to send it. The other day I heard an elderly and respected member of the Club (wouldn't you like to know if I am either?) complaining that fried curled whiting was never on the menu. A simple taste, quite easy to satisfy; and yet it is typical of you that you did nothing about it. So, as a sign, next Thursday there will be fried curled whiting for dinner. Just like that. You will remember, won't you?

P.S. Don't forget the water-bottle.

In a violent passion Ford put down the letter. So this was what Anstruther's silly schemes had led him to! To be the victim of a blackmailer! A low-down creature who was capable of black-mailing the secretary of his own club!

Well, it was quite easy! All he had to do was to ignore the letter and let the brute do his worst. He triumphantly put the water-bottle on to his desk. Let the fellow take a good look at that next time he came in! With a convulsive gesture of his fat hands he seized the letter with the intention of tearing it up, but, just as he had it firmly gripped, he stopped. After all, supposing he wanted to prove blackmail, wouldn't it be advisable to have his evidence?

Sitting down once more at his desk, he re-read the missive. Suppose he was to be brave and call in the police, and ask for protection against a blackmailer? Well, he would have to start admitting rather a large number of things, and certainly his correspondent was right; he would have to tell Anstruther first. Even if the doctor agreed, there was a further difficulty. From whom was he to be protected? That was a problem which had to be thought out, and rather carefully too. It would certainly mean losing his job if he accused the wrong man.

But after all, did it amount to blackmail? The writer of the letter was not demanding money with menaces, which Ford vaguely believed was the approximate definition of blackmail. He was not even trying to extort any property or valuable thing. He could imagine the scene in court.

'And was he attempting to blackmail you?'

'Yes.'

'To obtain a valuable thing?'

'Well, yes.'

'And that thing was?'

'A fried curled whiting.'

Laughter in court in which his lordship and the jury joined heartily. No, it would not do at all. He would probably find himself under restraint as a lunatic.

Taking a cigarette from his case, he struck a match and decided to think the thing over.

'Supposing', he remarked to the water-bottle, 'I give the fellow a little rope in the hope that he will hang himself? Or rather commit himself. Supposing that I use the time in finding out who he is and spying on him while he is spying on me?' He chuckled and lit another match, the first one having burnt his fingers. 'What sport it would be to see the engineer hoist with his own petard!'

Whenever Ford indulged in a quotation, which was distressingly frequently, it was never quite apposite and never quite accurate.

'Well, anyhow,' he went on, 'my mind's made up. To appear to yield and really to be "bold, bloody, and resolute". But all the same, I think I had better make it clear that he is not to wipe his boots on me as if I was the door mat.' He picked up the house telephone and talked to the chef. 'That you, Benson? Look, two or three people have been complaining to me that they never have whiting for dinner. Yes, I agree, a beastly fish. However, always humour them. Give it to them on Thursday, will you? What? Ordered already? Look here, I'm sorry, but I've practically promised it to them. Put it into the Club dinner as another alternative, but don't, on any account, make it fried curled whiting. Fried *fillet* of whiting, please.'

At the other end Benson was looking puzzled. It was unlike the secretary to interfere with his arrangements. In the opinion of the chef the secretary would do much better to mind his own business, namely acting as a dummy safety valve to which members could complain, while he and the steward got on with the job. As for fried fillet of whiting, it never looked well, he protested.

But to his surprise Ford was quite adamant. There was to be whiting for dinner on Thursday and it must be filleted.

Hughes, temporarily off duty from the library floor, chancing to pass by, was quite surprised to find the chef actually grumpy. It was so unusual that he stopped to ask him what the trouble was.

'Here's the secretary trying to run the Club!'

Hughes smiled. 'Well, after all, old boy!'

'Oh, I know, but he shouldn't interfere with the food. Especially not with the details. I don't so much mind his saying we must have whiting on Thursday if he must go and promise people things, but when he says it's got to be fried fillets, it's going beyond his province.'

'Fried *fillets* of whiting,' murmured Hughes. 'I wonder why? I thought I heard Pargiter – you know, one of my beauties in the small dormitory – saying he wanted a curled whiting.'

'Well, there you are. Now don't you hang about gossiping in my place any longer.'

The chef started pressing some spiced beef with more vigour than tenderness.

CHAPTER 7

THURSDAY'S DINNER

*

THE members' dining-room of the Whitehall Club was known as the coffee-room, a phrase faintly redolent of the age of Dickens. As the members of the Whitehall Club would have dissolved themselves as an institution rather than allow smoking in their coffee-room, and as the coffee stage of any meal usually synchronizes with a desire to smoke, the coffee-room might almost be said to be so termed because coffee was never served in that room alone.

When he was first appointed, the Committee had told Ford that he was expected to take most of his meals there, so that he might see from personal experience how things were being run – for the Committee very rightly considered that if the food, and especially if the drink was right, nothing else would matter so very much.

Ford never really liked it. Not that he was not made welcome. Grumblers such as Morrison, curmudgeons such as Pargiter, who managed to imply that he ought really to feed in the servants' hall, were rare, and their behaviour was not approved of by the rest of the Club. After all, most of the members, though they might be a little difficult about their own pet grievances, were perfectly rational about everybody else's, and were even ready to sympathize with Ford's troubles. Most of them liked Ford, though secretly or openly they expressed the opinion that there were better club secretaries. Still, he was always amiable and obliging. They admitted that he had a devil of a job, while privately considering that they could do it a great deal better themselves. Meanwhile, as a companion, they had nothing against him – a bit dull, perhaps, no more.

But what Ford himself disliked so much was the feeling that when he dined there he was still on duty, that everything that went wrong was his fault and must be corrected by him. He would sit there worrying until he had spoilt his own digestion and made all the staff nervous. Of course, if anything went seriously wrong, he never noticed it.

On this particular Thursday night his nerves seemed to be worse than ever. The head waiter was nearly in despair. He hurriedly moved to the other end of the room two of the younger waiters, who had only just been promoted from the ranks of the pages. They would probably do the wrong thing anyhow, but they had better not be put off by the sight of Ford fidgeting. He went up to the carver quietly.

'Apparently what's biting him is the fish. He keeps on looking up whenever anybody has any served, as if the end of the world had come.'

'The fish? Well, I passed some remark to Benson about the fish this evening and nearly got my head bitten off. It seems the old man ordered it himself.'

'Well, he doesn't seem to like it now he's got it. And he's still looking at everybody else's. Try to serve it so that it looks well.'

The carver looked at him pityingly. How could you serve fillet of whiting except, so to speak, flat?

Round the rather gloomy coffee-room with its massive cut-glass chandeliers, originally designed to hold candles and now looking rather out of date, dinner was proceeding quietly. Most of the members who were dining there that night did so frequently, did so normally, in fact, if there was no reason for being elsewhere. Gradually, as the years had passed on, they had slipped unconsciously into regular habits, not perhaps entirely from their own choice, but as a result of a steady pressure from the staff.

It worked in this way. A new member would come in. He would be shown to whatever table was unlikely to be wanted by anyone else. The next time he came, without thinking, he would go to the same table. From that moment his doom was sealed. Ever after, that particular table was reserved for him, and any attempt to go elsewhere would be greeted by such obvious disappointment that he would feel unable to break away. There was even a known case of one member who found himself, to his surprise, supposed to covet a particular seat, by which he was pushed into a position of more prominence than his essentially modest nature desired. In winter it was draughty; in summer the sun was in his eyes; but there he sat three hundred days in the year for six whole years before he summoned up sufficient courage to ask to be put somewhere else. It was another four years before the waiter who had looked after that table all the time ceased to look on him as one who had lapsed unaccountably into heresy.

With everything else it was the same. A member asked two successive nights for biscuits instead of toast, and the third night biscuits would be proudly brought automatically. It was a sign that he was known, and perhaps, too, it was the only way for the staff to while away pleasantly the rather dull hours, and maintain their personal pride that they were doing their job well. It must be sadly admitted that the younger waiters used to back their personal judgement with each other in pennies as to whether A would select jugged hare or roast beef, while the likelihood of B taking sprouts rather than marrow had been so hotly debated that sixpence had been known to change hands on it.

On the whole this largely unconscious system worked well. People got what they wanted quickly, regularly, and automatically, without having to think for themselves, while those who insisted on variety quickly established a reputation for eccentricity which eased the monotony.

Practically all the thirty or forty people dining that Thursday night were regular *habitués*, and all of them had known tastes. They were allowed, as a courtesy, to order their own dinner, but if the staff had done it for them, the results would have been almost identical. The head waiter looked round fairly happily. There were only two, perhaps three danger spots. The two newly promoted lads were in safe hands, looking after the most regular diners, men who were so constant that they would inevitably train the beginners. The chief danger was Ford (inadvertently) and Pargiter, a man whom the head waiter knew was always out for trouble. Cardonnel he expected later, but he did not so much mind about him – a precise man, it was true, given to asking awkward questions, but fundamentally kind-hearted, and prepared to make reasonable allowances if you took him the right way.

He moved so as to be at hand if Pargiter started being troublesome, and watched him neatly removing the bones from a herring. He was glad to see that he appeared to be reasonably happy. He would have expected Pargiter to have chosen whiting, on the absence of which he had been commenting for some time.

However, all seemed to be well. From where he stood he could hear anything Pargiter might say to Ford at the next table, and so, perhaps, discover why the secretary was more than usually on edge.

'Let me congratulate you,' came Pargiter's icy voice, 'on having at last adopted one of my unimportant suggestions.'

'You mean?' Ford walked straight into the trap and with two words gave away the fact that he had forgotten all Pargiter's suggestions. Moreover he should have known that the Pargiters of this world are always most dangerous when most polite.

'I feared you had forgotten my little wish. Merely that we should have whiting occasionally. I have, you know, asked you for it on several occasions.' He took a little mustard sauce before continuing. 'Yes, I see the direction of your glance. I am in fact, as you observe, eating a rather indifferent herring. I dislike herrings as a matter of fact, but having repeatedly requested the head waiter, and even, though you appear to have forgotten it, asked so distinguished a person as yourself, for fried whiting – fried curled whiting – I felt rather offended when I found that when for the first time for many months we have whiting – it is filleted.' He broke off for a moment and summoned a waiter. 'I have had all I want of this' – almost a sniff – 'herring. Are there any vegetables to-night?'

The head waiter looking at Ford saw him turn red, and then white, and then red again. To his mind the secretary ought not to be so thin-skinned as to let himself be upset by the sneers of a man like Pargiter. Everybody knew that he always went on like that, and would indeed be perfectly miserable if he had to admit that his dinner was perfect.

'But now,' went on Pargiter, 'that we shall no longer have to pander invariably to the wishes of, I am afraid I must say, that rather unpleasant person Morrison, perhaps the desires of some of the other old members may be occasionally considered. By the way, we have been electing some very unpleasant young members recently – but I fear I bore you. I see you are unable to give me your attention at the moment.'

'Not at all, sir. I was listening most carefully. A momentary touch of indigestion.'

Through Ford's brain was racing a problem. Was Pargiter deliberately telling him that it was he who had written the letter? If so, life would be unbearable for the unfortunate secretary! But then if he had, would he be so obvious? Would it not be more like Pargiter's character to keep entirely in the background, or had he found it impossible not to let his victim know whose claws were going to scratch?

Again, was it a double bluff? Supposing that Pargiter had written the letter, might he not think that Ford would assume that he would not give himself away, and therefore, that when he apparently did, the conclusion would be that it must be a co-incidence, and that Pargiter could not be the man who knew too much. Besides, Ford remembered now, Pargiter *had* been complaining about the absence of whiting. Was it possible that it was he who had put the idea into the letter writer's head? But then no one could ever have referred to Pargiter as a 'highly respected member' of the Club.

On the whole, Ford decided that it probably was not the sarcastic brute sitting on his left hand. With a mental reservation to keep him in mind nevertheless, he forced his attention back to his neighbour's conversation. Apparently, he had given so easy an opening that Pargiter considered it beneath his dignity to take the obvious chance.

'Indigestion, eh?' With a wave of his hand he implied how right in poetic justice it was that the secretary should suffer from his own maladministration. He remembered that his query as to vegetables remained unanswered. The list of those immediately available was recited to him. He shuddered realistically when he heard that mashed turnips were included. 'Really? Are there no swedes? Or mangel-wurzels?'

Another thought had occurred to Ford. Why had Pargiter sat next to him? He fancied it was not his usual table. Had he then come in order to drop his hint? Or just to make the secretary uncomfortable? Ford was quite aware of Pargiter's sentiments towards him and his position. Really either reason, he decided, might be right. He looked across to where Pargiter usually sat and saw a young newly elected member sitting there, blissfully unconscious that he had pushed his way to where he should not have been, and that he would not have been allowed to go there if the head waiter had not thought that as Pargiter was a little late, he was not coming.

Certainly the reason of his neighbour's remark on the subject of 'very unpleasant young members' was explained. But was that all?

Ford felt quite unable to eat any more. He left the coffee-room and went down the staircase. At the foot of it he found Cardonnel studying the menu. Apparently the lawyer was in a good humour. His eyes twinkled pleasantly behind the pince-nez which insecurely straddled his long thin nose.

'Ah, Ford, been dining? Hope you enjoyed it. Any sherry beforehand?' He laughed to show that he did not really mean to be unkind. 'On the whole` I must congratulate you on the dinner to-night. More variation in it. So easy to get into a rut in a place like this.'

He went up the stairs slowly, leaving the secretary gasping. Ford picked up the menu of the set Club dinner and read it through again and again. For the life of him he could see nothing unusual in it – except perhaps the whiting.

'The trouble is,' he said to himself, 'that I'm beginning to imagine things. I'm getting whiting on the brain. The times are out of joint. Ah! cursed spite . . .'

It may however be doubted whether Ford was exactly born to set things right.

CHAPTER 8

TWELVE POINTS

*

FORTUNATELY for his sanity, Ford was only to hear twice more of fried curled whiting before, as a worry, it sank into the background and was obliterated by the greater troubles that were to follow.

If there was one thing of which Ford at first felt certain, it was that his taskmaster would have come in to the Club during that Thursday to look at least at the menu, and see that his orders were being obeyed. It would have been easier, simply because it would have shortened the list, if he could have thought it certain that the man would have dined there, but Ford did not feel that that was an assumption he could make. However, if he got a list of all those who were in the Club on that day, he would at least have eliminated those who had not been in; and if he were to continue getting a daily list of those who had come in, he would be able to eliminate more and more whenever a similar incident occurred. Ultimately he might even be able to pin it down to the one man.

The Whitehall Club, fortunately for him, had a slightly expensive habit which made the preparation of such a list possible. At the beginning of each year a large sheet was prepared containing the names of all the members in alphabetical order. This was printed and the copies made into a loose-leaf block so that the hall porter should have available one list for each day of the year on which he could quickly and readily, and, it was hoped, accurately, mark each member as he arrived or left, so that if anyone inquired if a particular member was in, or anyone was rung up on the telephone, the hall porter could instantly say whether the member was in the Club or not. It was the hall porter's pride that he knew all the thousand or so members by sight, and could put a name even to those country members who only came to London once a year. He also boasted that he never failed to mark in any of the stream of those who flowed in rapidly at lunch time.

The preparation of a daily list then would be perfectly possible.

Indeed Ford could have done it himself, except that he disliked personal energy, and to make someone else do it he considered required some explanation. One of the reasons why Ford could not manage men was that he always found it necessary to explain his motives to his subordinates.

But chance again came to his aid. It is one of the mysteries of club life that almost every club periodically has at least one fantastic member who systematically steals the books from the circulating library. The books from the permanent library go less often, a fact attributed by the cynical solely to the fact that there is nothing really desirable. Even so the story is told of one well-known club who found their volumes of the new edition of the *Encyclopaedia Britannica* disappearing gradually in irregular order, and to the hero of that theft a universal though grudging admiration had to be given.

In the Whitehall Club this theft had recently been peculiarly virulent. For many years the thief, or thieves, had been content with detective stories – an odd taste perhaps, but one which only cost the Club seven and six a time. When multiplied by fifty – one a week was the average – that was a sufficiently large sum to drive the honest members into a state of fury bordering on frenzy, but when the thief changed his literary tastes and started on expensive volumes of memoirs and travel books, it was generally felt that Something had to be Done about it; only nobody knew what. Of course Ford had no practical suggestions to offer. He seldom had.

But at least it gave a grand excuse for requiring a nominal roll of those in the Club each day.

On the Friday, however, he had somewhat of a shock. He was descending the staircase after tea when he heard Laming's bird-like voice.

'Brill Choisy. I really must talk to Ford. Halibut, dory, brill – round and round – all unfit human consumption.'

'Come, come, Laming. It's not as bad as that. And anyhow, you're the chairman of the Committee.'

'Maybe, maybe. Not got power over everything, though. Always is one of those, or lemon sole. Pity Ford doesn't like fish. Might see to it otherwise.'

'Really, I think you're a bit hard.'

'Well, what was there last night? You were dining here. I wasn't.'

'Let me see. Herrings, I think, and – yes, whiting.'

'Oh, cheap fish all the time though, you see. All for economy. Must be economical, I know. But all the same –'

The other member laughed.

'I could not help laughing at one bit of economy last night. So as to save having to give each of us a whole whiting, we had filleted scraps of whiting.'

Ford could hear Laming shuffle.

'Really, really. Most extraordinary. You're quite sure? Fillets, eh? Most odd. Food's going down. Shall have to exert myself. Won't do.'

He turned away from the menu so that he faced the stairs. Ford pretended that he was just coming down. If anyone who came in on Friday could inquire so easily about Thursday's menu – well, what was the use of his carefully prepared list? He had not thought of that before. And why was Laming so interested? Was there anything sinister in the phrase 'exert himself'? Ford pulled himself together and tried to remember the price of salmon, mullet, trout and other such things. There was no denying it. It had been a nasty shock.

Late that evening the whiting was mentioned for the last time.

It was with a feeling of slight nausea that Ford recognized the typing on the envelope. He looked at the envelope to see if the postmark gave him any help. As he suspected, the letter had been posted in the same district as the Club.

Once more the writer came straight to the point.

I appreciate the fillets. On the whole I had not thought you capable of such subtlety. You will obey – more or less, will you? Oh, no, my friend! You will *obey*. However, for the moment we will let it stand at that.

It has been great fun, by the way, watching you the last few days. That haunted expression whenever 'whiting' was mentioned, that leap in the air on the word 'fillet', the deep blush with which you received the word 'curled' – I only wish I could have stayed with you all day and watched your reaction to each occasion. But of course I had to limit my joy. Still, I managed to look at you sufficiently often to enjoy myself and, for the rest, I sat back in one of the less uncomfortable arm-chairs in – I will not tell you what part of the Club – and enjoyed myself. You poor little worm; it is superb to see you wriggle!

But you have been very wrong about one thing – you have not told that hard-faced doctor; at least I do not think you have. I have seen no signs of *his* wriggling, and that is a sight I am going to enjoy more than any. You are poor game, but Anstruther, I fancy, is a quarry worth hunting. As time goes on I shall make him do some very odd things. So see him soon.

And now to start putting the Club to rights.

First of all you will abolish those tea-trays; old, battered, noisy bits of tin, unfit even to sit on and use for sliding down hills. Those will go – gradually if you like, but you must make a start at once. Also those dreadful glass bottles with dirty white metal tops, in which you put the salt, will be abolished. Woolworth's would refuse to sell anything so tawdry; and while you are about it you might see that the tea is not so strong as to be impossible to drink. Then, do not be so stingy with the butter. There's a note in the suggestion book 'That the muffins for tea be buttered'. Just bear that in mind.

Ford put down the letter and snorted with rage.

'Well, aren't they? Not buttered, indeed! If I only knew who this brute was I'd butter his muffin all right for him. With the very best perchloride of mercury!'

He resumed reading the offensive typescript.

Now, in case you think you know your job, you shall now have a list of twelve simple little things that an efficient secretary would put right without having to be told – far less forced.

1. The strips of news from the tape machine will be put up in the right order.

2. Look at the billiards balls. One of them is a perfect cube, unspoilt by any curves.

3. There are calendars which show just the date and the month. Why not have the right date always – instead of just sometimes.

4. The clock in the smoking-room is generally two minutes fast – a fault on the right side, perhaps, but still a fault.

5. Have you ever tried to work out which switch turns on which light in the libraries? Why not connect them on some coherent plan.

6. I happen to know that one of the bishops who is a member was translated to another see ten days ago. Why not correct the list of members? For that matter the list in the card-room does not show that Morrison is dead – and you do know all about that, or nearly all. You

might also cease to state that somebody called James was elected in 1997.

7. Incredible though it may seem, there are still goose quill pens to be found in the Club. Have you ever listened to one being used? The squeak which they make on paper is bound to set everyone's nerves on edge. You will have these removed. It may annoy Pargiter – he uses them to irritate other people – but I cannot help that.

8. There should be a flag flown from the Club house on certain public occasions – His Majesty's birthday, and so on. A proper list should be drawn up and adhered to.

9. You will devise some reasonably efficient system whereby books taken out from the library are returned to their proper shelves. It is useless to expect the members to do it. No doubt they should, but they don't and they won't. The result is chaos.

10. You know those bronze ash-tray bowls for cigarette ends? They are supposed to contain water. Please see that they do. Otherwise cigarettes are left to burn, and when they have called attention to themselves by a most offensive smell, it is quite difficult to get at them to put them out. One of the bowls leaks. Have it mended, or, if this is impossible, removed.

11. The bell on the left-hand side of the fireplace in the card-room has not rung for two years. Have it put right.

12. Finally, reorganize your sub-committees. The Card Committee never come into the card-room. The Squash Committee do not play Squash, nor the Billiards Committee billiards. It is believed the Cigar Committee do not smoke, and anyhow never meet. The Wine Committee alone is carefully chosen. In other words stop drifting.

Now I know you will tell me that many of these things are not your duty. Perhaps; but it is your duty to see that they are done. Nos. 2, 5, 6, 7, and 11 you will see to at once. You will give the necessary instructions as to Nos. 1, 3, 4, and 10. As to Nos. 8 and 9, you will start getting your organization together. No. 12 will, I know, take time.

So much, then, for the preliminary details. I think I have written enough to prove to you your own incompetence. We will turn to more important matters later.

I shall expect to see much of this done at once, and the carrying out of my orders will be the best proof to me that you are being sensible, but as a further sign, you will sit on the settee in the smoking-room on the right of the notice of candidates proposed for election on Sunday from 1.45 to 2.0 p.m. If possible, you will get Anstruther to sit beside you.

By the time Ford had finished the letter he was in danger of apoplexy. To be insulted in this way was bad, but to be insulted without any chance of answering back was intolerable. It was the calm assumption that all these things were wrong that was so infuriating. He lit a cigarette in the hopes of calming himself, and puffed vigorously at it. None of these things were wrong! At least, he didn't think so.

Standing with his back to the fireplace he ticked them off.

'Tape machine – I talked to the page-boys only recently. Bother, it's a new boy. Billiards balls. Believe they're all right. Calendars. Nonsense! Switches. I got a sub-committee to consider that once, but the General Committee vetoed the expense. Score to me!'

He chucked his cigarette end into the brass container in front of him and considered the list more favourably. There was nothing that needed doing in all of it – at least, nothing serious. 'Alteration to list – very well. Wonder which bishop, though? There are several. Quill pens. All right. Flag. That means preparing a list. I shall quietly forget that. Books. Quite impossible. Perhaps a notice asking people to assist? Useless of course, but it might fill the bill. Cigarette ends.'

He glanced at the bronze bowl into which his own had been thrown. The next two minutes were spent in trying to stub it out with the end of a match. He folded the letter up and took the resolution that though perhaps there were some details which might be improved in the general high level of efficiency of his management, nevertheless, he would not be dictated to. By way of proving it, with unconscious irony, he sat down to write a letter.

Dear Dr Anstruther [best to be a trifle formal].

There is a slight repercussion arising from the unfortunate circumstances of Morrison's death, which I think it is important I should talk over with you.

I must apologize for troubling a busy man, but the call of duty, you know! I wonder if you happen to be lunching in the Club on Sunday? I believe you often do. If so you will find me in the smoking-room – about a quarter to two.

Curiously enough, as you will see, the time is relevant.

                                    Yours sincerely,
                                        Leonard Ford.

CHAPTER 9

ON THE SETTEE

*

CLUBLAND is comparatively empty on a Sunday. But if the population is small, it is extremely regular and frequently quite different from that which is there on a weekday. The arrival of Cardonnel, for instance, to lunch on Sunday would have created a small sensation of about the same dimensions as would have been caused by his absence on a weekday.

With a sense of suppressed excitement Ford looked round the coffee-room. Anstruther was present, lunching as usual quietly behind a book, but the remaining half dozen members, Ford was certain, knew nothing, and cared less, as to Morrison's fate. He could check the matter from his lists, but he believed that not one of them had been in the Club except on a Sunday for the past three weeks. So whoever it was who wanted to see that the secretary was sitting on the settee would have to show himself, and with the aid of those lists in Ford's pocket, must become incredibly conspicuous.

'Leonard, my boy, you're in luck at last!' the poor harassed man confided to the mint sauce. 'They say every criminal makes one mistake, and now this fellow has made his. He's chosen an incredibly stupid moment, and you're bound to find out who he is. Then surely you ought to be able to think of something! Come to think of it, though, it's odd the fellow should have selected such a very stupid time.'

But if the coffee-room had been thinly populated, the smoking-room was completely deserted. Ford found himself sitting on the prescribed settee surveying an empty room, while slowly the hands of the clock ticked round to a quarter to two.

A couple of minutes later Anstruther came in and glanced first at the clock and then at his watch.

'Sorry if I've kept you waiting. Clock seems to be fast.'

To his annoyance Ford found that his own watch agreed with Anstruther's. He had meant to speak to the man who wound and regulated the clocks about that particular one, but somehow it had slipped his memory. He was annoyed too to find that he had got slightly red in the face about it.

'Time's before us,' he murmured tritely.

Anstruther came straight to the point.

'What do you want to see me about?'

It was not Ford's way to come so very directly to business. Nevertheless he managed without much fuss to produce both the letters. The doctor read them carefully and returned them without speaking a word; during the whole time the expression on his face never varied.

The silence was broken by Ford.

'Well?'

'Fairly well – yes.'

The secretary was surprised. He had expected Anstruther to take up one of two attitudes. He might well have shown alarm. After all, the situation was an even worse one for the doctor. But Ford's chief fear was that Anstruther, whom he believed to be a strong-minded man, would have taken up the line of 'let the fellow do his worst'; and, while between them they might have managed to bluff their way through, there was a risk, a very great risk, and Ford preferred safety. The committee they probably would be able to manage, but supposing the blackmailer went to the police and Morrison was exhumed? Even if it was ultimately found that he did die of heart failure, it would be a nasty scandal.

'If only we knew what he did die of,' he groaned aloud.

'Precisely. We should know the time then.'

'The time?'

'How long we have to wait.'

Ford looked puzzled.

'With every day that passes this fellow's hold on us gets less. If we knew what poison it was, I could tell you pretty accurately when exhumation would be safe. Meanwhile – play for time.'

'I see. Just deal with these little points sufficiently to satisfy him.'

'No.' Anstruther seemed annoyed at Ford's stupidity. Once before he had to stop him from being a chatterbox; now he had to prevent his being a fool. 'Much the best way is implicit obedience, so long as it is possible, and it probably will be. The man won't be so stupid as to drive you to desperation. After all, why not try to run the Club efficiently?'

'Well, really. I had an impression I did.' The more that Ford became convinced that criticism was justified, the more bitterly he resented it.

'Look at the list he gives you. So far as I know they are all true. Look at that clock, for instance. And this tray my coffee's on.' He pointed to two dents and several places where the paint had peeled off.

Silence fell for a moment while Ford swallowed his anger as best he might. Outside, the Sunday calm was broken only by an occasional omnibus passing close to the windows of the smoking-room.

Ford surveyed the bus angrily.

'So like the Crown to have put up our rent one day and then altered the traffic rules the next, so that buses stop immediately outside our windows and make this room nearly uninhabitable.'

'Yes. And so like you to have let them.'

'Like me. Why, what on earth could I have done about it?'

After a few seconds' consideration Anstruther agreed to the justice of this. Once more silence fell, broken only by the noise of the coffee tray which, being dented at the bottom, did not lie quite flat. Consequently, when the coffee-pot was picked up, the other end settled down with a slight clang and when it was put down, the motion was reversed, spilling some of the coffee into the saucer.

As the hands of the clock approached two, Ford's eyes became glued to the door. If the writer of the letter was to receive his sign, he must come in soon. Two minutes to two, and nothing had happened. One minute to, and still nothing. As the clock on the mantelpiece was striking two the door slowly opened. Ford half rose from the settee. A page-boy came slowly in and put coal on the fire. Then he crossed the room towards them and inquired if he should remove the coffee tray. As the door closed behind him silence reigned once more. It was broken at last by Ford. 'Just half a minute more; I'd forgotten that clock was fast.'

'For what?'

'For him to come in and see us here.'

Anstruther smiled.

'I don't imagine the man is quite so simple as that. He probably walked past the window some time ago, or perhaps went by on a bus. In fact that's almost certainly right. Here, come with me.'

With that he got up and walked out of the Club. The bus stop was not far round the corner. In silence he went to the top of the bus and took two penny tickets. As the bus went slowly past the Club smoking-room, the settee on which they had been sitting became plainly visible. Indeed it was the only part of the room where faces could have been easily recognized. He turned to Ford.

'You see,' was his only comment.

But his companion was red in the face.

'What fools we are! Who was that pretending to pick up a newspaper in the room? Somebody arrived, just too late, to see us. He won't know we've been there. And we've just missed seeing him. We've failed to catch him and he won't be satisfied. And all because you hurried us out.' He looked reproachfully at the doctor.

Anstruther smiled quietly.

'Now I wonder what is worrying you most? I should like to think that you were taking my good advice and were prepared to do just what you are told – within reason. But, as a matter of fact, I think you're wrong. After his remarks about the clock being fast, your friend would never have been late.' Abruptly he said 'Good-bye' and got up.

Before Ford had time to answer, the doctor was down the steps and disappearing round the corner. The secretary shrugged his shoulders and let him go. Then, making his way back, he interviewed the smoking-room waiter. So far as Johnson, the waiter in question, knew, no one had gone into the smoking-room since Ford had gone out; but then he had not been in there, and certainly no one had rung.

'But then, sir, I always hear footsteps going down the passage and generally go to see if anything is wanted. And I didn't hear anyone. Of course, sir, some members move more quietly than others.'

There was nothing for it but to nod and go. A good servant to the Club, Johnson – and so, thought Ford truculently, they all were. If this fellow tried to cause trouble about the staff, he really would have to put his foot down. For if Ford was lazy, he had the redeeming virtue of being loyal.

He went back to the smoking-room and found it still empty. Who had appeared just while he was out? He found himself looking round the room for possible hiding places. There were none – unless the fellow had concealed himself by crouching down behind an arm-chair in the far corner? It hardly seemed possible – and yet he wondered. He got down on his hands and knees to see, and then found himself trying to invent some plausible reason which might explain why he was there to Pargiter, who had just come in. In the end his suggestion that he was looking to see if the carpet was worn gave that gentleman an excellent opportunity to use his eyebrows and congratulate him on his energy on looking after every detail.

'And I hear, too, we are to have a new set of billiards balls.'

'Who told you, sir?' Ford was all eagerness.

'Now why this interest? I fancy it was the billiards-marker.'

His hopes dashed again, Ford started off to check up the list of the twelve points. He was quite sure his letter writer would not have been so foolish as to have hidden behind that chair at any rate. Anstruther was right. There was nothing for it but to fall in for the time being with all demands. He spent the Sunday afternoon making a very overdue inspection. It was not, however, until nearly tea time that he found which ash-tray leaked, but eventually he discovered it in the corridor outside the non-smoking library.

Standing in the iciest draught in that room he handed it over to Hughes with orders to see that it was mended. He was well aware it was not the waiter's business, but he was not quite sure how to set about it himself. Hughes looked at it doubtfully, and remembered that only a couple of days before, Benson had been complaining that the secretary was trying to run the Club. He suggested handing the offending bowl over to the steward.

Ford, gazing at the tops of the passing buses, wearily agreed. Anstruther was right. They must have been seen from a bus. A sound fellow, Anstruther, if a little abrupt and a little unkind in his comments. Best to do what he told him. Obey Anstruther, obey this letter-writing man – easiest course in the end. Comforting himself with the futile remark that it would all be the same thing a hundred years hence, he went up to his own room. A short snooze before dinner would be pleasant after such a busy day. It was, after all, Sunday.

CHAPTER 10

A QUIET RUBBER

*

"TAKE some sherry, and pass it on, would you?' Cardonnel had gathered three of his legal friends from the Club to dine with him and enjoy a quiet rubber of bridge. Not contract, which Cardonnel's live mind would have preferred, but auction, owing to the prejudices of Skinner, the County Court judge sitting on his left. His Honour had stated that auction was a gentleman's game, but contract was not. Nobody had thought of a sufficiently polite rejoinder as yet. Besides, Judge Skinner's game had been described as 'a triumph of hope over experience', and with him as a partner contract might have been too exciting. Apart from anything else, he was far too absent-minded ever to remember which suit was trumps.

Opposite to his host, Gladwin the K.C., who was generally regarded as having turned one of the best of juniors into one of the least successful of K.C.s when he took silk, sipped his sherry attentively.

'This seems familiar; isn't it the one we used to have on at the Club?'

'Let me see if I know before you answer,' put in the fourth man.

He took a little and put his head on one side, an attitude which is recognized to help greatly in the proper appreciation of wine.

'I think Gladwin's right, though I should never have spotted it myself.'

'Quite right,' Cardonnel purred. He liked his guests to take an intelligent interest in their wine. 'I got in some when the Club put it on to the wine list, many years ago now. Shan't pay the new one the same compliment, though.'

'No. Too sweet for me.' The Judge shook his head wisely.

As a mere solicitor, Knight, his opposite neighbour, did not like to express his opinion too freely. Privately he thought the new Club sherry a trifle bitter. He compromised by remarking that it was not a patch on the old one.

'I can't help thinking that Ford made rather a fool of himself.

Didn't he ignore the Wine Committee and follow the advice of self-appointed experts?'

The Judge, who considered himself an expert, but whom Ford had failed to consult, agreed heartily that the wrong experts had been consulted.

'Sauce with your turbot, Skinner?' Cardonnel scented slightly dangerous ground.

'What I can't make out is what's come over Ford these last few days.' Gladwin helped himself to salt. 'He seems to be an absolute bundle of nerves.'

'In what way?'

'Well, Laming was talking to me about the fish the other day, and I admit we were both grumbling a bit. As it happened, Ford overheard it. Sorry, of course; wouldn't talk at a man on purpose. All the same I was amazed to see how upset Ford was about it.'

'Perhaps,' suggested the Judge, 'it was because Laming's the chairman this year.'

'May have been. I must say I do think that while he *is* the chairman, he might keep his complaints to himself, or say them straight to Ford. Rather a bad show, grousing to me or any other member.'

'Quite right. Never did think much of that twittering little Laming. So like the Civil Service.'

The three other legal heads nodded in agreement with Skinner.

'But just come back to Ford,' Cardonnel came in. 'I think Gladwin's quite right. He has been very odd the last ten days.'

'Ever since Morrison died,' put in Knight.

Cardonnel gave him a sharp glance and continued: 'Yes. Especially the last few days. He's in a state of nervous activity instead of being his usual self. I like Ford. He's courteous and obliging, but all the same I have always thought he was a bit lazy, and I must admit I have occasionally seen to it that he stayed awake.' (A smile passed over the faces of the other three – Cardonnel's little ways were well known.) 'But the last few days his temper has been thin – which is unusual. He has been very touchy, which is strange, too, and he's been going round and round the Club looking at all the tiny points and trying to find out what was wrong and put it right, which is definitely odd.'

'Why odd?' The judicial mind disliked being hurried.

'Because it's so unlike his character. He's usually placid, urbane and all that sort of thing. Not exactly tactful, because he's trying to be too tactful, but the kind of man who always agrees with you, because he hasn't got the courage to disagree, and then does nothing about it; always putting off all the awkward things until another day and never facing a difficulty squarely. And now he's running like a bull at a red rag at all sorts of things. Wants the Committee to have new tea-trays of some artistic pattern; [the Judge snorted] and he's even trying to reorganize the Card Committee. Some more saddle, Knight? There's only a savoury coming.'

'No, thanks. I know the size and excellence of your savouries.'

'Nor for me, thank you. Just in parenthesis what is this Burgundy? Apologies for being so inquisitive all through about my drink.'

'No need to apologize.' Cardonnel smiled at the K.C. 'I like people to take an interest in what they are drinking, as you know. It's a Chambertin 1923. Bit young yet, I'm afraid.'

'Not a bit. It's magnificent.' The Judge looked at it with increased respect and tried to disguise the fact that he had not been considering it properly up to that moment. He took advantage in the turn of the conversation to refill his glass and look wise while he drank it. Then he fixed the solicitor with his well-known glare. 'Granted that the man is behaving a bit peculiarly, as Cardonnel tells us, why did you say just now "Ever since Morrison died"?'

Cardonnel echoed the query. 'Yes, why? I meant to ask you too. Thank you, Skinner.'

'Oh, just, I don't know. Nothing special. Only that it was a day or so after that, that like you, I began to notice the change. I suppose it's only a coincidence.'

'I wonder,' Gladwin said quietly.

'Why, surely you don't suggest –?' Skinner looked at him severely.

'No, I'm suggesting nothing.'

'Well, do you mean that it just gave him a bad shake-up?'

'Perhaps that was all I meant.'

'Well, I really can't see why because a fellow dies of heart failure in a Club, it should make the secretary object to someone criticizing the fish. Still less why it should make him change the composition of the Card Committee.'

Cardonnel laughed, and with a half pleading look at Gladwin to let the old man have his way, suggested some more mush-rooms. These being a particular weakness of the Judge's, he conveniently, and apparently genuinely, forgot that he had had any at all and helped himself to a further generous double helping. The suggestion had the additional advantage of causing the subject to be changed to that of food. It is difficult to say which is the best theme for conversation, food or drink, for while the remarks which can be made about drinks are of a more cultured nature, and the very mention of a good wine is a pleasure, there is more variety in what can be said about food, if less subtlety. Perhaps only such a man as Cardonnel would have tried to combine the best of both by saying that the Cox's apples of 1934 were the best he had known since 1911, and during that year he had to admit he had been in a part of Hereford where the drought had not been severe.

And so, inevitably, though for once at the end instead of the beginning of dinner, the conversation turned on the weather. When at about a quarter to twelve the party broke up, his guests were prepared to agree that if Cardonnel was a bit too sharp sometimes, he certainly made a most perfect host, and even the terrors of the Judge's bridge were worth facing for so pleasant an evening.

Catching his host's eye, Gladwin stayed behind on the excuse of a final drink.

'Help yourself,' murmured the ever hospitable Cardonnel.

'No, thanks. All I want, thank you. I fancied, though, you wanted to say something.'

'Yes. I thought you had something on your mind really about Morrison, but very wisely didn't say it to Skinner.'

'You're quite right. I had, but, dear old boy though the Judge is, there are moods when it is best not to argue with him, or really to tell him too much.'

Cardonnel smiled and waited for Gladwin to go on.

'I used to know Morrison fairly well. I didn't like him and I didn't want to know him. In fact I did my best to avoid him, but he was never rude to me, and apart from trying to escape, I had no reason to be offensive. After all, one must show common civility.' Gladwin seemed almost to be apologizing.

'Tiresome for you, no doubt, but all the same, of course you had to.'

'It certainly was tiresome. Anyone other than Morrison would have realized that I didn't want him, but he seemed impervious, and the more I edged off, the more he would talk. I suppose he was lonely.'

'I think he was. I don't believe he had a friend in the world. Did anyone go to his funeral?'

'No idea. Anyhow, he used to confide his sorrows to me a bit. Mostly little personal bits of spite – very dull and sordid. I used to suffer abysses of boredom when he caught me. He's often driven me out of the Club. But the one subject that was most dreadful of all was his health. He suffered, according to himself, from every known disease – *except that his heart was perfectly good.*'

'And yet he died of heart failure!' Cardonnel whistled.

'Precisely.'

'He may have been wrong, though?'

'Undoubtedly he might. I am sure he did not have half the things he thought he had, so it is quite likely that he had in fact got the one thing he thought he had not. That's why I have said nothing.'

'I don't quite see how you could have said anything. *Was* Anstruther his doctor, by the way?'

'Yes, I think so. He certainly attended him once, because I remember Morrison telling me that though he loathed the sight of him, he was at least certain he could keep his mouth shut. He went on to make the most unwarranted – and dull – comments on the medical profession.'

'Well, if that is so, it seems to me there is nothing we can do or say.'

'No, except keep our ears and eyes open.'

Cardonnel grinned. He was perfectly aware of his own character.

'That is a thing I always do. I find it – entertaining.' The last word was thrown out, almost a question, as if the speaker was in search of the exact adjective, and was not quite sure he had obtained it.

CHAPTER 11

'PALMER'

*

THE sitting-room of Anstruther's flat near Wigmore Street led out of his consulting room. Like its owner, it was a severe room. Each end was covered by a long bookcase, one containing medical books only, the other standard works of literature. There was some fiction included, but nothing light, little even that contained much humour. Apparently his favourite type of novel was by authors such as Henry James, Meredith, Louis Couperus, Hardy in his most analytical mood, while Dickens was considered frivolous, and Scott too elementary.

On the right of the door was a small gas fire giving out far too little heat in view of the two foot or so by which the large window opposite had been opened. Despite the slight fog of the winter evening, the curtains were not drawn across it, and the papers on the desk below were inclined to blow about. Ignoring such comfort as was offered by a not very inviting arm-chair, the doctor was sitting at the desk reading a letter.

He turned it over, glanced at the end, and then pressed a bell by his side.

'How did this arrive?' He held up the envelope.

'I found it in the letter box, sir, about half past four. By hand, I suppose, sir, but I heard no ring.'

'I see. Thank you.'

He returned to reading the letter. When Ford received letters from this correspondent, they came through the post, because, of course, clubs do not have convenient letter boxes. Apparently, however, the blackmailer was sufficiently economical to save the three halfpence where possible. A slight point in his character which might help to trace him.

Sardonically he received the blackmailer's congratulations on his having had the good sense to sit quietly on the required settee for the whole quarter of an hour and not move away until after two o'clock. It had made it easier, so his correspondent informed him, to see from outside. All this was interesting. He had guessed at the time, more or less, from where he would have been observed. With the slightly bored air of one who expected something better, he let the first page flutter down on to the desk and started on the next. Here he was glad to see the man was coming to the point.

And now to tell you exactly where you come in.

Of course I do not deny that you are very useful in keeping Ford in order. There is no limit to the possible folly of fools, and a sensible man to keep him on the straight path of obedience is undoubtedly useful. Firstly, then, you will make quite sure that you see all letters that I write to him. On second thoughts, perhaps, it would be best if I sent you a carbon copy by hand.

So it was the postage! With a barely audible chuckle, Anstruther went on reading.

I wish I knew more about you as a doctor. I have been making discreet inquiries as to your abilities as a matter of fact, but nobody seems to know much about your particular bent. Is this professional etiquette, I wonder? Or ignorance? Or are you in fact incapable of doing anything in particular and conceal your incompetence under a cloak of silence, and an air of extreme wisdom?

'I wish he'd mind his own business and not talk so much,' Anstruther muttered.

I hope at least you are fairly expert in the matter of poisons. If you are, well and good. If you are not, you will set to work at once to read up the subject, a most useful one professionally, since that is how you are going to be useful to me.

You see this Morrison business has intrigued me. Apparently it is possible to poison a man and get away with it, provided one has a complacent and helpful doctor handy. And if one murder can be managed, why not others? I am sure an occasion will one day arrive when the ability to do so will be useful.

But for the immediate future, I am not so ambitious. Have you, by the way, ever read a novel of Stevenson's called *The Wrong Box*? I fear it is too light for your taste. Anyhow, there is an admirable reflexion of Michael Finsbury's, 'Anything to give pain', which I have adopted as my motto. Like him also, I shall probably only consider driving to Scotland Yard without, I hope, actually going.

To give pain to you, to Ford, to anyone, mentally or physically, that is one kind of amusement, and on the whole the mental form gives the most refined, the most exquisite pleasure; but it is a little difficult to arrange daily. The giving, then, of mere physical pain can also be used as a substitute. And here you, with the knowledge you have or soon will have, will be useful. A little something to be slipped on to a plate, or into a glass or a cup, and I shall see some normally unpleasantly healthy man giving the most amazing exhibition, all the more intense because he is so unused to pain; and then on top of that there will be a suspicion of carelessness in the kitchen – after the perchloride of mercury neither you nor Ford will welcome inquiry – and there will be the added pleasure of seeing what arises from that.

So you see I shall want to know several good poisons. A suitable one for killing somebody perhaps, easy to administer and hard to detect, although of course, as you will fake the death certificate, that will not be so important. And another with which to hurt strong, healthy people. Here I shall not have the advantage of having you to shield me, so it had better be something which might reasonably occur in food, and something not likely to be fatal.

On this kind of point, I shall require you to coach me, and remember, please, that your safety will depend just as much as mine on your keeping quiet. Quite how you are to communicate with me, I have not decided, nor how you are to convey the various ingredients that we may jointly decide that I shall require, but that I shall settle later. By the way, I do not insist on your using expensive drugs. You will know best, too, what you can get most easily.

'Thank you,' murmured Anstruther, with grave irony.

For the moment then, you will merely start to read (if necessary) and be prepared to write. Perhaps you will be good enough to convey to me your acquiescence in this matter through what I believe to be the usual channel in these matters, the personal column of *The Times*. Sign your message 'Palmer' after our old friend from Rugeley – an admirable man, in advance of his time, but a bungler. I leave the exact wording to you. There is no need as in the case of your colleague, Ford, to leave nothing to the imagination.

Rather sadly Anstruther got up and prepared to go out. There was just time to reach *The Times* sub-office in Regent Street.

'What I object to most,' he said, 'is being bracketed with Palmer.'

He walked steadily down towards Piccadilly Circus, and with no sign that he was doing anything unusual, or was under the influence of any particular emotion, took the proffered sheet of paper and wrote 'Fillets to you, Palmer'. Then, after a moment's consideration he tore it up and substituted 'Fried and curled within reason'. Attaching the same signature he pocketed such change as he got and went on down to the Club, more surprised on the whole at his lapse into the humorous in the wording, than at having sent the message at all.

In his opinion one thing was very unfair. His correspondent economized on stamps, but expected him to choose a very expensive way of writing. 'At any rate,' he thought as he went up to the secretary's office, 'I don't see why Ford shouldn't pay half the cost of advertising – and of drugs, for that matter.'

CHAPTER 12

UNUSUAL ACTIVITY

*

THERE is no more popular target for abuse than the committee of a club. It would be worse than inaccurate, it would be dull, to belong to a club, or for that matter to any other society, and admit that it was at all times perfectly managed. If a body of angels, endowed with perfect wisdom and all the gold wherewith the streets of Heaven are paved, were to take over the government of the country, they would undoubtedly be defeated at the next election, but if they took over the management of a club, all the members would resign out of pure boredom.

So then, complaint being necessary, it is essential to find someone on whom to put the blame, since, after a while, the attribution of every moral and social failing to an abstract 'they' becomes unsatisfying. To be the butt of such criticism is one of the main duties of a club secretary, but since he must, if he is to remain sane, have someone behind whom to shield, a committee is selected annually.

Not, of course, that they really manage the club. It has, in fact, never been discovered who does. Perhaps, after all, it is really the page-boys, the only people who have been a sufficiently short while in the institution to retain ambition, even of a local nature. There was once even a boy who delivered a telephone message correctly, but he went off and joined the Royal Corps of Signals, and never did such a thing again.

But as to the Committee there are various accepted axioms. First, it is assumed that they are a narrow, self-electing and self-elected clique. Secondly, they are known to desire to control the club for some sinister if undefined purpose, which may be love of power, self-assertiveness, a desire to thwart their fellow members, or merely a constitutional inability to mind their own business, but anyhow is very obscure and very wrong. Thirdly, it is recognized that they wish to run the club as badly as possible.

It is none of it, of course, in the slightest degree true, but it serves as an admirable *point d'appui* from which to let loose pet stalking horses. Moreover those on the Committee forget that they held such views before they joined that august if reviled body. They forget, too, that in a few years' time they will hold them again.

Of course in fact nothing of any real importance occurs at a committee meeting. You cannot expect twenty-four people to meet together and arrive at a sensible decision; the number is far too high. The proceedings, therefore, are in the nature of a formality.

In the Whitehall Club the meeting was usually opened by the reading of some highly complicated figures as to coffee-room receipts which included the average sum spent per head both at lunch and at dinner. As this included sums spent on entertaining guests, it was generally a little higher than the ordinary member spent on his own entertainment. The Committee were therefore able to start the meeting with a virtuous feeling that they were not doing themselves too well, but with little other information.

The next item was the reading out of the 'backed' bills, the recognized method by which members would express complaint or even gratification about the food. These invariably were referred to the secretary to refer to the chef, or perhaps the steward, or the head waiter, which Ford, with his customary desire to avoid trouble, generally neglected to do. However, a little amusement could always be derived by trying to guess the identity of the writer.

At this point, Laming, during his year of office, usually tried to declare the meeting closed. Otherwise – who knew? – someone might go and propose something, and before you knew where you were a decision might have to be made and responsibility taken.

On this day, early in December, however, he was not so lucky. He cleared his throat, and in his reedy, tenor voice began:

'Well, gentlemen, if that is all – you have read the minutes, Ford? – yes, well then –'

The pause given by the question about the minutes had been fatal. Cardonnel had come to the meeting without having quite made up his mind – an unusual state of affairs with him. If Laming had closed the meeting promptly, he might have remained silent, but during the momentary check, decision came to him.

'I am afraid, Mr Chairman, there is a point I wish to raise.'

A sigh went round the meeting. Cardonnel's points so frequently were unanswerable.

'A great many things seem to be being done in the Club without the authority of the Committee.'

Laming, glancing round the faces at the table, saw that this was not a matter to be brushed aside lightly. The Committee were quite prepared to let things be done in fact without their authority, but not in theory.

'Such as?' he queried.

'Well, first, this rather peculiar notice which I found in the library. May I read it?'

Barely waiting for silence to imply assent, he went on: '"In view of the difficulty which is occasioned by books being inadvertently returned to the wrong shelves, members are requested to hand volumes they have finished with" – I shudder at the grammar, Mr Chairman – "to the librarian or the library waiter." Apart from the fact that I have yet to be convinced that Hughes, our excellent library waiter, is any more capable than I am of returning a book to its proper place, I should like to know on whose authority that notice was put up.'

Ford turned a little red. It would have been a little difficult to explain how his hand had been forced.

'I will certainly take the notice down and reword it if Mr Cardonnel would assist me, sir.'

Cardonnel was a little annoyed that the secretary should think that he could be deceived by so transparent a red-herring. He returned to the charge.

'But has this Committee decided that a notice of such a kind should be put up?'

'Mr Cardonnel is quite right, sir. I thought the matter was too trivial to trouble the Committee with. *De minimis non curat lex,* you know, sir.'

'But Cardonnel, though a lawyer, does care, Ford. Your quotation's misleading,' came good-humouredly from the far end of the table.

Seeing his chance, Laming took his opportunity.

'Well, well. Don't want to fetter initiative. Quite right, though –

put point in order. Authorize notice now? Perhaps, Cardonnel, you would help draft? Well, gentlemen, if that is all –?'

'Sorry, Mr Chairman, but there is a further matter.'

This was really getting annoying! Laming openly looked at his watch.

'I have an appointment quite shortly, Cardonnel.'

The remark was unfortunate. Cardonnel was the mildest and kindest of men when it came to realities, but it was always advisable to let him go about things in his own way. The attempt to stifle discussion merely served to rouse his blood.

'I'm sorry,' he remarked acidly, 'that you thought it unnecessary to allot more than so very short a period of your time to the affairs of the Club. I know our meetings are often brief, perhaps too brief, but just occasionally things do arise. However, sorry though we shall be to miss your guidance, perhaps the vice-chairman –'

'Well, well, perhaps can manage.' Laming became more jerky than ever. 'Short time more. Your point is?'

'I hear that arrangements are being made to do away with the tea-trays in the Club and replace them with wooden ones, said to be more artistic and less noisy. I am by no means certain to be opposed to such a project. There is much to be said against the old ones; in fact I consider them a disgrace to the Club; but again I ask, Mr Chairman, under whose authority this expense is being incurred, or who has decided upon the new pattern? I do not think the House and Furnishing Sub-Committee has met. I might say I do not think it has met for several years.'

At the mention of the word 'expense' every man sitting round the table stirred slightly. It is an established tradition in the minds of all such Englishmen, vaguely associated in their minds with Magna Carta, Simon de Montfort, and the British Constitution, that the control of expenditure cannot be devolved. Even Laming looked a little reproachfully at Ford. After all, why should he worry to try to defend what appeared to be a little peccadillo of the secretary's? Especially as apparently such a defence would not even gain time.

For a moment there was silence. Then Ford hurriedly tried to explain the matter away. No decision, of course, had been reached. He fully realized that it was one on which he could not act by himself, but he had received numerous complaints about the trays, and so he was merely getting a few samples just to let the Committee see. No question of expense was yet involved.

'But at least one is in use. I saw it yesterday.' A hitherto silent member spoke.

'Oh, yes – yes. A free sample – just to see. An ounce of practice, you know, sir, is worth –' His voice trailed off, the rest of the sentence having deserted him. He could only think of 'a pint of theory' which he was sure was wrong. Privately he hoped he could withdraw the other three trays he had issued, and with luck nobody would find the rest of the dozen in his office. If the Committee approved in the end all would be well. If not, he would have to pay for them himself. So much for doing what he was told too readily! Once more he vowed not to give way so easily to all and sundry. There was, however, no more chance of his keeping the vow than there had been in the past.

'Quite, quite. No expense as yet, you see, Cardonnel. Examine the sample after use at our next meeting. Agreed? Good. Well, gentlemen, if that is all –'

'I hear a rumour, Mr Chairman' – another member had plucked up sufficient courage to make himself slightly conspicuous – 'that the composition of the sub-committees is to be reconsidered.'

'Nothing so definite as that. Ford raised the point with me. Sounded a few people. Nothing decided.'

With alarm Laming noticed that Cardonnel was turning over the pages of the Club bye-laws. The combination was invariably ominous.

'I much regret, Mr Chairman, that according to Bye-Law 43 such a reorganization is impossible. You see it stated there that certain Sub-Committees must be elected annually by the Committee from amongst its members, power being given to add other gentlemen belonging to the Club who are not on the Committee – obviously where technical advice is required. But you see we only have power to elect them annually; we have no power to change them in the middle of the year. Of course we can put on additional members, I presume.'

'Besides, Mr Chairman,' the bald-headed man who had raised the point continued, 'that annual election takes place early in the spring –'

'May,' murmured Ford.

'Well, in the spring. Why worry till then?'

'Quite agree, quite agree. Point merely being considered. No action being taken. Well, gentlemen, if that is all –?'

At last Laming had had his way; the meeting was closed. He deliberately walked out with Cardonnel, anxious to restore peace after the slight acerbity which had arisen.

'Ford getting very active these days. Quite unlike him. Proposing all sorts of new things. Vigorous, too – all sorts of details. Odd, very.'

Cardonnel looked surreptitiously at the little bald-headed man bobbing along beside him. He agreed with him both as to present energy and past lack of it, but he somehow felt that it was slightly bad form for the chairman to be so ready to disparage the secretary. He left him as soon as possible. All the same he was puzzled. What was the cause of this sudden burst of activity? His nose wrinkled as he made his way through Covent Garden towards New Square. He seemed to be snuffing up the scent of something other than oranges.

Two other members of the Committee were walking away together.

'Do you suppose,' said one of them, 'that it is possible to imagine a worse chairman than Laming?'

'Difficult, I should think. Tactless. Anxious to avoid responsibility. And that perpetual effort to stifle all discussion and close the meeting at once.'

'I know. Some chairmen let people like Cardonnel talk on for ever, but Laming never lets anyone say anything.'

'Afraid of anything coming up. And I don't think he quite plays the game by Ford, either.'

'Which is his worst crime. When you think of the sort of people who have been chairmen in the past. The Whitehall has usually had the good luck to get hold of absolutely first-class men; it's bad luck that one of our three years should be with this fellow.'

'I agree. If Ford, by the way, is trying to do a job of work, which I must admit is a bit of a change, I'm all for backing him, despite Laming, and for that matter despite Cardonnel.'

'Oh, Cardonnel's all right really. He just has to have things done the right way or he won't look at them. Ever been to dinner with him? No? Well, do, if you get the chance. It's a little precise and formal, and perhaps unoriginal, but you always get good food, the exactly right concomitants and the wine that goes correctly with it. In the same way in life the details have to be right for Cardonnel, but the main idea's right too. He'll keep Ford up to the scratch, and perhaps worry the life out of him, but he'll get the right thing done in the end. You know, but for him, the Committee would have no say in the running of the Club at all.'

The other nodded.

'Perhaps you're right. And as to getting things done, it's more than I'd say for Laming.'

CHAPTER 13

THE PARTING OF THE WAYS

*

STANDING in the street, his bowler hat in need of being brushed, and tilted slightly too far forward, Ford looked at the club of which he was secretary. It had never occurred to him before to look at it from outside, either physically or mentally. He came to the conclusion that it needed cleaning. For a moment he had a vision of scaffolding covering the long, shallow building, and jets of steam playing all over it until it emerged almost white.

'But only for a week or two,' he reflected sadly, 'and anyhow, as usual, we can't afford it.'

In his own opinion, Ford was a very economical manager, but in his own opinion alone. His only real idea was to put off spending any money until the last possible moment. He then usually found that double the amount had become necessary. As to buying in the cheapest market, it never entered his philosophy. He bought in the easiest market or let someone else do the buying – on their terms.

But mentally he was trying for the first time in his life to see the institution as a whole, trying to visualize what sort of an appearance it must present to the outside world. People – especially his female relatives – he had found, had very odd ideas about clubs. They thought they were places of the highest luxury and considerable extravagance. Well, there were clubs where you could get the best of everything and where money was apparently not considered, but the Whitehall, like many others, was not that sort of place. Its ambition was to provide something as near as possible resembling the kind of home to which its members were accustomed, at the lowest possible price. It was, for instance, rather proud of the fact that its set club dinners cost only three shillings, so that its members could justly tell their wives that if they dined at the Club, they were not being extravagant.

It was, moreover, a very friendly institution. If you wanted solitude and quiet, you could, as Anstruther did, obtain it, but if you wanted companionship, that too, after your first few visits, could be obtained. On the whole, Ford liked an extraordinarily high percentage of the members – extraordinary because, though nearly all the members were likeable, as in fact they were, yet as the secretary, Ford was bound to see their worst side.

Standing in the street, and trying to recollect all his grievances, all the moments when people had been most unkind to the staff (an action which he never could stand), all the occasions on which they had been most trying and irrational and vexatious, he could hardly think of any whom he would gladly even contemplate handing over in the way which Anstruther apparently was prepared to surrender them to the mercies of some unknown person, who was clearly a sadist and who would enjoy giving pain for its own sake. He shook his head. Perhaps, on the whole, there were none. Not even – a face, sneeringly polite, presented itself to him – no, none. He could not understand it.

Not only could he not understand the mentality of his correspondent – he did not expect to fathom that; in fact he was glad he could not – but he also found Anstruther incomprehensible. In his heart of hearts, Ford knew that he himself was a weak man, but he had thought that the doctor was a strong one, and yet apparently Anstruther had fallen in with the orders of the blackmailer quite as readily, if not more readily, than he had; moreover was falling in by doing things which Ford believed he never would have done.

'Though so far I have not been asked to do anything that it has been really against my conscience to do. A few minor improvements in the Club – things I might have consented to do anyhow, though perhaps I should not have worried about, and certainly should not have hurried so much over. In which case I should have had less trouble about them. Heigh-ho,' he solaced himself with an original reflexion, 'it's a weary world.'

'But the worst of it is, this business is not over yet. It's all very well for me to say that I should not have been so ready to do what Anstruther did, but I have not been asked as yet.'

His mind went back to the scene a few evenings before when the doctor had arrived in his office and told him what he had put in the personal column of *The Times*. He had tried to express his

horror and amazement at the readiness with which Anstruther
was falling into line.

'But you aren't going to do what he says?'

'Possibly.'

'But – but, are you going to help him to torture people, and
even possibly kill people?'

'Well, I don't know that it will come to that. I'm playing for
time.'

'But if once you give him any poison, you can never be free of
him.'

'Only if he can prove I gave him the poison – and he won't be
able to. At least, not without giving himself away.'

'But – but how do you propose to gain time?'

'For one thing, I need know nothing about poisons as yet. You
see that loophole in his letter?'

'But, don't you?'

'Just the ordinary amount of knowledge one has to have –
nothing specialized. I think I shall take his advice and learn
about them really thoroughly. Have to start by getting a few
books, by the way. I have always thought poisons must be a very
interesting study. Useful knowledge too, professionally. Yes, I
think I shall take his advice and work the subject up.'

Ford had breathed a sigh of relief.

'Oh, if that's all –'

Once more, however, the doctor's taciturnity had destroyed
the feeling that all was well. He remembered how Anstruther, in
telling him that Morrison had died of heart failure, had made
him believe that he had not, and now, although all the doctor did
was to look at him and walk out of the room, he managed to
convince Ford that learning about poisons was by no means all.
If it came to a pinch, Ford was certain that the doctor would
calmly supply anything he was asked to provide.

'Now why is it,' thought Ford for the hundredth time as he
prepared to cross the street and return to his office, 'that I am
contemplating putting up a fight (naturally), but that he is not?
Of course it is true that he is in a worse position than I am if it
comes out, or so he seems to think, but that does not seem enough.
Perhaps it's his medical training. Some of them do not seem to

mind if things do hurt. I suppose Anstruther must naturally be a little hard and callous and indifferent to other people's sufferings anyhow, but all the same – I should have thought there would have been limits, even with a doctor.'

With this sweeping slander on the medical profession, Ford returned to his office to read a ten-page letter containing a most elaborate scheme for saving the library books from being stolen, a suggestion so complicated that it would not work even if the Committee could have screwed up the courage to face the storm of unpopularity which would descend on them if they ever put it into execution.

On one point he had definitely made up his mind. However much he might be ordered in the letters to tell Anstruther, he was not so sure he would. The desire to be hand in glove with the doctor no longer remained. Above all, he had no wish to receive any confidences as to the transfer of poisons to someone else. So far as possible he had but one object – to have nothing more to do with it.

CHAPTER 14

THE TURNING OF THE WORM

*

'FOR the life of me,' snapped Laming, 'I can't make out what's come over you, Ford. When I consented to act as chairman, I never thought I should have all this difficulty with you. Thought you were at any rate an inoffensive sort of person. And now, here you are setting people by the heels!'

Ford had never before seen Laming angry. Somehow it seemed unnatural, and gave him the same shock that he had suffered when he had been pecked by a canary. Moreover he had no idea what his chairman was talking about. Surely he was not going back once more to the points Cardonnel had raised at the committee meeting? With a vague idea that it might appease Laming's wrath, he got up and produced one of the suggested new tea-trays.

'What on earth!' Laming looked at him as if he had gone mad. 'I am not referring to that sort of matter at all.' He dropped back into his more usual jerky sentences, anger having for a time made him almost grammatical. 'Talking about this letter. From Pargiter. Distressing man, Pargiter, but must be humoured. No point in being rude to him. In fact, have to take extra care about him.'

Ford nodded. It was part of his philosophy, that, if a member was troublesome beyond the ordinary, an extra effort must be made on his behalf. He would have been very surprised if he had been told that those who like grumbling will always complain, and that those who do not lose their temper over every little detail, are really worthy of much more attention. In an unfair world the Pargiters and their like often get an undue share of attention, and then regard it as their due.

But so ingrained was Ford's habit of complete subservience to the sarcastic and irritable Pargiter that for a moment he could not imagine that he had ever been anything other than almost too civil to him. He faced the chairman with an expression of completely vacant surprise. Laming was holding up a letter.

It appears,' he chirped, turning over the paper, 'that Pargiter met you on the stairs last night and made what he describes as "a completely inoffensive and humble suggestion". He goes on to say that he is aware that his suggestions are not usually considered very seriously, since "it has been carefully pointed out to me by many members of the committee for some years past that despite the fact that I have been a member for nearly half a century, I am of no importance in this club".'

Laming shook his head. 'Idiot, isn't he?' he commented brightly. 'All the same, I don't think you ought to have been quite so rude to him. Apparently you told him that you were doing your best, but you wished to goodness he would not want everything done at once. Rather grumpily, too, it seems.'

Under the stare of Laming's hard, birdlike little eyes that contained so little sympathy, Ford, to his annoyance, felt himself beginning to blush. How could he explain to the chairman the incessant badgering he was undergoing at the hands of this malicious fiend with a typewriter? How he was told to do this, and abused because the other was not being carried out quickly enough, until by now he was half mad with the worry of things. Last night, too, he had received the worst letter of all, the one with which he could not comply.

Under the shock of it he had walked downstairs in a trance, his mind full of one thing only – the fact that he must refuse, and that refusal might mean exposure, and with that on his mind he had heard a voice say:

'And when will you have the lights in the library put right?'

Without thinking, his mind had instantly assumed that this was an hallucination, and he had snapped back to what he had thought was only the shadow of his tormentor, his plea for consideration and for time, and passed on without looking back. Unfortunately, as it now emerged, it was not a shadow, but the very real substance of Pargiter, and all that was wrong was that the connexion controlling the reading-lamp was out of order – nothing to do with his tormentor's fifth point.

With an effort he brought his mind back to Laming.

'I'm very sorry, sir. I had a headache and hardly realized what Mr Pargiter said. Indeed, I thought it was not him at all.'

'All very well, but I hope that is not the kind of remark you would make to any member.'

Trying neither to feel nor to look like a naughty little boy, Ford promised to apologize in writing to Pargiter and to be a good boy in future. It was a relief to him when Laming went.

Very carefully, and with a furtive air, although he was all alone, he drew out from his pocket the bundle of letters from his anonymous correspondent and cursed the day when the fellow had become so proficient a typist. If only he would not write at such length! The very fact of their physical existence was becoming a problem in storage too difficult for Ford to solve.

He could hardly put them in a folder in the filing cabinet in his office. He could not leave them lying about. If he put them with his bank he was afraid they might read them (a thought which was definitely unjust), and anyhow, he needed them for reference. He would have liked to have destroyed them, but he might one day want to produce them if he ever found out who the fellow was, though so far, he had to admit, he had made not the slightest progress along those lines. Besides, he was being ordered to do so many things that he was afraid of forgetting one of them entirely. Consequently he was reduced to carrying them about with him always. He dare not leave them when he went to have his bath, and he had even considered sleeping with them under his pillow. But sleeping or waking, never, for one moment, was he quite free from them. And now the packet was getting so large that it had ruined hopelessly the sit of his best coat, had bulged out one pocket and overflowed into another, and still the spate of letters arrived. He took them all out and for the hundredth time tried to put them in order.

He had headed them neatly, so that he could get at once – in theory – the one he wanted. 'The Twelve Points.' 'The original Warning.' 'Vegetables and Ventilation' – an impossible request. You could draw up rules till you were blue in the face as to what temperature the rooms were to be kept at, but still one room would be at eighty because some *malade imaginaire* was afraid of catching a chill, while another would be dominated by a fresh-air fiend. And as for vegetables, it seemed impossible. However, he was doing his best. Perhaps his correspondent was right and steaming them *was* a mistake. 'But if,' thought Ford, sadly, 'the members start eating the vegetables in quantities instead of rejecting them sadly and scornfully, the coffee-room will show a loss.' (Vegetables were included in the table money without charge.)

Still more piles of letters. 'Furniture.' How could he refurnish the Club in a day, even if there were only two chairs in the whole building fit to sit on? 'Polishing handle of front door.' In point of fact it was lacquered and nothing could be done about it. 'Provision of scribbling pads.' A glad 'Done' had been written across this – the best idea the man had produced yet; Ford really believed it would actually prove in the end to be economical. 'Country Membership, Consideration of Scheme.' Well, that was not his business. Besides, to his knowledge, successive Committee after successive Committee had tried to evolve something practical and had failed.

And so on. And so on. At last he came to the letter for which he was looking.

My Dear Ford.

I am glad to see that you are making occasional progress. Allowing for your incompetence ['Why be so rude?' Ford remembered that he had ejaculated, and then, as an afterthought: 'Why be so untruthful?'] I must not complain.

But there is one thing I will not stand. When Morrison was killed – or shall we say when he died of heart failure? Which do you prefer? – besides yourself and Dr 'Palmer', there was one other witness, the waiter Hughes.

I have never thought that he was a very good waiter, though you, I know, regard him as the apple of your eye. For a light man he has an incredibly heavy footstep, for instance, and he is far too officious all round. He thinks he owns those library floor rooms, I believe. All of this, however, I would have passed by if I had not observed the very curious way in which he has been looking at me. If I go into the library, if I pass him in the passage, always I find the same fishy eye staring at me, trying to penetrate what is in my mind, and I WILL NOT HAVE IT!

Understand that once and for all. The man has become a positive menace. To you, which matters only because I like controlling you. To Anstruther, who is more important to me, and by the way, *much* more sensible. And above all, to me. That Hughes should dare to suspect *me* of having something to do with Morrison's death is a piece of impertinence which I will not tolerate or allow for a minute longer.

You will therefore not only dismiss him, but you will sack him with every circumstance of ignominy. You will arrange somehow within the next month that he is short in his cash, or that he is found drunk – surely Anstruther can provide you with a suitable drug? – or whatever other crime your ingenuity can suggest, but anyhow he will go, and he will go characterless and pensionless.

And if you don't, there will be more trouble for you.

'Even,' said Ford to himself, with unconsciously more accuracy than usual, 'a worm will turn.'

Standing in his rather dingy little office he worked himself up into a passion. It was one thing to force him to overhaul the machinery of the Club, to worry the Committee into making this or that change, to make his own life restless, but when it came to interfering with the staff – that, in his turn, he would not tolerate. The members could look after themselves – after all, he was not responsible for them; they elected each other; but the staff –

'Damn it all!' he burst out, 'I hand-pick them myself.'

And Anstruther? Well, Anstruther must look out for *himself*. Forgetful of the fact that it was at his request that the doctor had signed the death certificate, Ford decided that he would not even tell him of the letter. Judging by the way that he seemed prepared to assist actively in any poisoning enterprises that might be about, Anstruther might even be capable of advising him to tell Hughes to go, at any rate for a time. No, his mind was made up. He would do no more. Hughes should stay, let the consequences be what they might! Perhaps, with luck, the time for which Anstruther had been playing was already gained. Perhaps it was safe and the blackmailer's hold had already rotted away?

With a sudden rush of relief, Ford realized that the decision freed him from all the tyranny under which he had been suffering. He looked at the bundle of letters.

'From this time on, I don't care how badly cooked the vegetables are, or what the temperature of the rooms is, or how fast the clocks may be. The pettiness of it!'

Logically he should have ended by giving three cheers for the old and happy golden age of incompetence which was now to return. Actually, he merely sat down, lit a cigarette, and went into a daydream. From this time on, he decided, he would, if possible, do nothing. It was a very soothing decision.

CHAPTER 15

OVER COFFEE

*

IN a corner of the smoking-room a number of members had gathered, as was their custom, after lunch, to take their coffee and smoke for a while before returning to their chambers, offices, or consulting rooms.

The conversation had turned on the Club book thief. The members as a whole hardly knew how to take it. They all felt that it was so very disgraceful that there should be such a person. For a long while it had been fondly hoped that the occasional disappearances could be put down to absent-mindedness. It was easy to believe that someone wanted to finish some story he had started, and fell to the temptation of 'borrowing' it for an evening, with every intention of returning it, and then forgot. Or that a book read in bed by someone sleeping in the Club had been accidentally packed the next morning; perhaps unpacked the other end by a housemaid and carefully put away in a shelf without the reader having any idea that he had by mistake acquired a book that was not his. It was easy to imagine such a train of events or many similar ways in which such a thing might happen, easy and soothing to the feelings.

For after all, no one likes to think that he belongs to an institution which contains a thief. Besides, a deliberate thief was so improbable amongst the members of such an institution as the Whitehall. For many years the theory of accident held the field. It was reinforced from time to time. There was, for instance, the slightly improper novel posted back anonymously. True, it was postmarked from a distant town in the West in which only one member of the Club lived, and the anonymity was therefore very thin. But as the member in question was so very respectable, the incident went round as a joke, the point of which was not that he should have taken away the book in question, but that he should have read it at all.

Then there was the sad case of Mr Geoffrey. There was no doubt about it; Mr Geoffrey had been so anxious to finish that thrilling story, *The Mystery of the Poisoned Banana*, that he had taken it home one evening. The next morning he had been unable to return it first thing, so he had put it on his hall table to remind him to bring it back that evening. But he had forgotten that by this time a book-marker with the name of the Club on it had been tied into every book; forgotten, too, that he shared a flat with a well-meaning man, an individual who, seeing the book and the marker, had gone straight round to the Club and returned the book with the message that Mr Geoffrey had asked him to bring it back. That, the unfortunate Geoffrey had been quite unable to explain away. Fortunately, however, the Committee, after delivering a homily on his wicked ways, had been unable not to see the funny side.

But the introduction of these book-markers had taken the thing a stage further. It was just possible still to imagine that people took books away accidentally, or with intent to return, but it was no longer possible to believe that they kept them in ignorance as to where they belonged.

The subject had been raised after lunch that day by Cardonnel.

'One would like to think that it was an accident that the books go, but after all the notices about it, lists of books missing, and entreaties to all members to help in stamping it out, can you imagine anyone borrowing a book for a night or taking one by mistake?'

'Have you heard the latest about it?' Knight the solicitor chimed in. 'An official memorandum from the Commissioner of Police (Lost Property Office in fact, of course), saying that the following book has been discovered in a public vehicle plying for hire in the Metropolitan Police District, viz. *Murder in the Morning*, which contains a book-marker showing the name of the Whitehall Club. I forget the exact wording, but Ford's put it up on the notice board.'

'Left in a taxi, was it? That's pretty good.'

Cardonnel turned to the last speaker.

'Did you write it, Henry?'

There was a general laugh at the novelist, which he managed to turn in his favour.

'Certainly not. My books are *not* left in taxis. They are never put down until they are finished.'

'As a matter of fact, nobody ever starts them. When they come in here, they lie about looking so lonely and dusty that he's reduced to stealing them himself.'

'My own theory,' went on the novelist, 'is that it's the publishers. We've got as members here –' (He mentioned the names of several well-known publishers.) 'Now has anyone ever thought of classifying the books that are stolen according to who publishes them? If you found that they all came from the stables I have mentioned, you'd know who it was.'

'I've got another theory,' put in Cardonnel. 'Eh! here's Laming. Come and join us. We're talking about book thieves.'

The little man came jerkily up.

'Tiresome subject, very. Your theory?'

'Well, we know, don't we, the dates on which they have gone? I mean, Ford could give us a list, couldn't he?'

'Believe so – coffee and milk, please, Johnson.' The smoking-room waiter, who knew perfectly well what the order would be, had in fact already produced it. 'Yes, Cardonnel. What then?'

'Take the list of dates and find out what events happened on those days. I believe it would give you a clue.'

'I don't understand. What sort of events?' Knight looked interested.

'Well, if a large number went just when the Courts ceased sitting, one would look for a member of the Bar.'

'Or a judge.'

'That would be *lèse-majesté* – but to go on. If the disappearance always coincided with the Varsity rugger match, or a Test Match, one would look for someone who came up from the country regularly to go to those sort of things.'

'But when,' put in the novelist, 'you found that it always corresponded exactly with the meeting of the Church Assembly, you would not dare draw the conclusion.'

'The trouble as I see it –'

Cardonnel winked. 'Now this is going to be depressing. The eminent chartered accountant, who has not previously spoken, is now going to tell us exactly why the scheme will not work. It's

the sole and invariable contribution of all his profession towards
the revival of trade and industry.'

The speaker thus objurgated continued quite placidly – 'is to
know where you are to stop. You have mentioned sport and two
professional activities. But supposing it's a film fan who comes
up from the country every time, say, Marlene Dietrich has a new
film, and takes a book back with him to last till the next time he
has the chance to see that very charming lady. Are you to keep a
record of every first night of Marlene's?'

'He mightn't go to the first night.'

'Exactly. And you would have to do it with every film star.'

'Or stage star.'

'And why stick to that sort of thing only. It may be somebody
who comes up for dog shows or horticultural shows.'

'And why assume that it is a country member. Are the London
members more honest? There is, for instance, one member who
breeds Pekingese in London. He wouldn't have to come up for
dog shows.'

'But he would, my dear Henry, know how to spell it. Not
Pekinese, as you did in your last novel – with a 'g' in future,
please.'

'As I thought,' sighed Cardonnel, 'the eminent chartered
accountant has carefully destroyed my theory. It's no good,
Laming, we shall have to think of something else. Why not intro-
duce a detective into the Club?'

'Hate detectives.' Laming took a gulp of coffee. 'Won't have
them in the house.'

'Besides, it would be so difficult to do. A strange waiter would
excite the curiosity of all of us. Or do you propose to disguise a
retired member of the C.I.D. as a page-boy?'

'I've got a much brighter idea.' The novelist sat forward. 'Why
not appoint my learned friend, Mr Cardonnel, as Club House
Detective-in-Chief. Think, just think,' he turned wickedly to
Laming, 'of how much trouble would be saved for everybody if
his activities were fully occupied, instead of, shall I say, restlessly
seeking an outlet.'

'Henry,' said Cardonnel solemnly, 'one day someone will
punch your face.'

'Besides,' went on the novelist, totally ignoring the slight interruption, 'he might find out who it was. You all know what he is, bloodhound on the scent, and all that.'

The Chartered Accountant saw his chance to get his own back gently.

'Do get up and do your stuff, Cardonnel. I'm longing to see you go sniffing all over the carpet on the track of a book-marker.'

'Do you usually trail the book you are going to steal along the carpet first?'

Laming looked at his watch. This flippant conversation was not in his line. The Home Office was made of sterner stuff. It was only his desire to show that he really got on well with Cardonnel that had made him join the party. With a great appearance of activity he hustled to the door.

In a few minutes Cardonnel was left alone.

'I'm not at all sure that I shan't,' he remarked to his coffee-cup.

CHAPTER 16

A REALLY MERRY CHRISTMAS

*

Of all the miserable things to do, the most miserable is to spend Christmas Day in a Club. In the first place anyone who does so is obviously a depressing person without family, without even anyone who wants him. At the very best he will be somebody whose arrangements have broken down at the last moment, and who is suffering from all the irritation consequent on such an event.

The very tables in the smoking-room proclaimed the desolation. There were no papers. One copy of yesterday's *Times* with the crossword partly and inaccurately filled in was to be found lying about disconsolately, suggesting that the would-be solver had either happily left and joined his family, or had in despair stabbed himself in the billiards-room with the half-butt, the latter event seeming the more probable.

Beside this derelict copy was placed neatly the pile of Annuals which everybody had finished reading in November and the previous day's evening paper, full of photographs of others departing. It was almost a comfort to observe how crowded the trains were.

All over the Club house the depression was the same. The Tape machine found no news that was worth recording, or if it did, as it ticked its message out letter by letter, the click resounded through the empty hall and emphasized the fact that no one would read it. Hughes, sitting in the little cupboard allotted to him on the library floor, was vainly endeavouring to drive away boredom and forget how much happier he would be at home trying to induce his children to believe that he was Father Christmas. He had been there all day and had served one tea and one slice of plain cake. If only someone had wanted him to mix them a cocktail or find a book for them, it would have been a relief. But no one was there, and hours more had still to be passed away somehow.

In his lodge by the door the hall-porter dozed away uncomfortably. To his mind Christmas Day would be bearable if it fell in the New Year. He would have had something to do then. Every year he amused himself by learning the list of members by heart, and at the end of each year the few resignations and the election of new members would give him something to do. But on 25th December –! He had become word perfect months ago.

Drearily spreading his long legs in front of him in the smoking-room, Ford was wondering whether to get drunk. He resented bitterly the fact that, as he had no family himself, he had allowed the steward to go away to his home, while he stayed on duty to see that 'things were all right'. He had an uneasy suspicion that his presence only deepened the gloom of the staff. To get drunk would have three advantages: it would pass the time away; it would soothe his nerves, frayed by the worries of the autumn, and it would help him to forget that his month of grace was nearly over. If he had not sacked Hughes by 1st January, something was to happen, and judging by the violence of the threats he was receiving, something pretty nasty.

But it would not make him cheerful. Sitting there, the ash of his cigarette dropping all over his waistcoat, he did not feel that he could ever be cheerful again. He looked back on the few other occasions in his life when he had had too much to drink. They had been dull at the time, and incredibly dreary in retro-spect. Getting drunk, he decided, was the most overrated form of amusement in the world. But then all forms of amusement were dull. Still, he might as well have a drink. He ordered a small whisky and soda, and decided after the second sip that he disliked the taste of whisky.

Just as he was finishing it, he was annoyed to see Anstruther come in. Since he had made up his mind to disobey, and to risk the consequences both for himself and the doctor, his conscience had driven him away from Anstruther. If he talked to him, he must either tell him that something vague in outline, but definitely unpleasant, was going to occur, or he must lie, and Ford was well aware that he was a very poor liar.

Gulping the rest of his whisky he fled to the coffee-room. Usually he found it a cheerful, pleasant room, but to-night its primrose walls struck him as chill, its red curtains as garish. The touch of fog which had drifted in made it worse. Besides, it was deserted, except for the cashier twiddling his thumbs behind his pay-desk, and one weary-looking waiter with a cough which sounded as if it might turn into bronchitis at any moment; and the emptiness added to the sense of unreality. It was usually a room humming with life.

He turned to the menu apathetically. It was much too early for dinner, and the conventional efforts which Benson and his assistants had made to provide a real Christmas dinner seemed only to increase the depression. To eat plum pudding by yourself in a mournful manner is almost more depraved than to drink alone. Turkey Ford had never liked, and as for obtaining a happy month by eating a mince-pie, a happy month January was likely to be for him, so far as he could see! He flopped down on a chair with such violence that nothing but solid Victorian carpentry would have stood up to the onslaught. There was no evening paper; he seldom read a book; in the tone of one demanding a small prussic acid, he asked the bronchial waiter to bring him *Punch*. While he waited for it to come, he thought of a remark that seemed to him original. '*Punch*,' he desired to say, 'is getting worse than ever.'

As it arrived, some member, exiled in fact owing to his cook's influenza, crawled in, looked at him, shuddered slightly, and sat down in the opposite corner. Silence reigned. Five minutes after, a very old man, slightly bent, with an air of having been mislaid by his relatives, wheezed slowly across the room and sat in the corner opposite to Ford. He complained instantly about the draught, but seemed grateful when, coughing himself, the waiter went through the motions of shutting an already closed window. Not long after the old man, Pargiter came in. He stood in the middle of the room, apparently absorbed in a mathematical calculation, before selecting the seat which kept him as far as possible from all the other three occupants.

Ford pushed away his unfinished turkey and pretended to eat some Stilton. What he really wanted to know was whether Anstruther was going to dine or not. If not, he would linger over dinner. If he was, he would get away as soon as possible. For a moment his attention wandered, and during that second the doctor sat down next to him.

Very much to his surprise he saw that Anstruther was looking pale and haggard. In his eyes there was a look that almost seemed to amount to fear. Turning his back on the rest of the room the doctor spoke in a hushed voice.

'Must talk to you sometime. This fellow, worrying me. Keeps on demanding things. Threatening. Apparently there is something you won't do.'

'Me?' Ford tried to show surprise. At the same time he tried to convey by a glance that the silence of the room made it impossible that their conversation would not be overheard.

'Yes. Says he has written to you and that he believes you have taken no notice. Tells me complete exposure possible, that something awful is going to happen. Don't know what it is you are to do, but remember this fellow is not a man with whom you ought to trifle. Do what you are told, whatever it is. By the way, I got this.'

He flicked across a piece of paper on which one sentence was typewritten. Ford was at first glad to see that it was not the typescript which haunted his dreams. On second thoughts, however, he was not certain that he was not sorry. Apparently someone else was taking a hand.

The message ran: 'Look out for Pargiter.'

He read it again, completely puzzled. 'Look out for Par – What do you think this is? A friendly warning?'

'No idea. Better say no more now; the man himself might hear. But – don't go on keeping this fellow's letters from me as he says you are. Show them. And whatever it is you're told to do, do it. I am.'

How much more of this Ford would have stood is uncertain. The strain of conducting a conversation of so peculiar a nature only just above a whisper was beginning to break his already frayed nerves. Momentarily an intense curiosity to know what it was that Anstruther was doing in accordance with the instructions he was receiving, overcame him; then it was followed by a desire to know nothing. Whether the doctor was supplying irritant poisons or deadly poisons was no concern of Ford's, and he did not intend that any particle of such knowledge should become part of his responsibility.

Just, however, as the strain was getting too great, two interruptions occurred, apart from the inquisitive glance which Pargiter himself was throwing in their direction. Pargiter was the kind of man who always listened to other people's conversations, but, even if he had not been, the faint noise of two people whispering would have been enough to arouse (and slightly irritate) anyone's curiosity.

The first interruption was a big breezy one. A cheerful hearty member of the Club had just arrived, and was looking round the room with boisterous mirth.

'Good lord, what's this place? A morgue? Here am I just back from abroad – boat held up by fog, and so I've missed my train – but I'm not going to be miserable. Heavens, waiter, aren't there any crackers? Can't we make the party cheerful somehow? After all, it is Christmas Day.'

Pargiter turned in his seat and fixed a malevolent eye on him. On the words 'Christmas Day' he raised his eyes to heaven in mute protest. Ford was well aware that the next day he would have to answer a letter of complaint. Anstruther looked at his plate. He had not joined the Whitehall to talk to strangers. Only the little old bent man seemed pleased. With a silvery little chuckle he beckoned the hearty man towards him and went on to explain that he would love to pull a cracker. He did not think that he had pulled one since the Jubilee of '97, and now that his family had all gone, he had never hoped to pull one again. It emerged too, that he was longing to take a glass of wine, and hoped that his newly made friend would join him to celebrate his return to England. With a bottle of Ruinart 1914 in front of them, they settled down to make friends, the old man talking away garrulously in his shrill piping treble. He might be ill the next day, but who cared for his doctor, anyway? He would have a happy Christmas Day after all. He felt friendly to this young man, a trifle noisy perhaps, but then all young people were – they were little the worse for that. As for the 'young' man (he was thirty-seven), he felt a little strange, a little condescending, perhaps, as he listened to the funny little senile platitudes coming from his neighbour; but, after all, poor old boy, he was delighted to cheer him up – and, 'come to think of it,' he added to himself, 'the old buffer's doing me a power of good.' Whatever else may be said of the hearty, they have a heart.

But now the second interruption was about to occur. For an event which afterwards was to prove so definitely important, it took a small form, being nothing more alarming than the arrival of a page-boy to say that Ford was wanted on the telephone. Secretly relieved at the opportunity to escape, the secretary tried to keep up appearances, and, as usual, rather over-acted.

'Can't even leave me alone, you see, on Christmas night,' he remarked resignedly to Anstruther as he got up. 'Do you know who it is, boy?'

'He didn't give a name, sir, but I think it was Mr Cardonnel's voice.'

Anstruther looked slightly surprised. So much intelligence was unusual for a page-boy. His own experience, which, as a doctor, was extensive, was that the page-boys were not too good on the telephone.

'Cardonnel?' he asked. 'What's he likely to want, Ford?'

'Oh, some wild idea of his which he's gone mad about. Thinks he's a detective or something. Of course, it's all absolute nonsense. I wish he really was some use.' Then, realizing rather late that he was expressing his opinions rather freely before the boy, and possibly before Pargiter, he added: 'Very able man, though. Very able indeed. Most useful to the Club. May help us in this matter, too,' and walked away trying to look official and business-like.

Below stairs the atmosphere had changed. All the staff were busily rushing about searching in the most unlikely places for a cracker. There was a belief that one had come in accidentally, or had been left over from the previous year's staff dance. Anyhow, someone had expressed a wish for a cracker, and a cracker they would produce. The staff of the Whitehall prided themselves that they had never been defeated by any request, reasonable or unreasonable. One page achieved temporary popularity by announcing that he could make one. His fame, however, was short-lived, as in the same breath he added a desire to be supplied with gunpowder.

Eventually two were miraculously discovered and solemnly

served on a plate. The strangely assorted pair of diners had by
then forgotten all about the remark that had brought them
together. The young man was just trying to persuade his companion to join him in a glass of port. The arrival of the crackers
finished it. The old boy, casting his doctor and caution to the
winds, was on for anything. With tears pouring down his cheeks
he gaily pulled both crackers and placed a purple paper cap on
his head.

Fortunately (or perhaps unfortunately) Pargiter had finished
his dinner and left. He would have resigned from the Club the
next day.

CHAPTER 17

THE LITERARY SHERLOCK

*

'THAT you, Ford? What a long time you take coming to the telephone!' Cardonnel's voice did not sound really annoyed. He happily accepted the apology that was offered to him with a good-humoured complaint, clearly not to be taken seriously, that his arm was aching with holding up the receiver.

'However,' he went on, 'really the apology is due from me for troubling you on such a night. I do hope I haven't spoilt your Christmas dinner.'

On that point Ford had no qualms about reassuring him. He managed not unreasonably, and quite truthfully, to imply that the fact that he was at his post at such a moment was highly creditable. By this time, however, his own arm was starting to ache, and he began to think it was desirable to bring Cardonnel to the point. Characteristically he dropped what he thought was a gentle hint, but which was in fact an almost direct question.

'What do I want?' came the voice from the other end. 'Oh, simply to know this. Do you keep a record of who occupies the bedrooms?'

'Yes.'

'Could I look at it?'

'Why, certainly. That is,' Ford went on, his voice losing his assurance, 'if it is still in existence. I'm not sure, but I think that after a certain time we destroy it.'

Cardonnel was not surprised. It would be like Ford to do away with what might be useful evidence to him. It was even more like him not to know what happened under his own management. He listened with a slight smile, while Ford stumbled along and contradicted himself as to the system. Eventually he cut him short.

'Well, never mind. Would you mind putting together what you can get and handing it to me to-morrow at lunch time? Or, if you will not be in there yourself – and I suppose you do take a day off sometimes – leaving it so that I can pick it up? I want it of course for my little enquiry.'

'And how's that getting on?' The enquiry was more polite than hopeful. Ford had little expectation of catching his book thief as the result of anything Cardonnel might do, an assumption which was foolish, for if anyone should have been aware of Cardonnel's uncanny trick of finding things which it was hoped would escape him, it should have been the secretary of the Whitehall Club.

'Oh, not so badly. There is, as they say, some progress to report. I can't actually *name* the man yet, but he lives in Nottinghamshire, has a sister-in-law whose birthday is in May, is between sixty and seventy years old; I think he is a Socialist in politics, and his favourite musical composer is Beethoven. If he is married, of which I am not quite sure, he probably plays bridge. But I'll explain it all to you to-morrow. Good night, Ford. Oh, and by the way, a merry Christmas to you.'

'And to you.'

'Don't worry about me. I've had the most amusing one I've had for years. Good night.'

Ford addressed his 'Good night' to an irresponsive receiver. At any rate there was something he could do that night. Before Cardonnel was due to arrive the next morning he had a complete list of all those members whose addresses ended 'Notts'. Somehow from what he knew of their characters he could not imagine any of them being the man for whom they were looking. Still, as Ford said: 'You never could tell. Even in the best regulated families –' which was a peculiarly inappropriate remark even for Ford. One thing was quite certain. If any of Cardonnel's deductions were right, it was a matter of system and *not* of accident. Nor were there any grounds for believing that the man belonged to a family regulated in any way whatever.

In the course of the morning of Boxing Day, however, Cardonnel rang him up again. He had, he said, the very slightest chill – nothing in any way infectious. If Ford would be good enough to lunch with him, he would be charmed to point out the steps by which he had arrived at his conclusions, 'and if you could bring the information as to bedrooms?'

Ford would be charmed to do both, but unfortunately the hall-porter who kept the bedroom list, so that members could be told the number of their room immediately on arrival, was off duty. The secretary therefore had been unable to get all he wanted. In this way he disguised the fact that he had forgotten to take any steps about it during the previous evening.

Arrived at Cardonnel's flat, he found his host's sitting-room covered with past files of *The Times*, which Ford now remembered he had given him leave to take away from the Club over the Christmas holidays – a permission which he was quite unentitled to give, and which he strongly suspected Cardonnel would have been the first to have objected to his having given to anyone else. Besides *The Times*, there were sporting calendars, the book from the Club showing what books were received and what were returned to the circulating library, a volume which had no right itself to have left its place in the smoking-room; a theatrical annual or so, *Wisden* for the past two years, while the pile was crowned by the *Oxford University Calendar* for 1934, and the *Cambridge University Calendar* for 1934–5, the difference in date offering a silent commentary on the respective outlooks of those two seats of learning. On the writing desk in the corner were sheets of foolscap covered with commentaries and columns in Cardonnel's neat, legal handwriting.

The lawyer was clearly in very good form. Standing on his own hearthrug, his grey hair neatly brushed, his sparse figure clad in a carefully pressed suit, he made a startling contrast to his tall, ungainly guest, whose clothes always looked as if he had slept in them.

'Sherry, my dear Watson? You know my methods, I think? At least you don't, but I feel so like Holmes that I forget you are not the learned doctor. We ought to have had that odd bird, Anstruther, whom I have seen you talking to so often recently, along to play that part. At least, on second thoughts, not so often recently as a month or so ago. But I wander from the point. It's the greatest fun playing the detective, a most amusing role. I'm quite absorbed in it. I thought, you know,' he cocked his head on one side, with a twinkle in his eyes, 'of receiving you in a dressing-gown and refusing to talk until I had played two sonatas, or whatever Holmes did play on that violin. But, unfortunately, I have no musical accomplishments.'

Ford, not being well versed in his Holmes, but having a slight doubt as to the exact accuracy of the picture, contented himself with a grin.

'Now I see no reason to keep lunch waiting while I do explain my methods,' went on Cardonnel laughingly, 'so I propose to bring down some of my notes and talk to you over lunch. Some sherry first, though?'

It was one of Cardonnel's little tricks as a host that he never said 'more sherry'. It was also typical that he could not resist a little dig.

'You recognize the wine, perhaps? The one that was recently finished at the Club and the finding of whose successor gave you so much trouble. Come, come, my dear Watson, and now to lunch while I tell you everything. Though I am sure that the real Holmes would have kept you in suspense much longer and I really don't see how I am to get any food at all if I indulge in a monologue all the time.'

Partly over lunch, but partly also for a considerable time afterwards, Cardonnel explained his 'methods', which, as he said, 'might fairly be said to run on the deductive lines of the late Sherlock Holmes, or is he late? I always forget. He returns and comes to life again so often. However, let that be. This is roughly my idea.

'I took the dates on which the books were stolen, and then I set to work to find out exactly what was happening in every sphere of life, not only on those days, but also on the days preceding and following them. You see, I had no idea whether the man lived in London or came up for the day, or came up and spent the night and took back something to read in the train, nor whether whatever brought him to London took place on the day of his arrival or the day after. It's a little confusing, but if you think for a minute, you will find I could not safely exclude either to start with.'

Ford thought for very nearly fifteen seconds, at the end of which he decided it was quite impossible to comprehend but that he was perfectly prepared to take Cardonnel's word for it.

'That of course was to begin with. Later on I began to understand his habits. His usual technique is this. He comes up to

London, generally on a Friday night, stays probably at the Club –
we are going to find out from your bedroom records if that is so,
and we shall also be able to add the detail of his name from
them – steals his book on Friday night or Saturday morning,
goes to a professional football match in the winter, or a cricket
match in the summer, and returns home.'

'But the books don't always disappear on Saturday.'

'Not always. That's the beauty of it. I said generally, but if
they go in the weekday there is always either a professional
football match or some cricket on in London on that day, or
one day either side.'

'But there's cricket going on in London almost all the summer.
I don't know much about professional football, but surely there
are never three consecutive days in the winter free of it.'

'Oh, yes, quite often. You look at my list. But – and this is
the real point – the days in the summer correspond each time
with the matches of Nottinghamshire in town. Each time a book
goes Notts are playing either Surrey or Middlesex or the M.C.C.
at the Oval or Lords, except once, and then they were playing
Essex at Leyton.

'The winter was more difficult. I didn't get it at first, because I
had not realized how many league teams there were, nor, I must
admit, was I quite sure of the geographical centre of each team. I
wasted a great deal of time,' Cardonnel shook his head sadly,
'owing to a mistaken idea as to the locality of Tranmere Rovers.
However, once I had got on to Notts, it was all plain sailing. On
each occasion either Notts Forest or Notts County were playing
a London league team. At least, I think Clapton Orient is in
London. That I have still to confirm.

'But leaving that one occasion aside as the possible exception,
that is my reason (and I will prove it to you in detail) for saying
that the man lives in Nottingham, or at any rate, Nottinghamshire.'

Ford thought a minute. 'Supposing he was born there or used
to live there, but had now gone to live in Surrey, but still took an
interest in his old county and took the opportunity of seeing
them when they were in town.'

'Most improbable.' Cardonnel brushed it aside airily and then, remembering his manners, hurriedly substituted: 'At least a very interesting idea, and though I think it will prove to be wrong, one we must bear in mind in case we find ourselves at fault. But to continue.'

Once more he got into his stride.

'In the same way it cannot be a coincidence that the loss of the books always coincides with the dates on which there is a concert which includes at least one item of the works of Beethoven.'

Having very little idea of how many concerts there were in London, or what proportion of them were likely to include that particular composer as an integral part, Ford contented himself with looking as wise as he could and nodding his head.

So far as his rather confused mind could follow the argument, it seemed to mean that Beethoven was always performed whenever Notts played. Well, perhaps it was a good thing, but it seemed strange. He gave it up and went on to the next point. 'But the sister-in-law?' he asked.

'Ah, that I must admit is a slight flight of fancy. It might be a niece, or even – though that is less probable – a nephew. But it will be someone of that kind.'

'Because?' Ford prompted.

'Every spring, at varying dates, but never later than 10th May, one novel of Dorothy Sayers goes. During the rest of the year the works of that excellent authoress are spared. Therefore we may, I think, safely assume that our thief does not desire them for himself, but gives them away – clearly a birthday present as the time is not Christmas, and clearly to a relative since a second-hand copy is considered adequate. I suggest, after some thought, a sister-in-law, since I think that Miss Sayers appeals on the whole more to women, but, as I say, the exact relationship is not certain. One should never jump to conclusions.'

He folded his hands judicially, and seeming more incapable of irony than unconscious of it, continued calmly:

'Last spring he obtained his book on the day that he went to watch Notts County play Millwall somewhere near the Docks. Rather a rough game, I gather. The London club got into trouble on account of its spectators, and incidentally were relegated at the end of the season to the Third Division. I gather that they

were, in fact, deserving of a very great deal of sympathy, but then
I hardly know anything of these things.

'But to resume. Much the same line of reasoning applies to the
wife and the card playing, though here, definitely, we are in the
realm of conjecture. You see, if he has a wife, he must explain
somehow how he is able to obtain so readily a supply of second-
hand books, many of them having perhaps some mark identifying
them with the Club. The most ready suggestion is that he buys
second-hand packs of cards from the Club in the usual way, and
explains the second-hand books as being a similar convenience.
But that, as I said, is perhaps stretching the imagination rather
far.'

Ford thought it was stretching it a good deal, but he hardly
liked to say so. Instead, he enquired as to how Cardonnel had
decided on the man's politics. 'Because,' he said magnanimously,
'I don't think one ought to assume that because he's a thief he's
necessarily a Socialist. Of course, I know, give a dog a bad name,
but still –'

'Oh, no. That isn't my reasoning at all. As you have noticed,
there have been many books of memoirs, biographies and so on
amongst the list of those books that are missing.'

'And very expensive too,' the secretary interposed.

'Quite. And all written by staunch Conservatives.'

'Well, but – wouldn't that show that he supported them? I
mean, if he wanted Conservative memoirs?'

'Not at all. He did *not* want them. One or two of them were so
dull that nobody could possibly have wanted them. Quite the
contrary. He wanted to destroy them as *poisonous propaganda* –
from his point of view, of course, from his point of view.'

This seemed definitely confusing to Ford. After all, if you
went on those sort of lines you could argue in any direction, but
Cardonnel's voice recalled him again.

'Much the same line of thought has given me his age. All the
memoirs are largely concerned with the "naughty nineties" –
obviously our thief was a young man then, and the period
interests him.'

'But isn't that exactly the opposite method to the one you have
just been advocating – I mean about his politics?'

Cardonnel looked at him pityingly.

'How could you dislike a period so much that you wanted to destroy all traces of it? No, no. I think you'll find when we catch our man that I am right. When we get those full bedroom lists of yours we can move on a stage. Meanwhile, I'm studying his hobbies.'

'Hobbies?'

'Yes. Chiefly negative results so far, judging by some of the books he has *not* taken. It is almost certain, for instance, that he does not collect coins –'

'Very few people do.'

'No, but I do know one member of the Club – a highly suspicious character to my mind, too – who *does* collect coins, and possibly on that fact alone we ought to delete him from the lists of suspects. I think, however, that he may be thinking of travelling in the East Indies – two travel books about that part of the world have recently gone.'

'At the age of sixty or seventy!'

'A good point, my dear Ford, a good point. Perhaps he is studying aboriginal customs. Keep an eye out to see if anyone is reading Frazer's *Golden Bough*, will you? I remember both these travel books, as it happens, and if my memory serves me in each there was a chapter on native poisons. Now do you happen to know anyone in the Club who is interested in poisoning? Why, what's the matter, Ford?'

The word 'poison' had produced its usual effect on Ford. He was looking slightly sick. With some remnant of presence of mind, however, he managed to make the usual conventional suggestion that perhaps it was the fire at his back which had upset him. In a few minutes he had recovered.

'The only trouble though, sir, is that so far ı can't think of anyone who answers to your description. Here is a list of all the people who live in Nottinghamshire, and none of them are about that age. Nor do I think – though this is only my memory – that they have been up in London on the days when the books have gone.'

'Then I expect the man lives just over the border of the county; or perhaps there is some detail wrong. I am sure that if I go on on these lines, eventually we are bound to get our proof.'

'Proof will be a bit hard, won't it? Moral certainty perhaps.'

'Oh, once we know who he is, we can set some trap.'

Ford shuddered. He did not like traps.

'Oh, well,' he said, 'first catch your thief –'

To his credit, Cardonnel just managed to refrain from saying that he never cooked thieves.

'There is one point, you know,' went on Ford, 'where the latest results do not seem to bear you out.'

'And that is?' Cardonnel's voice sounded a little disapproving.

'The books that have been going recently.'

'They are still going?'

'Oh, yes! I am afraid I have not put up the list for some time, nor told you about it.'

A shade of annoyance crossed Cardonnel's face. It was so like Ford not to give him all the information! He had probably not kept the list up to date for weeks!

'Well, what has been going?'

Ford produced a rather crumpled piece of paper.

'*A Frenchman in Khaki* by Paul Maze, the last volume of Lloyd George's War Memoirs, *A Village in a Valley* by Beverley Nichols, and *A Letter to a Young Lady on the Occasion of her Approaching Marriage* by Ambrose Hoopington. It's a varied selection,' he broke off to comment.

'But very sound and all interesting.'

'What would so old a man want to know about the war?'

'Well, a young one would not be interested at all.'

Finding no answer to this, Ford contented himself by remarking that the last-named was said by the *Morning Post* to be disgusting, cynical, immoral, 'which was why I got it in,' he added, apparently without irony, 'and then there is *The Serial Universe* by J. W. Dunne, which I believe is incomprehensible, *How Like an Angel* by A. G. Macdonnell, and two detective stories.'

'Which are also incomprehensible,' Cardonnel chuckled.

'Well, let me have the complete list some time, would you? It's a line I must follow up.'

CHAPTER 18

IN BEDROOM NUMBER 4

*

As the days went on Ford began to wear a more harassed expression. Not a day passed but that he was reminded that he had still taken no action about dismissing Hughes, and each reminder told him that, if he did not, something would happen which would automatically raise the question of how Morrison had died. To add to his other worries he was almost sure that Anstruther was getting similar letters, and was even more frightened than he was. Indeed the doctor seemed now to be an absolute bundle of nerves.

The second of January was to be his final day of grace. The day before he was so much on edge that even Laming thought that he must be on the verge of a nervous breakdown, and attributing it with a good deal of accuracy to his having been compelled to stay too much in the Club and getting too little fresh air, induced him to get out into the country for the day. It was hardly the time of year for a country walk, but nevertheless, the change of scene was some use, or would have been if for one minute Ford had been able to stop asking himself what on earth would happen next, and how soon it was to happen.

Perhaps, fortunately, he had not long to wait. He had managed to keep away from the Club until after dinner time, and it was nearly ten before, rather muddy and tired, he had come in to be greeted immediately by a message that Dr Anstruther wanted to see him at once in Number 4 bedroom. Mr Pargiter had been taken ill.

Directly he opened the bedroom door he saw that there was something very wrong indeed. Anstruther was standing, a syringe in his hand, with a look of wild terror on his face. On the bed Pargiter was lying, apparently unconscious. His usually florid face was rather pale, but otherwise he showed no particular expression.

'It's no good, it's no good. I can't get any further sign of life out of him.'

To his surprise Ford found himself rather calmer than the doctor.

'Don't make such a noise, man. You'll attract the whole household.'

Unexpectedly a nervous giggle startlingly left the doctor's lips.

'What! Keep it quiet again? It can't be done, man. Can't be done.'

'Keep what quiet?' Then, seeing the hysteria on Anstruther's face, even Ford realized. 'You don't mean to say Pargiter's dead too.'

A nod. 'And I didn't mean – I didn't mean to let him out of my sight this evening after that warning. You know, I showed you the warning.'

Though he strongly resented what seemed almost an attempt to drag him into something from which he was fondly hoping that his day in the country excluded him, Ford could not deny having seen the warning. He brushed it aside and asked what had happened.

'I had gathered – as no doubt you did – that this was the dangerous day for Pargiter, and so instead of being away all day – where *have* you been, by the way? – I have, as far as possible, been keeping an eye on him. All went well until after dinner – at least, Pargiter seemed quite well – but during dinner I must have eaten something which disagreed with me. I've been sick and dizzy ever since, and so I couldn't go on watching him.'

'You've been ill? Do you imagine you've been poisoned?'

The doctor seemed startled. 'I suppose I must. I never thought of that.'

'Who was sitting next to you?'

'I don't know. I was too busy watching Pargiter. Besides, it might have been before dinner.'

'Well, I can find out from the head waiter. But go on about' – he pointed to the bed – 'him. I say, oughtn't you to be doing something?'

'No good now. But to go back. I remember now saying to Hughes that the glass of sherry I had before dinner tasted a trifle odd.'

'Let's go into that later. About Pargiter.'

'There's very little to say. I returned from one of these attacks to find him sitting exactly where we found Morrison. Of course I suspected at once, and I've been doing everything I can to bring him round, but' – he indicated the syringe – 'of course it was useless from the start. Hyoscine's absolutely deadly in big doses.'

Ford looked at him curiously. 'I don't know what hyoscine is; but how did you know that it was hyoscine and that it was in big doses?'

'Can't you guess? My God, I thought I'd made the doses weak enough, but this fellow must know more than I gave him credit for.'

'What! Do you mean to say that you have been supplying this stuff, and now Pargiter's been murdered by it. But, heavens, doesn't that make you an accessory before the fact?'

'Yes. And you too.' Anstruther sat down and was suddenly violently sick.

By the time that he had more or less recovered physically, his nerves seemed to have gone to pieces more completely. He seemed to be in an abject mortal funk.

'How many more times are we two going to have to meet, and go through this scene? How much more have we got to put up with before we find out who this fellow is? Aren't you doing anything to find out who it is who is torturing both of us?'

Without thinking exactly what was implied Ford answered quite literally.

'Cardonnel's nearly found out who the book thief is – at least he thinks he has – we might get him to help.'

'Cardonnel? *Cardonnel?*' The doctor seemed appalled. 'I wouldn't trust him if I were you.'

'Oh, I think he's a decent fellow. But, look here, there's no question of trusting anyone or finding anything out. We've got to go straight to the police.'

With a stifled shriek Anstruther jumped up.

'You fool! You fool! Don't you see that this fellow has got us – got us absolutely. Call in the police and I get penal servitude for life I should think, if I am not hung, and you get – I don't know what – but a good long sentence.'

The threat did not appal Ford. He might be careless, lazy,

weak, but as he had shown when he refused to sack Hughes, there was a limit, and this idea of trying to frighten him by telling him what the unpleasant consequences were for himself was beyond that limit.

But Anstruther was no fool. He very quickly saw that by appealing to fear, he was arguing on the wrong lines. He shifted his ground to that of loyalty. After a while he appeared to quieten down and went on in a quieter voice.

'I see. Your conscience won't let you. You prefer to let me down – to let me in far worse than you will be involved yourself, and remember, too, that it was you who originally induced me to help you to keep it quiet in the first place. So much, however, for relying on other people. Very well, then, go and ring up Scotland Yard. I'll stay here.'

Despite the touch of theatricality, the implication of disloyalty stung Ford to the quick. It was the one virtue on which he really prided himself, and prided himself with justification.

'But my dear fellow, what can one do? It isn't as if he was your patient this time.'

'As a matter of fact he is. But, if you've made up your mind, of course that's quite irrelevant.'

For a moment there was no sound in the small bedroom except Ford drumming with his fingers against a wardrobe.

'But could you do it? You said yourself just now you couldn't. I mean is it safe? I mean two deaths from heart failure in the same chair, and both your patients?'

'I know I did say it couldn't be done, but I was a bit hysterical at the time. Forgive me, Ford. I think I can manage a similar certificate. Not, I think, heart failure this time. A clot of blood or a haemorrhage, described in the proper medical terms, and no one will notice the coincidence. After all, why not? Quite a lot of the members of this Club, though you may not know it, are my patients. I attract them to me by saying nothing. It's a sort of self-hypnotism. And many of them are old and have weak hearts.' A curious look passed over the doctor's face as if he were considering other elderly patients of his. 'I think, yes, I think that it will be safe for me to sign the death certificate again. There may be talk, but after all, supposing the talk gets so bad that we *are* found out, are we any worse than before? You see, we're committed already.'

At the time Ford believed him – he always did believe what people told him.

'You mean,' he said, 'that we may as well be hung for a sheep as a lamb?'

Anstruther gave a slight shiver.

'Not hung, I hope.' Then seeing that Ford had gone rather white, he added: 'It'll be all right, my dear fellow. You leave it to me. I'll see you through.'

At the time Ford did not notice that the doctor seemed to have completely recovered his nerve. Before he quite realized what he was doing, he found that he had agreed that once more he would help to hush the thing up.

'But this time,' he added, almost as an afterthought, 'we must find the fellow and deal with him.' He did not specify, even in his own mind, how the dealing was to be done.

'We'll start on it to-morrow – and I think we'll start from that glass of sherry.'

Ford drew himself up. 'If you think it was Hughes, you're quite wrong. I *know* it's none of the staff. It might of course be any of the members, they elect each other. But I hand-pick the staff myself.' It was one of his favourite sentiments.

'Quite so, quite so. We'll discuss it to-morrow. You know I think we're rather forgetting –'

With a start Ford realized that he had completely forgotten Pargiter. As he made his way down the passage towards the library, he thought of the peculiar relationship he had just entered into with Anstruther. A nasty muddle, and a nasty man with whom to be involved, he was beginning to think. 'His honour,' he quoted to himself, 'rooted in dishonour stood. And faith unfaithful kept him falsely true.' He reached the landing and absent-mindedly picked up a weight from the weighing machine.

'I really think that that man should show more respect for the dead. At any rate he ought not to be sick. It's all wrong.' He shook his head sadly. He weighed, he found, thirteen stone five. Angrily he got off the machine. He was letting his mind wander.

CHAPTER 19

THE AMATEUR POISONER

*

IF Ford had been able to see into Anstruther's mind, or had even been able to glance for a second at his face as he stood in bedroom Number 4, he would have been even more surprised.

As the door closed behind the clumsy figure of the worried secretary, the expressionless mask had fallen from the doctor's face. He had suddenly exploded into uncontrollable, if silent, mirth. It was all right! Despite his error it would be all right after all! Once more he had bamboozled Ford, and once more the very incompetence of that worthy man had come to his rescue. The fit of laughter over, he mopped his brow with a blue silk handkerchief, the excellence of whose quality did not quite succeed in disguising the garishness of its design. It had been a near thing – too near a thing to be pleasant. He glanced at the syringe, still lying on a table, and put it carefully away.

'Doing everything he could to bring him round,' indeed! He wondered Ford had swallowed that! Of course he had at one time, but not with that syringe, and not just before Ford had walked in all unannounced. Unconsciously sharing one sentiment at least with the secretary, he considered that Ford, merely as a matter of good taste, should have knocked on the door before he came in.

Carefully Anstruther checked over each word of the interview. When he got home he would commit as much as he could to paper, in case any detail should escape him and cause him to make some stupid slip. He even let his mind wander back to the day that Morrison died, and he had rapidly examined him in that very bedroom as being the most conveniently situated to the library.

Both then and now he had very little doubt as to how Morrison had met his death; never for one moment had the secretary's fear that Benson had flavoured the *soufflé* with the contents of the wrong bottle worried him. For years he had known that Morrison was suffering from a bad heart, the extreme weakness of which he had in pride concealed from all the world. As to his having died from the results of perchloride of mercury, or any other poison for that matter, he had been able to feel a moral certainty from the very first that that had never happened. At any rate, so far as perchloride was concerned, there was not a symptom to suggest it. Of course, without a post-mortem he could not be absolutely certain, but lacking the evidence that that would give, he was as sure as made no difference.

He well remembered his feelings as he had looked at Morrison that night. Of all his patients he was the one who had given the most trouble, had caused him more work, grumbled most at being charged a fee which Anstruther considered was below his proper scale, and had rewarded him merely by occasional disparagement. He had felt that Morrison owed him something. That had been the meaning of his remark at the time, when he consented to sign the death certificate because he was 'thinking of the dead man'.

And then, suddenly, as he had stood there irresolutely turning the matter over in his mind, he had seen how Morrison dead could repay some of the debt due by Morrison living. What an opportunity there was to square so many accounts! The temptation had been too much for him – and it had seemed so harmless. After all he was only going to certify what was probably true!

He remembered his intense delight as the whole plan had formed in his mind. He had always longed to take Ford by the scruff of his neck and shake him, and go on shaking him until it hurt, and until he had got some sense in his head. Even now, standing in the bedroom in the Club, he felt his blood quicken at the mere thought of what joy the physical sensation would have been when he saw Ford's fat head wag from side to side, and his knees gradually begin to give in. There was a roll of fat at the back of the secretary's neck from which several times he had hardly been able to keep his hands.

Alas! that the shaking had been only moral. Still, the pleasures of the mind, as he had written one day when he had been unable to concentrate his thoughts so as to exclude his fingers from typing too much, were more subtle, more keen, if not so entirely satisfying as those of the body. Carefully playing on the nerves of a weak man he had been able to get complete control, and at the same time to watch the unconcealed reactions of his victim to the twists of the screw. It had been a stroke of genius to manoeuvre himself into the position of both the torturer and the confidant on whose shoulder the victim sobbed, and at the same time to put right all the grievances as to the Club which he had so long cherished, and so fortunately never mentioned.

The first suspicion of a fly in his ointment had been Hughes. It had always seemed to Anstruther that there was a very real danger that Hughes might know too much. At first he had felt that he could rely with confidence on the waiter's stupidity, but as the days went by, he thought he detected a curious look in the man's eye. He seemed to be always watching him, and he made up his mind that it would be better and safer if he went.

Well, that matter was not yet finally settled, but Anstruther flattered himself that it was by now well on the way to being disposed of; what between the pressure he could exert through his typewriter, and the direct spur he could add by his alleged doubts about the glass of sherry, with which of course there had in fact been nothing the matter, he was pretty sure that Ford would have to obey. It was quite time, by the way, that this disobedience was ended. He must devise some additional punishment for that lack of good discipline.

Then the play-acting had been fun. He had enjoyed nothing so much as writing those letters to himself, letters so violent that when he got them next day they had actually hurt. He had hugged them to himself and let their taunts sink in. After the first time he had decided that it was well worth the three half-pence to post them to himself late at night. The next day they came to him as something fresh, something new and barbed with points dipped in irony. The reading of them had been even finer than the writing of them.

Then he had at any rate forced himself to learn more about poisons. A useful and profitable study, that of poisons. Besides which the alleged compulsion under which he worked might serve other purposes. It had helped to throw dust in Ford's eyes for one thing, and, if by any chance anything should subsequently emerge, it might serve as a screen to save him from hanging. He was not quite sure of the law as regards people who supplied poisons either knowingly or carelessly – he expected that it earned a pretty severe sentence – but if you could manage to get a judge and jury to believe that it was the result of blackmail, he strongly suspected that you stood a very good chance of being dealt with leniently. The popular prejudice against blackmail was so strong!

But – he looked at the syringe – he must get his facts a little better if he was to continue along the charming path he had mapped out for himself; if he was frequently to have the fun of watching the reactions of arrogant men to the doses he could insidiously insert into their food or their drink, or inject into them. There must be no more mistakes as in the case of Pargiter! For one thing he had not in fact, whatever he might have said, so very many more patients in the Club whom he could use as victims in his experiments, and it would not be safe, since he could only sign certificates for his own patients, to select any member of the Club casually.

It had been annoying in the first place to have had to do anything about Pargiter at all. He had never really intended to. He had merely taken his name in vain in order to frighten Ford, and if Ford happened to get into his head the idea that Pargiter was the blackmailer, well, so much the better. But he had all along expected the secretary to give in and sack Hughes.

But when he had not, he had fallen back on the idea of giving him a good fright. It would be a very good moral tonic for that disobedient man if he found one of the members for whose safety he ought to consider himself responsible, lying lightly poisoned in the library. But only lightly poisoned. 'Death,' Anstruther repeated to himself as if there was some magic in the phrase, 'was entirely accidental.'

He had spent the whole evening watching Pargiter, and waiting for his opportunity. He was sure it would be offered sooner or later because of his victim's habit of sitting in what had been Morrison's corner, and of turning the chair round so that he got a better light, which involved turning his back on the room. And sure enough eventually the chance had come, and he had been there to take it. Of course he had not been ill. That had been a brilliant afterthought, suggested to him by the presence in his pocket of a strong emetic – another experiment! – and a very convincing corroborative detail he had made of it!

And so, when the chance came, he had been all ready, ready with the syringe containing the hyoscine he had taken from its normal *ampoules* of a two-hundredth of a grain. The maximum dose, as he knew, was a sixtieth of a grain, and that was what he believed he had got in the syringe. Had he not used just three and a third of the *ampoules* that contained a two-hundredth of a grain each, so that just a sixtieth of a grain had been shot from behind into the unseeing and unknowing Pargiter? As he had expected, the man had stiffened as if he had been knocked out. That was exactly as he had planned it, and then that little touch more that he had given him, just for fun. It could not have amounted in all to more than a fiftieth of a grain, and surely that ought not to be fatal?

It had been in a considerable state of alarm that he had gone through for Pargiter exactly the same process, except for the absence of Ford, as had been enacted for Morrison. Sending Hughes away, he had for a while genuinely done what he could for the man who was so unaccountably dead, done what he could, that is, for a while, until he had finally realized that it was hopeless. Then, with a spasm of blind rage, completely out of control, he had allowed his elementary feelings of pure brutal violence to dominate him and had dug the syringe in again and again long after it was empty, and had only just stopped, panting and terrified, as Ford came in.

It was not until several days later that he realized that he had founded all his calculations on the *ampoules* containing a two-hundredth of a grain, and that in fact he had got hold of *ampoules* containing one-hundredth of a grain each, so that his first injection had been double the strength that he had intended, in itself the maximum dose.

At first he was inclined to blame the chemist, but a little calm reflexion convinced him that the mistake was entirely his. He was inclined to take up the attitude that it was an unfortunate error which had nearly had regrettable consequences for himself. With a resolution to be more careful in future, he dismissed that detail as a mere incident. So far as Pargiter was concerned it was, no doubt, bad luck, but beyond that he did not go. Indeed he was rather indignant. Had he not been deprived of the results and pleasure of a very interesting experiment?

But now a second fly was threatening to get into the ointment. At least to call Cardonnel a fly was an understatement; a positive blue-bottle! One, moreover, who would be difficult to suppress, but who must be kept out at all costs. That Ford should dare to try deliberately to bring him in! The impertinence of it! That was another cause for reading the secretary a much needed lesson. He had had to do it once before and at that time his hypnotic powers had not failed him. So far as he knew, Ford had kept his lips tightly sealed.

As Anstruther wended his way quietly up Regent Street, he began to consider the problem of Cardonnel. By the time he was home, several plans had occurred to him, but as yet, none of them seemed quite satisfactory. However, no doubt with the morning new inspiration would occur.

CHAPTER 20

CONCERNING THE SHERRY

*

IT was going to be a very delicate matter, and delicacy was
scarcely Ford's strongest point. He even suspected the fact himself. Nevertheless he must somehow or other talk to Hughes
about the sherry, and somehow or other he must manage to do it
without suggesting that Anstruther's glass had been deliberately
doctored so as to get him out of the way. Considering that Hughes
was a bit touchy, it was not going to be too easy. In addition to
that it was most important to find out from him who had been
on the library floor that evening. Moreover, he had to frame his
questions in such a way that they might appear to be quite casual.
It would never do for Hughes to suspect that there was any reason
why the secretary was particularly anxious to know. He could
not have Hughes thinking that there was anything fishy about
Pargiter's death!

Ford sighed as he realized what a muddle he was getting himself into. Not for the first time, he complained bitterly that it was
all Benson's fault. If the chef had not got it into his head that he
had made a muddle over the vanilla bottle, Ford would never
have tried to keep quiet the mystery of Morrison's death, and if
he had not done that he would have been free to go straight to
the police when Pargiter died without having to make the odious
decision (to him) of ruining the doctor whom he still thought he
had lured into being his innocent accomplice.

In fact, as he summoned Hughes on the morning after Pargiter
died, he had reached a state of mind which almost exceeded
Anstruther's fondest hopes. He began by a question which he
regarded as leading up to the subject in an indirect manner.

'Did anyone say anything to you yesterday about the sherry?'

'No, sir. At least, sir, nothing special.' With the privilege of an
old servant, Hughes went on. After all, surely the man he was
talking to knew something of the ways of members by now!
'You know how it is, sir, about the sherry, since we got the new
one, there's some of them always have to say it isn't as good as

the old one. Sort of convention, sir, I never takes any notice
of it.'

Ford frowned. He did not want to discuss the respective merits
or demerits of the two wines. 'I do not mean anything of that
sort. I think the members are gradually beginning to realize that
we chose an excellent wine for them.'

'Yes, sir.' If the secretary wanted to get on his high horse, let
him! Hughes, himself a very pretty judge of sherry, knew perfectly
well that not only were the members unconvinced, but that they
were perfectly right.

'I mean,' went on Ford, still under the impression that his
approach was indirect, 'did anyone make any special complaint?'

Hughes considered for a moment. 'No, sir.'

'Are you sure?'

'Quite, sir.' Was this a catch? If so, he could not see where the
point was. No one had said anything special about the sherry.

The secretary was compelled to start a more frontal attack.
'Didn't Dr Anstruther say something?'

Ah! So that was it! Hughes was not a clever man, but he had
a very shrewd idea that he had an enemy there. As he went about
his work in the library, he had often caught the doctor looking at
him in an odd, almost malevolent manner, and yesterday he had
noticed the glances had been more frequent and more peculiar,
but he was quite sure he was speaking the truth when he told
Ford that Dr Anstruther had made no complaint. If the secretary
had not been quite so official that morning, he would have liked
to have added that if the doctor had thought there was something
wrong with it he might have said so sooner. To Hughes's mind,
one, or at most two, of the club's large glasses, which he knew
quite well only went six to the bottle, was quite enough before
dinner for a gentleman. He had his own ideas as to which members
of the club were gentlemen and which were not; there were some
rather surprising decisions and some that were very far from the
mark, but so far as Anstruther was concerned, it must be admitted
that he was perfectly right.

Still Ford persisted. He was almost sure that the doctor had
told him that he had actually mentioned it. But perhaps Dr

Anstruther only thought that the taste was odd and said nothing?
'At any rate, he thought it was unusual in taste, and something
must have upset him. Certainly something made him ill. While
he was examining Mr Pargiter too. Very awkward.'

'Yes, sir.' It was no business of his, but if his opinion had been
asked, he would have given another suggestion as to why the
doctor was unwell. He would find out what the fellow had drunk
during dinner in addition to his generous ration of sherry. Meanwhile Hughes remained mute, but with a gradually growing con-
viction that he would have to do something about Anstruther
soon. The man was clearly trying to get him into trouble. Besides
he could not help wondering why the secretary was talking solely
about a glass of sherry. He had imagined that he was wanted to
say all he knew about Pargiter's death, but still the conversation
went on about the same subject. He was beginning to get annoyed.

He continued answering the questions put to him as briefly as
possible.

No, no one else had complained. Mr Gladwin had been in the
library and had been talking to Judge Skinner. They frequently
went there before dinner and always broke the rule about silence.
Could Mr Ford speak to them, did he think? One or two of the
junior members wanted to complain but did not have the courage,
being rather afraid of the Judge. Had anyone else been there?
Only, he believed Mr Laming.

A train of thought ran through the secretary's mind. Laming
who complained about the fish, Laming who had repulsed his
half-confidences when Morrison had died, Laming who would
never take responsibility for anything and was always prepared
to let him down, Laming who was so often there and seemed
always to have been about when any of these odd events occurred
– so he was there once more last night! Could he be the man who
preferred to work indirectly? Was that the solution of his mystery?
He began to cross-question Hughes rather obviously as to Laming's movements.

The waiter was clearly surprised, but on the whole not very
helpful. After dinner there had not been many people in the
library, and most of his time had been spent in looking after the
billiard room on the floor above, which it was also part of his

duty to attend to after dinner. He had no very clear idea of who
had been there. 'Except, of course, sir, Mr Pargiter.'

'Yes, yes. Poor Pargiter. A tumour on the brain, I believe, or
perhaps a clot of blood. I am not sure. But anyhow Dr Anstruther
is investigating. I was too upset last night to take it in fully. So
Mr Pargiter was alone in the library – very sad. A little difficult
at times, but *de mortuis*, you know, *de mortuis*!'

'Yes, sir.' Despite the Latin, Hughes did know. 'But I think
Dr Anstruther was there too. At any rate he had coffee there, sir,
and brandy.'

The slight emphasis was wasted on Ford.

'Yes, so he told me, but he was rather disturbed unfortunately,
something, as I have said, having upset him. I am afraid he
thinks it was the sherry.'

It was on the tip of Hughes's tongue to say 'Probably'; but he
managed to stifle it and to confine himself to saying that he knew
nothing of what had happened to the doctor. While he was up
in the billiard room anyone might have gone in and out of the
library without his being any the wiser. 'Indeed, sir, when I am
in my service bar, I usually shut the door. The place looks untidy
from the passage for one thing – so that anyone might pass and
repass without my knowing.'

Ford sighed. It was perfectly true. At the same time it was
exactly the same lack of evidence as he had received from
Johnson on the smoking-room floor when he had been made to
sit on the settee that Sunday afternoon so long ago now.

'Well, anyhow, I think you had better bring me up the rest of
that bottle of sherry just in case –'

'Very well, sir.' Hughes turned and went out in a blinding rage.
There was nothing whatever wrong with any sherry he served,
and he very much resented that any whipper-snapper of a doctor
who ought never to have been elected to his club should say that
there was, and he even more resented that the secretary should
support him. *He* ought to know better! On the way back from
his bar he made up his mind. It was not his usual habit to give the
members away. 'Loyalty all round' was his motto, but a time
did occasionally come when it was essential to speak, and, to his
mind, that time had come. He returned triumphantly carrying

three empty bottles and a nearly empty decanter, and placed
them all on the secretary's table.

'Three?' Ford blinked at them.

'Yes, sir. One was used the night before, but I could not say
which bottle was which. Yesterday one whole bottle was drunk
and nearly another. The rest is in the decanter.'

'But you said there was only Mr Gladwin and Judge Skinner
besides Dr Anstruther.'

'Yes, sir – and Mr Laming.'

'But that's only four people. I suppose Mr Gladwin must have
had a second glass.'

'Yes, sir, he had two, and so had the Judge. Rather unusual, but
Mr Gladwin seemed very pleased about some case he had won.
And Mr Laming had two, which is also unusual, sir.'

Through Ford's mind went a picture of the birdlike Laming
nerving himself up with an extra glass. 'But even so, that only
accounts for one bottle, and apparently the second one was nearly
finished.'

'Yes, sir. Dr Anstruther. I am not quite sure if he had four or
five glasses.'

'What!'

'Oh, nothing unusual in that, sir. Nothing at all.'

Ford made a slight deprecatory noise. He had a vague feeling
that he ought never to discuss the characters of the members with
the staff and he was quite unaware that he frequently implied
more by his expression or even by his silence than he really
meant. All that he intended to convey was that having unfortunately stumbled on something that it would be better that
he should not know, at any rate officially, it would be wise to
change the subject at once. As actually he was surprised by the
revelation, having always thought Anstruther the most temperate
of men, he merely succeeded in looking incredulous.

The effect on Hughes was, not unnaturally, unfortunate. He
disliked being grunted at in such a way as to imply that he was a
liar, as much as any other man.

'Nothing unusual at all, sir,' he repeated. 'And there's another
thing I should like to say, sir. I do think, sir, that it's odd when
the books are going like they are, that a member should be

untying the marker from one of them – the marker with the club name on it, I mean, sir – as he goes downstairs. And doing it in a very secretive way, too. And that's what I've seen Dr Anstruther' – there was a wealth of contempt in his tone – 'doing with my very eyes.'

'Oh, surely not, Hughes, surely not.'

'Yes, sir. You may not believe me, sir, but I saw him.'

'I didn't mean to doubt your word, but I'm sure there is some explanation. Do you happen to know what book it was?'

'I am afraid not, sir.'

'That makes it rather more awkward. I'll turn it over in my mind, but I think I shall not mention it to Dr Anstruther on the whole. A little vague, you see, a little vague. A miss is as good as a mile in such a case.'

'Yes, sir.' Hughes refrained from pointing out that he meant 'as bad as a mile'. Besides he saw now that an unsupported accusation might have unpleasant repercussions for himself. He added that he thought it was his duty to mention it.

Ford agreed. As he sent Hughes away, he came to the conclusion that he was no further on than before; but then he was a past master at the art of failing to see the point.

CHAPTER 21

A NICE CHOICE

*

AT about the same time Anstruther was trying to carry out his ordinary duties, but with a feeling hanging over him that life was very difficult.

It was not alone the effects of the drinking of the previous day – the emetic, if it had done nothing else, had cleared off most of them; it was not at all the reaction to having killed Pargiter. That he had already been through, and by now had almost recovered from it. Pargiter had been of little use to a world to which he had given no pleasure. Pargiter was now dead, and Anstruther was at least sane enough to see that in strict fact there was no cause for tears in that. It was true, of course, that he had killed him, but he refused to regard it as wanton or cold-bloodedly deliberate. It was nothing of the sort. It was not even premeditated. In fact if Pargiter had been a perfectly fit man, Anstruther believed he would not have died under the first injection of hyoscine. There must have been something else wrong with him, or he would not have done so. In fact the doctor had a shrewd suspicion that if he could have followed the normal procedure and got someone else to hold a post-mortem as well, it would have been found that there *was* already a cerebral haemorrhage or something of that sort. From that it was an easy step to consider that Pargiter had no right to be unfit. Within a very short while Anstruther was regarding his victim as largely responsible for his own death.

But the serious matter – to his way of thinking – was the possible consequences.

However discreet Ford might be, and his fears for his own safety ought for once to make him so, it was bound to strike somebody as peculiar that two people should die in the same chair within two months of each other and that both should be patients of the same doctor whom no one should be asked to assist in examining the causes of death. It was so odd that someone might go and comment on it, and when once people started talking, there was no knowing what might happen.

The only hope, to his mind, was that the events had occurred where they had. There is no place where people mind their own business more, where there is less vulgar curiosity, than a London club. A man may go there day by day and form quite a close friendship with another without even knowing whether his acquaintance is married with six children, or a bachelor living with a widowed mother. Nor is it regarded as being of any great importance. The facts often leaked out casually, but that again was considered as trivial – an attitude of mind which slightly annoyed and completely baffled the wives of members.

It is true that there was gossip – there always is anywhere – but it never spread very far and was mostly confined to the particular man's ability to play billiards or his fatal partiality (from his partner's point of view) for declaring grand slams which could never be made, his habits of snoring every afternoon or of talking in too aggressive a voice.

But when it came to dying in the club, it was a nice point how much notice was likely to be taken of an act so contrary to the best traditions of the place. There had been singularly little interest aroused when Morrison had died. It was passed round as a piece of news, and that was all. On the whole, so far as Anstruther had heard the matter commented upon, it was re-garded as a piece of rather bad form typical of that retired nuisance.

So then there was a sporting chance that the death of the more unpopular Pargiter would be similarly regarded. All the same, if anything did happen, what was his line of defence?

Well, firstly, he might try to get them to exhume Morrison. They would find nothing wrong with *him*, even after the passing of two months or at any time. Anstruther could not help smiling as he thought of his ridiculous remarks about 'playing for time'. As if time had anything to do with it! If there had been poison, which there never had, substantial traces would have lingered for a very much longer time than he had implied. To talk about playing for time, therefore, had been unsafe, even to so stupid a man as Ford.

But there must be other methods of defence, and if possible, better ones. He began to consider who were his chief dangers.

Well, first there was Hughes. It had by now become an absolute obsession with him that the library waiter knew more than he should. Well, that must be dealt with once and for all.

Secondly, there was a possibility of a revolt by Ford. That he considered unlikely. After the previous evening, in his opinion, the secretary was under his thumb more completely than ever.

Thirdly, there was just general gossip. As to that, he must meet it as and when it arose. There was no good in trying to meet trouble halfway. If he did, he would probably disclose in the process that there was some trouble to be met.

But finally and worst of all, there was Cardonnel. Despite his warnings and orders, he gathered that Ford was not only allowing but actually encouraging this most undesirable man (from Anstruther's point of view) to continue to go on prying about the club. Had Ford forgotten the trouble Cardonnel had caused about the sherry – how difficult he had been about the tea trays? And how always he could be relied upon to raise difficulties? He would probably start the matter by pointing out that there was no bye-law under which members were allowed to die on the club premises.

And this was the man whom Ford, in his lamblike ignorance, was allowing to play the detective! About the books, apparently. Well, that mattered very little. He had, it is true, borrowed a book which rather interested him by describing in considerable detail the exact methods adopted by Papuan savages for torturing the wrongdoers of their tribe, partly by extremely effective and painful wood poisons, but this could be returned. That was nothing serious. But what other matters had Ford encouraged Cardonnel to investigate? Morrison's death? Well, Anstruther smiled, there was no harm in that.

But it would never do for so pertinacious a man to start taking an interest in the little matter of Pargiter's hyoscine, nor in Anstruther's own private affairs. He must never, for instance, see the old typewriter, which he kept secretly locked away and used only for his letters to Ford – and to himself! It would indeed be best if Cardonnel found himself slightly ill – if he could be induced to think that a little sea air was good for him. If only Cardonnel had been his patient, how happily and convincingly he would have recommended a very long sea voyage – right round the world – twice if possible.

Perhaps then the best thing to do would be to see to it that Cardonnel *was* ill – a trifle, quite light poisoning. There must be no mistake this time. A third death would never be explained away, however ingenious he might be! No, there must be just enough to make Cardonnel feel that he was really ill, something administered quietly and unobtrusively, in small doses, repeated, if necessary, until the tiresome lawyer fled from the effects of the English winter which this year was trying him so very severely.

Suddenly a bright idea occurred to Anstruther. Why not arrange matters so that it would look as if the poison had been administered by Hughes? An admirable thought! With a double advantage too. It should make certain, if any question arose, of Hughes's dismissal, and if further inquiries were made about Pargiter's death, it might even throw suspicion in the wrong place.

On further thought, though, not even Ford, far less Scotland Yard, if they were called in, could imagine for a moment that anyone in Hughes's position could have got hold of so much, or indeed any, hyoscine. Still it was not a bad idea. It could be used if Ford were still obdurate about dismissing the waiter.

So then it only remained to decide on which poison to use to encourage Cardonnel to move to another continent rather than another world.

By the time he had got thus far in his meditations, Anstruther had finished his day's work. During all the time he had managed to conceal his often interrupted thoughts from his patients and had indeed even managed to feign an interest in their sufferings. It was difficult work. He had positively to relieve pain, when all day and every day he had but one thought, to give it! Now and then he was lucky and managed to force a particularly painful operation of doubtful necessity, but generally it was impossible. He had, after all, his reputation to consider.

But now he could sit back in his still chilly, austere sitting-room, in which he mortified even his own flesh with trivial discomforts, and could allow himself the luxury of thinking of the effects of various drugs.

On the whole he favoured the more actively irritant poisons and the more common ones at that. Hyoscine had been almost a flight of fancy.

Of course there was always arsenic. It had the great merit, from his point of view, of giving gradually increasing pain. But then, if you were careless, and after the recent incident he was afraid of being careless, it might be fatal. Besides, arsenic was such a platitude. Everybody knew about arsenic. There was nothing new, nothing intelligent, nothing *witty* about arsenic.

Now what about oxalic acid? That was a good irritant poison. The objection was that it acted almost at once, and if everyone who sat next to him at dinner was invariably sick – well, somebody might notice it. Especially as it would always be just as he finished his own dinner or lunch as the case might be. Besides, the crystals were large, awkward, clumsy things.

There drifted back into his mind the original trouble from which everything had started – the perchloride of mercury that Benson feared he had confused with the vanilla, a powerful emetic, even more powerful than the one he had used the night before, one which was readily obtainable in nice small crystals, a poison the use of which was not hackneyed.

Now what was the best way to administer it, not only to Cardonnel, but to the club in general? Suddenly an idea struck him, a method so simple and so very difficult to detect. True, he could not always be present to see the effects, but no matter. He would no doubt hear of them. Oh, admirable subchloride, he meant perchloride of mercury. Subchloride! The slip of the tongue had given him another idea. Calomel, the subchloride, was not a poison, but it was also a fine white powder; a little greyish in tinge perhaps both of them, but not noticeably. With the two of them, something should really be possible.

Moreover, the method would once more call attention to those detestable tea-trays which he loathed so heartily, and which were still not entirely replaced. Of course there was the difficulty that any member of the club might be the victim, even Anstruther himself, and not Cardonnel in particular. But then he could probably manage somehow a little extra for that gentleman. Besides, it would not be so conspicuous if Cardonnel was only one of the crowd; and as for himself – well, if it came his way, it would add an artistic touch of innocence, and he would have to put up with it.

For a moment, resembling Ford, he reflected that he would have to take the rough with the smooth. That he might ruin the club in the process, was a matter of no consequence to him whatever.

CHAPTER 22

THE WEARING OF THE GREEN

*

'AND what, young man, is the bright idea?'

Judge Skinner was slightly out of breath. In his opinion, only the elderly or decrepit ought to use the lift. Nevertheless he considered that he had a grievance that the secretary's office should be up so many flights of stairs and he conveniently forgot what his comments would have been if a more easily accessible part of the club had been set aside for that purpose. With a growing sense of injury, he put his left hand immediately under the secretary's nose; three of the fingers were stained a startling shade of sap green.

'I have tried, let me tell you, every kind of soap in the club, but apparently nothing will get it off. We have, by the way, no pumice stone soap. Why not? I have put a request in the suggestion book to that effect.'

Later Ford was to become quite well aware that he had. What he had actually written was: 'It is suggested that pummy stone soap be supplied'; and the rather harassed secretary had to hope that the Judge would not notice that some irreverent member, neglecting to sign his name, had added: 'It is suggested that "pummy" be spelt "pumice".' But for the present, in happy ignorance of this slight contretemps, he hastened to assure his visitor that the soap was usually available. It just so happened by bad luck to have been used up or lost or something of that sort when the Judge had needed it.

His fingers still spread out in protest, the Judge puffed at him solemnly. 'Finished, eh? Am I to understand then that this green mess has been plastered all over the hands of all the members?'

Ford politely indicated that he hoped it was not quite as bad as that; only certain members.

'Indeed! And may I ask what I have done to be so – distinguished?' Once more the vivid green fingers were prominently displayed.

This was getting harder and harder to explain. 'Well, sir, I was trying – I am afraid with very unfortunate results – to see if it were possible to – to identify the man who' – (this was getting more and more difficult) 'who was – was borrowing occasionally the library books from the Club.'

As an explanation it was hardly tactful. The Judge fairly snorted. 'Do you mean to say, young man, that you have the impertinence to suggest that I, a Judge of His Majesty's County Court, am a common thief? It's a libel, sir, a positive libel – or a slander,' he ended weakly. Who could say offhand whether smearing a green dye on a man's fingers was a written accusation or a spoken one? It was a nice point, requiring consideration. He must consult the Clerk of his Court.

Faced with the direct result of his trap, Ford ran away. The idea, when it first came to his mind, had seemed so clever, so automatic and neat, but now it hardly seemed so convincing. Long ago in an attempt to eradicate pure absent-mindedness, the Committee had decided that in every book in the circulating library a short cord was to be tied with a running noose down the back of the binding, hanging from which was a celluloid tab with 'Whitehall Club' clearly stamped on it. The label would serve as a convenient marker, and unless the cord were deliberately untied, the marker would remain in the book as a reminder of where the book belonged. It had only been on that part of the cord which he had been confidently certain ought, under all normal circumstances, to be well inside the space between its back and its binding that he had put the dye.

In order, therefore, to get the dye on his hands, the Judge must have untied the cord – at least that was the theory – and the idea had been that whenever he saw a member whose hands had gone that very peculiar shade of green, he would be able to ask him why he had seen fit to tamper with the marker. But now presented with the first fruits of his handiwork, he found it quite impossible to carry out the programme. And yet – how had the Judge contrived to get his fingers on to the dyed cord?

As a speculation, it was interesting, but from a practical point of view, Ford certainly lacked the courage of his convictions. In fact he ran away from them as fast as he could. He hastened to explain that the idea that Judge Skinner might be the book thief was too ridiculous to be considered for a moment. It was, *of 'course*, not a man like him for whom he was looking. But he had hopes all the same of finding out something from the device.

Nothing seemed less probable to the Judge, and he said so. Nevertheless, as a reasonable man, he was prepared to give the secretary credit for having made an effort. 'For, young man, it's quite time someone took this club in hand. Allowing members to die twice in the library! It's disgraceful.'

It passed through Ford's mind to suggest firstly that he was being taken in hand far too much by his anonymous correspondent, and secondly that no one had died twice, but it would never do to be funny at the expense of an indignant man. He contented himself with saying that it 'was most regrettable'.

'Regrettable, eh? Hardly the word I should use about Pargiter. Careless, that's what it is – careless. When you see a man's ill, send him off home. At once. That's the right thing to do.'

Ford wondered what the Judge would have said if he had started the interview by saying: 'Sir, in my opinion, you are in danger of having apoplexy. Go home'? Aloud he muttered a non-committal affirmative.

'And how long will it take before this has gone?'

Normally, Ford explained, he had been told that it took about a week before the dye disappeared, but with a person of such scrupulously clean habits as Judge Skinner, perhaps four days would see the end of it. For the fact that the dye had got on to the Judge's hands he could only offer the humblest apologies.

It was a bit obvious, and Skinner was not for a moment deceived. All the same, it was clear to him that Ford was doing his best to repair the damage done, no doubt by accident. After all, what else could he do other than apologize? Wisely he decided to make the best of it, and went off to tell the story against himself as often as he could. It seemed the only way of preventing other people from telling it behind his back.

Left alone, the prospect seemed drearier than ever to Ford. His attempt to find out something for himself had started badly, and if he was going to have as little success in the less important and less difficult matter, what chance had he got in the bigger and more complicated problems? He picked up a sheet of paper, and heading it idly 'Men I would like to know', wrote underneath:

'1. The man who killed Morrison.
2. The man who killed Pargiter.
3. The man who steals the library books.
4. The man who sends those anonymous typewritten letters to me.'

He sighed wearily. It would be a help if he were sure whether it was four men he wanted to know, or three, or two, or possibly only one. Certainly not more than three, he thought. Surely it was reasonable to assume that numbers 1 and 2 were the same? Hearing a step outside, he hurriedly crumpled up the paper and threw it in the fire. It was no document to leave lying about!

Cardonnel came in chortling with laughter and gaily singing 'They're hanging men and women now, for wearing of the green'.

'Watson, Watson, my dear fellow, you have excelled yourself. If the club laughs, and I think it will, all will be well, but heaven help you if they don't see the funny side.'

With tears trickling down his cheeks, he waved in the air three fingers resembling a chestnut tree in spring. 'I've just been talking to the Judge and I think he's all right now, but did it never occur to you that that dye would spread? For heaven's sake take all the markers out before someone covers his clothes with it.'

'But do you mean to say that *everyone's* getting it? Surely it's only if you untie the cord?'

'Did you suggest to the Judge he had?'

Ford blushed. 'Well, no, as a matter of fact, I hardly liked to.'

'I'm not surprised. But do go and take them off. Everybody's getting covered with it. Laming's absolutely furious; says he'll never live it down in the Home Office.'

'Heavens, why?'

'Who knows? But, man, don't waste time. Get on with it.'

Ford picked up the house telephone and gave instructions to each floor that the markers were all to be untied from the books and brought back to him.

'I suppose you *are* right,' Cardonnel said thoughtfully, 'if half

the members of the club are going to be bright green, we may as
well have green waiters to match.'

'What?'

'Well, they'll all get smothered bringing them up. And has it
occurred to you, too, that probably most of the books will be
smeared. You'll probably have to pay for new copies of most of
them. Do you know really it seems to me that it would have been
cheaper to have let them be stolen. But, my word,' he added
meditatively, 'what an efficient dye!'

There comes a moment even in the life of a club secretary when
it is impossible to go on giving a realistic imitation of a doormat
any longer.

'Dash it all, sir,' Ford broke out, 'I was trying, and, come to
that, if you will excuse my saying so, other methods have not
helped us very much. I mean, I have been through the bedroom
list I gave you, and we don't seem to be any nearer to fixing our
man from Nottingham.'

It was perhaps fortunate for Ford that Cardonnel was at
heart a good-tempered man. No one likes being told that he is
indifferently competent at his hobbies. It is worse than being told
you are incapable in your profession. But Cardonnel's character
was not only sufficiently big for him not to take offence where no
offence was intended, it was sufficiently big for him to appreciate
if there was any truth in the criticism.

'I know. You're quite right. There's something wrong somewhere. Perhaps you were right when you suggested that the man
did not live in Nottingham now, but only used to do so.'

'Well, I've been through the addresses again and not only the
present addresses, but the old ones for the last five years, and I
can't find anyone who comes from that part of the world who
was in the club on those dates.'

'I suppose I must take that as conclusive. All the same, I give
up my idea of a Nottingham man with the very greatest reluc-
tance. All those cricket and football matches could not have
been pure coincidence, could they?'

As a matter of fact, in Ford's opinion, they were probably
exactly that, but it was almost impossible to say so. It is never
very easy to convince anyone that a theory he has built up is

founded on a fallacy, and when the labour of building up the theory had been so very heavy, it is doubly difficult. Besides, if it was only a coincidence, it was a very extensive one. All he could do was to suggest feebly that there must be some curious and unexpected factor which had in some way vitiated the conclusions. '"The best laid plans of mice and men", you know,' he ended.

Cardonnel nodded. 'That is one of the quotations that is never finished, and if it should be, is almost invariably finished incorrectly.'

The rather legitimate indignation and the entirely incorrect assertion that he could finish the quotation quite accurately if he chose, which had both risen simultaneously to Ford's lips, caused him to stutter. Before he could say anything, there was a knock at the door, and after the briefest pause a page-boy came in.

Cardonnel gave one look at him and burst into fits of laughter. In his hand the boy held some fifty or sixty of the book-markers which he had apparently been sent to collect from floor to floor. His palms and all his fingers were a vivid green; even the dirt of his nails was mercifully obliterated with it. Smears of apple green covered his uniform, and, to add to it, he had apparently sucked the book-markers on his way upstairs. His lips, his forehead, even his hair and ears proclaimed the efficiency of the compound. He turned rather an angry look on Cardonnel. What was the old man laughing at him for? He hadn't done anything that he knew of to be laughed at like that.

'Help,' came faintly from Cardonnel. 'And the Judge says you told him that it took a week normally to get it off. It's a lucky thing, young man, Guy Fawkes Day is over. Just look at yourself in that glass. There's only one thing you can do with him, Ford. Send him round to the makers of that infernal dye of yours as an advertisement. It might pay for his uniform. Look out! Don't put those infernal markers near me, boy.'

Ford turned to the rather sulky-looking page. 'All right, boy. Not your fault. Go and see the steward and tell him I said you were to be put on duty for the next week where you will not be seen.'

The lad gave one last look in the glass. 'They won't half laugh at me, sir.'

'And at me, boy. You can tell them you're not the only one. Plenty on the members too.' Cardonnel showed him his hands, and sent the boy off reasonably happy. Anyhow. he was going to get a new uniform out of it. He liked to look smart, and the one he had inherited from previous page-boys was not, in his opinion, worthy of him.

As he went, Cardonnel got up and looked in the glass. 'Ah, I'm glad to see that, unlike our young friend, I did not suck the cord. Hope that stuff isn't poisonous, by the way.'

CHAPTER 23

SPIDER OR FLY?

*

'WE can't have the staff poisoned.'

'*What?*' Cardonnel swung round quickly from the looking-glass. 'What on earth do you mean by that?'

'Why, just what I said. It would be very awkward if one of the boys was upset by that dye. Their parents do make such a fuss – even about the most trivial things. Do you know, that the other day –' Ford tried to cover his unfortunate slip by starting to recount the extensive bullying he had recently received from a large woman, no respecter of persons, on the subject of the food given to her son. He had decided, he said, for the future to employ nothing but orphans or those whose parents lived at a safe distance in one of the remoter distressed areas.

But so obvious a red herring was useless against Cardonnel. That astute man was almost sure that Ford had stopped his sentence abruptly, and had swallowed the word 'too'. It was a good opportunity to bring up the point which Gladwin had made to him about Morrison's heart, and to that matter he started to bring the conversation round. The animadversions of little Billy's mother on the subject of rabbit as an article of diet were merely boring. He swept them all aside.

'I want to talk to you about Anstruther, and please understand' – his legal caution prevailing – 'that what I want to say is entirely confidential.'

With a feeling that if he did not, far too much might emerge, Ford made another desperate attempt to switch the conversation.

'I am so glad you have brought his name up. I want to tell you something that I was told the other day. It might help you in your inquiry about the books.' With that he plunged into such an account as he could remember of Hughes's accusations. As repeated by Ford, it did not sound very convincing, but at least he managed to suggest that there was some evidence for thinking that Anstruther, at any rate, borrowed books. To Ford's joy, Cardonnel seemed to be taking quite an interest; he followed the

story, such as it was, carefully, and began to cross-examine him
about it, a process which served to show how many links in the
chain of evidence were missing.

As a topic of conversation it could not last for ever, but there
was always a chance that it might last long enough. Like Anstruther himself, as Ford fondly thought, he was playing for time.
At any moment someone might interrupt. For once he wanted to
hear the telephone bell ring; even an angry member dripping
green dye from every finger would have been welcome. But
nothing happened.

'This is all very intriguing,' Cardonnel summed up, 'if hardly
conclusive. I think I shall give myself the pleasure of making the
acquaintance of Dr Anstruther. I hardly know him, you know,
and he seems to be a man well worth cultivating, a curious character, so very reserved, of whom so very little is known. I must
find out more about him, more about his antecedents, for instance. He may yet,' he added hopefully, 'prove my deductions to
have been right. But this is not what I wanted to talk to you
about. I wanted to talk to you about his patients.'

Ford's last despairing effort to make a feeble joke on the subject of its being unprofessional, was brushed ruthlessly aside.
'No doubt it has struck you as odd that two of them should have
died here recently. So far as Pargiter is concerned, I have nothing
to say. I have thought for a long while that he hardly looked a
healthy man. That he should have had a cerebral haemorrhage
seems to me quite likely. But what I cannot understand is
Morrison.'

'Heart failure,' remarked Ford woodenly.

'So I was told,' was the dry comment. 'The only trouble is that
Morrison used to talk about his ailments to a friend of mine *ad
nauseam* and the only thing he never mentioned was a weak heart.'

'Ah, that so often happens. People are so ready to talk about
their imaginary ills, but seldom about what is really wrong with
them.' Ford shook his head wisely. He had for once in his life
spoken the truth rather shrewdly, and the trifling fact that he did
not believe a word of it himself must not be allowed to detract
from the merit of the performance.

Not that Cardonnel believed a word of it either. He merely

shook his head and continued. 'Now there were two people, and two only as far as I can make out, who knew anything of what happened after he died – yourself and Dr Anstruther. And after that, what do I see?'

He paused rhetorically, and gave Ford time to hope that he had seen nothing.

'Why, that you two, who previously had exchanged very few words, suddenly became as thick as thieves. Moreover, you suddenly start a burst of activity over all sorts of little details of the management of the club which you have previously studiously neglected for years, and then you start getting nervous and jumpy, and hoping that the staff will not be poisoned. And now you tell me that this doctor, this newly found colleague of yours, is taking to drink, and is stealing the books. Well, perhaps he is. But why, tell me? Obviously because,' he shook his head solemnly, 'I was going to talk about Morrison's death and you wanted to lead me away from the subject.'

He paused for breath, and then continued. 'But, of course, the oddest point is this: why, when Pargiter died, did Anstruther not get a *second opinion*? It would have been the most obvious precaution in the world. So there must have been some reason. We know, don't we, that there was nothing wrong with Pargiter's death, was there?'

'No, nothing at all.'

'You said that rather too quickly. As a matter of fact you and I know nothing of the kind. I wonder now if there was?' He leaned back in his chair and considered the point. As for Ford, he could only hope that he did not look as nervous as he felt.

'Well, that is a point that can be considered later,' Cardonnel went on. 'Mind you, I am inclined to think that there was not, simply because no one would risk the exact duplication of a crime. Still, it will be wise only to let the matter stay in abeyance for the time being. Let us go back to the beginning. Obviously something was definitely wrong with Morrison's death, possibly something that might have come out, though I can hardly see how, in a post-mortem on Pargiter. But the point is this, you know quite well what happened about Morrison. Now then, what was it?'

The last sentence was thrown out suddenly and rapidly. Faced with the direct question, Ford made the fatal yet ultimately fortunate mistake of hesitating. He might have pretended a bland ignorance, have replied readily: 'Why, nothing so far as I know. It upset me at the time, that was all; naturally,' and gone on to talk about feeling responsible for anything that happened in the club.

But with Cardonnel's steady gaze, he did not for a moment believe that he could get away with it, nor did he feel that he could make a clean breast of the whole thing. Instead, with a devastating weakness, he adopted a middle course, which was completely untrue and very unfair to Benson. He placed Cardonnel in the position in which he had found himself when the chef had arrived to say he had muddled the two bottles, and he had then gone on and found Morrison dead in the library.

'But consider the position I was in. To this day I do not know how Morrison died. It may have been heart failure. It may have been the perchloride of mercury. There was Benson to consider – there was the club to consider. If it was heart failure, there was no more to be said. But if he had been poisoned, it was a pure accident, and one very much better kept quiet. And so I induced Anstruther to help me to do so. Really I have felt rather sorry for him. Now that this second death has occurred it's very awkward for him.'

'But doesn't he know how Morrison died?'

'No idea in the world. You see as he had decided to say it was heart failure, he could not make a complete post-mortem.'

For a moment Cardonnel leant back in his favourite judicial attitude, with the tips of his fingers touching. 'Not being a doctor, I speak with some hesitation, but I should say that that was unmitigated rubbish.'

Ford's mouth fell open. He had no desire to explain that, after the certificate had been signed, both he and Anstruther had become aware that the vanilla was nothing to do with it, nor was he going to talk about the blackmailing letters. He plunged deeper into the mess.

'I suppose you are right. He must know. But as you yourself have said, Anstruther is like the proverbial oyster. He impressed on me very firmly that it was heart failure, but in such a way that I was inclined to think that he knew it was not; so that whether *he* knows or not, *I* do not. But after all, sir, what does it matter? If it was heart failure, there's an end of it. And if Benson did – did actually poison him by mistake, wouldn't it be much better to leave it at that?'

'Do you realize that if he did, you are making yourself an accessory after the event to the crime of manslaughter at the least?'

'But it wasn't a crime, it was an accident.'

'Not in the eyes of the law.'

'Then the law's –'

'No, the law is not an ass. That is the silliest remark anyone ever made.'

'But isn't it in Dickens? Well, sir, anyhow, there it is. Personally I shall stick to it that it was heart failure, and so will Anstruther, and I really with all respect suggest that if you could possibly leave it at that, it would do no harm. But there is one thing I do beg of you, and that is that you will not worry Benson. Whatever happens to law and justice and all those sort of things, we cannot have the cooking upset.'

'Worry? Worry? I never worry anyone. But as to the main matter, it all depends.'

'Depends on what?'

'On what I think of Anstruther. I shall first take the trouble to cultivate *his* acquaintance.'

When next Anstruther and Cardonnel met it would be a little hard for a dispassionate observer in possession of all the facts to decide which was spider and which was fly. But as for Ford, there was very little difficulty in describing his position. His mentality resembled with considerable fidelity that of a rabbit which has been mesmerized by two snakes simultaneously.

Moreover, by way of making quite certain that his position was an unenviable one, he decided to give both of them good cause to dislike him. Having already given Anstruther away to a considerable extent, he considered it only fair to warn him that Cardonnel was after him. He wrote him a very carefully worded note.

In it he implied that some danger was liable to come from that direction, but he worded it so carefully and so obscurely, from a desire not to put Anstruther on his guard about the books for one thing, and for another to avoid committing himself in any way on paper, that it was almost incomprehensible. On the whole the impression on the doctor's mind was that Cardonnel was hard on his track in the matter of the death of Pargiter. He did not like it at all.

CHAPTER 24

'THE WAYS OF MELANESIA'

*

WHEN it came to a display of agility, as it were, with foils, Anstruther had one advantage over Cardonnel. He did know that he was on the defensive as well as on the offensive. He knew that he had to conceal everything connected with Pargiter's death, and he also knew that he intended to produce an actual physical counter-attack. Moreover, though he was undoubtedly impeded by having committed a murder, he had the advantage of having discarded all the recognized rules and of allowing himself the choice of any and every weapon. His only limit – but it was a very material one – was that he must not be found out.

But if Cardonnel suffered from a complete ignorance that he was in any danger, Anstruther was under the disadvantage of misunderstanding entirely the object at which his adversary was aiming. He thought he had to ward off an investigation into the crime he had committed. Actually Cardonnel, a man who liked to deal with one thing at a time, was so immersed in his investigation into the disappearance of the circulating library books that he had relegated even the matter of Morrison's death to a secondary place, but then Cardonnel was a man who was always in danger of attaching too high an importance to trivialities.

It was this lack of a sense of proportion that caused any conversation between the two of them to be extremely confused. In the most casual question, Anstruther would imagine there must be some deep trap, while the questions which, to Cardonnel, were really full of significance were answered readily enough; in fact sometimes so glibly and with so unexpected a reply, that Cardonnel, the victim of a preconceived theory, was apt to think that they were answered untruthfully with the definite object of throwing him off the scent.

There was, for instance, the question of Anstruther's female relatives. When he discovered that the doctor was a bachelor and never played bridge, Cardonnel had had to abandon the point, which was not one as to the accuracy of which he had ever been deeply committed, that the presence of the books was explained away by the analogy of the second-hand packs of cards. But there was still left the birthday present in May.

With the absence of a wife, went also some of the possibilities of a sister-in-law actually existing. It was with regret, too, whilst trying to lead the conversation to the subject of cricket and the exploits of the Notts eleven via the subject of village matches and practice in the garden, that Cardonnel learned that no cricket was ever played in the home of Anstruther *père*.

'What, didn't you knock a ball about with your brothers?'

'I had no brothers. Besides, I was brought up in London.'

This was doubly annoying. An absence of brothers eliminated the last chance of the existence of a sister-in-law, and if the man was brought up in London, he did not live in Nottingham. It was almost trebly annoying, since Cardonnel, prizing his reputation for intelligence, objected to fishing with quite so inane a question and bringing up a net that was not only empty but more than empty, if such a thing were possible. Even Anstruther seemed to feel the conversation was futile. He stirred in his chair, and added:

'And even my sister never played tennis.'

Suddenly he noticed that the remark had interested Cardonnel extremely. He appeared to be asking, with a complete lack of gallantry, how old the lady was. At least he seemed to want to know something about her birthday. Anstruther became suddenly cautious. It was years since he had seen his sister Violet, and as to when her birthday was he had no idea, nor had he in fact sent her a birthday present for years and years. But since it was impossible that such a point could ever interest his questioner in itself, there must be some deep reason for it.

Finally he decided that Cardonnel must be developing a theory that Violet Anstruther in some way provided a motive for his having wanted to murder Pargiter. As there was not the slightest chance that the two had ever met, he had no objection to so perfect a mare's nest being completely explored. The more time Cardonnel wasted on that, the better! And since the best way to arouse curiosity was to withhold information, he became acutely mysterious.

Of course the more enigmatic he became, the more Cardonnel

felt convinced that he was on the right scent. He frankly did not believe that anyone could have forgotten the date of his sister's birthday. He had never done so himself. But then Cardonnel was the kind of man who knows his own size in gloves and is amazed to find that others are not equally well informed.

Eventually, driven nearly desperate by Anstruther's evasions, he was forced to go to Somerset House for the information he required, and when he found that the lady was actually born in May, he became convinced that his theory was perfectly correct. As to her brother's denials of any knowledge as to her literary tastes, he simply did not believe them.

So far Anstruther had detected no signs of danger in the frequent and rather boring conversations to which he was subjected. He had no great objection to making Cardonnel's acquaintance, and that the first steps to doing so should be taken by the lawyer was all to the good. It would make it seem more natural that he should be near him if, later on, he wanted to be. For the present, though, he had postponed the administration of even the smallest dose of poison. It would be better to let things die down, if possible, first.

He had just practised occasionally the insertion of an occasional grain of calomel so as to acquire the knack of salting his neighbour's food and drink, but so far as he could make out, he was only improving Cardonnel's health – which was irritating. Still, what was practised with the subchloride could be carried out later with the very different perchloride. Meanwhile he listened patiently and, if possible, alertly to Cardonnel's conversation.

It was a curious form of conversation. It seemed to consist more and more of questions, and of questions without the slightest point. There was, for instance, an insistence on Nottinghamshire, which, to his dying day, Anstruther never understood. He gathered that Cardonnel was deeply interested in everything connected with the county. One evening he had even gone to the length of commenting on the fact that the evening paper mentioned that a reserve centre-forward had been transferred from Torquay United to Notts Forest – a matter which could not possibly have been of the slightest moment. As Anstruther had, as far as he knew, never set foot in the county, or taken the slightest interest in professional football or any other sport, he found it incredibly dreary. Still it was better than a discussion on the works of Beethoven.

His final conclusion as to Cardonnel's motives reflected credit on his ingenuity and on his respect for his companion. Cardonnel, he decided, was lulling him into a sense of complete confidence by applying the drug of utter and complete boredom. Finally, when he was weary beyond belief of this senseless chatter, the real questions would begin to come; and by then he would be so accustomed to answering, that he would do so again without thinking.

And when at last the significant question did come, he was more than ever convinced that he was right. It came so naturally and easily. He had been for once off his guard, half dozing, and when he found Cardonnel searching for the name of a book, without thinking, he had automatically supplied it. *The Ways of Melanesia*, it was called, by J. S. Christie.

It seemed such an innocent remark; he had, of course, returned the book to the club long ago. As he said it, he could think of no reason why he should pretend not to know it. It was not until he saw the carefully erased smile that flickered across Cardonnel's face, that he became certain that there was danger. Too late he remembered that in it was that fascinating description of the effects of wood-poisons. Even his impassive face must have for a moment showed his horror at the slip, for he was almost sure that in Cardonnel's eyes was triumph.

And so indeed there was. Not that Cardonnel, never having read a word of it, was able to connect its contents with the events that had happened, but simply that it was a moral certainty that this was the book from which Hughes believed that he had seen Anstruther removing the marker. That the suspected 'borrower' was familiar with the name of it and of its author was a very strong link in the chain, and when you added the obvious discomfiture from which the man was suffering as a result of having admitted so trivial a fact, well, it was time to report progress!

The only person to report to being Ford, Cardonnel did so. He even took the trouble to write it.

'I think', he wrote, 'that I have made several strides in my investigation. At any rate, I am now quite sure that our friend was responsible for the temporary disappearance of *The Ways of Melanesia* – it was away for some weeks, was it not? – and I have also found out that it is to a sister that he presents the novels. Do you think you could arrange to have him discreetly *watched*, or is that impossible? I fear that it is. In which case, I shall have to go on talking to him. I find him a very dull companion.'

The receipt of this note put Ford into a very considerable state of alarm. He had got it into his head that it was most undesirable that Anstruther should be watched in any way; supposing that the blackmailer was forcing the doctor to do something? There was no knowing what Cardonnel might not find out! He cursed the day that he had so inadvisedly placed any confidence in that pertinacious man, and, in his turn, sat down to write a friendly warning. It was rather a difficult note to write, because he had no proof that Anstruther was taking any books, and he therefore did not like to make too definite a statement. Comforting himself with the reflexion that a wink was as good as a nod, he wrote to Anstruther:

'Our friend seems to think that there is some significance in *The Ways of Melanesia*. Of course I am quite sure that he is following a dead scent. Still, I thought that I ought just to tell you that you cannot be too careful in the matter.

'Very mild weather for this time of year, is it not? Our friend, by the way, was saying that he found it rather relaxing, but personally I have not noticed it.'

He signed it 'Yours very sincerely', and decided that no one was better at controlling a very delicate situation. To Cardonnel, he wrote his congratulations, adding that as to convicting the thief, he feared that they were far from proof, and ought not to count their chickens. He was afraid that it would be impossible to have Anstruther actually watched. Did Cardonnel think that if a discreet warning were conveyed to the doctor, it would be possible that the trouble would cease?

Cardonnel's reply was almost a telegram. 'Certainly not. I have nowhere near concluded my investigations.'

CHAPTER 25

A BREACH OF CONFIDENCE

*

ON Anstruther, however, the effect of the correspondence was far more pronounced.

He had entered into the affair of baiting Ford so light-heartedly and once he had found how easy it was to force one man to do his will, he had thought that so many other things would be easy. Gradually, bit by bit, he had allowed himself to fall into one temptation after another. He had removed one by one the repressions which custom and fear had previously imposed on him, until the picture of the entertainment he was going to derive had become all-absorbing. In the future his victims were to be, not only Ford, not only all the members of the Whitehall club, but all the world with whom he came in contact.

So that, when his first experiment had ended apparently disastrously in Pargiter's death, he was constantly swaying between two opinions. At one moment he was full of caution. Nothing mattered except to conceal what had happened. The next, convinced that there was no danger, he was once more envisaging the prospect of further experiments and so fully by now was he under the control of his own illusions, that he found it impossible to relinquish them. It was hard enough to postpone his revenge on a world that did not fully appreciate him. That quite considerable number of conceited members who had seen him come into the Club house, sit there, and go, neglected and alone; who had avoided him deliberately and insultingly; why should they, simply because of the inquisitiveness of one member and one waiter, not suffer the inconveniences he had planned for them ?

In a white heat of hatred, but with a mind steadily clearing, he sat down to plan. The second objective should be Cardonnel, but the first should be Hughes. He would tolerate that man no longer. With nervous fingers he tapped on the typewriter with unnecessary violence. For the first time he allowed a note of hate to creep into the letters written to Ford.

So now you see the effects of your folly. Hughes is still with you, but Pargiter is dead, the direct result of your disobedience.

Why?

Why have you disobeyed the orders I have given you? There can be only one reason. Hughes, I imagine, has some hold over you. You would never risk the consequences of disobedience merely for the sake of standing between him and his deserts unless there were some valid cause.

He may have some hold on you, but he has none on me. Hughes will go within the next forty-eight hours or there will be another accident. This time it will be your precious doctor friend who will suffer, and it will be of no avail if you tell him to avoid the club. I shall get him sooner or later.

I shall not trouble you to give any signal that you intend to obey on this occasion, I shall expect to find it done.

Anstruther sat back in his chair. It was, he knew, despite what he had just written, unlikely that Ford would crumple up at once, though why he should be so obstinate about so unimportant a matter as the dismissal of one servant, even if the grounds for dismissing him had got to be manufactured, he could not imagine. Still, it had to be done, and if the secretary did not do it, he had, he thought, a plan to force his hand.

It was not a plan that at first he liked, because it involved inconvenience to himself. Thinking of what he would do, he fell into a brown study. His eyes, always close together, seemed to get closer still. His mouth became a tighter and thinner line, and his hand gripped convulsively on the arm of the chair until the knuckles stood out white.

By now he had turned his mind to his other objective. Cardonnel might have to come second in point of time, but very surely he was first in importance. He could not get the thought of Cardonnel out of his mind. Without taking sufficient reflexion, he rashly let his fingers start tapping the typewriter again.

And there is one other thing. I observe you, and I observe Anstruther even more, taking that man Cardonnel far too much into your confidence. You should be careful of Cardonnel. He knows too much already.

He was grimly amused when that night Ford rang him up.

The secretary was clearly alarmed, but at the same time was

rather mysterious. Had Anstruther, he enquired, received a letter from a mutual friend?

This was a point which the doctor had been thinking over carefully. On the whole he had decided to say he had not, since, despite the fact that on all previous occasions he had caused his blackmailer to send off a copy to himself, it was perhaps natural that he should not do so if he himself was the person threatened.

Anyhow, natural or not – and it was a little difficult to decide how, in his capacity of imaginary blackmailer and poisoner, he ought to act towards himself in his equally imaginary character (in reality), of harassed medical man, driven by harsh fate and a cruel taskmaster – he had decided to feign complete ignorance.

It was a risk, but it would have several advantages, of which the most important was that it would force Ford to talk. It would be interesting and instructive to see how open the secretary would be. Also, in order in fact to carry out the threat he had delivered to himself, he had to go to the Club and he wanted to tell Ford that he was coming. He could almost say that he saw no reason why he should be forced to resign because one waiter was being kept.

He was prepared, therefore, when he heard Ford's voice speaking from a public telephone box, to enjoy a grim ten minutes or so of cross-purposes. He had worked out the right reaction, as he thought, to every line that Ford might take if he should speak to him. Silence, of course, would have been perfectly easy. He had merely to go to the Club after the forty-eight hours were over, and carry out his own plan against himself with the additional advantage of being able to complain afterwards that Ford had not warned him.

But when he put down the receiver, he was no longer amused. Ford had not warned him, Ford had not played fair! It was no longer safe for one moment to trust a man who would allow himself to adopt such a feeble device. A man, moreover, who, when he decided to act a part, acted it so badly that no one could be deceived.

He had not been surprised when Ford had opened the conversation by suggesting to him that it would be wise for him not to come into the club for a while. That was easy and proper.

Ford was going to warn him of the contents of what was actually his own letter, and, being Ford, he would prefer to do it in some absurd, roundabout way. It implied, of course, that he was refusing to sack Hughes, which was annoying. Ford should suffer for that later. Still, if it showed that the recipient of his letters was disobedient, it did prove that his nominal ally was still reasonably loyal.

But when in reply to his very natural question as to why he should not go to the Club, Ford had gone on to give his reasons, the doctor had been seriously displeased. Ford had produced the most ridiculous cock-and-bull story which, as an excuse, would have deceived no one.

He had begun by going back to the question of books being stolen from the club – a subject which did not interest Anstruther. He had gone on to say that Cardonnel was conducting an inquiry. Anstruther had refrained from retorting that Cardonnel had much better stick to that as his only subject for investigation. In view of what he intended to happen to Cardonnel, the less he seemed to be interested in him the better.

So far Ford's remarks, if irritatingly irrelevant, were no worse. But when Ford went on to suggest with much humming and hawing that Cardonnel thought that he, Anstruther, was taking away the books, and was trying to prove the fact, and that therefore it would be a good plan if he stayed away for a while, because, if in his absence a book went, it would prove that he was not responsible, and so Cardonnel would be convinced and would turn his activities elsewhere, then Anstruther really was angry.

A futile performance. Book thief indeed! It was an insult to suggest that he was, and he had no intention of staying away from the club. So much was easy to say and, indeed, helped his plan. But when, despite his denials, Ford only protested the more and at the same time absolutely refused to admit that he had any other motive, Anstruther found himself not only angry but more than ever determined that he must waste no time in putting both his plans into execution.

That Ford was disobedient, disloyal and untruthful, he was quite prepared to discover. That he was a bad actor, if it was a cause of contempt, was certainly no surprise. But the serious part of the revelation was that Ford was plotting with Cardonnel, and so far advanced were their plans, that they had now realized that the fact that they were trying to find out something must be obvious to him, and were accordingly trying to cover the fact of their investigations into Pargiter's death by pretending to be working for something else.

Save for the one book, *The Ways of Melanesia*, he had never even borrowed a book from the Club. Clever, by the way, of Cardonnel to have introduced it into the conversation the other night; it served to give an appearance of verisimilitude to his wild accusation.

Safe in the knowledge of his own innocence, Anstruther disregarded it as a serious inquiry. It was clear to him that Ford, frightened by the possibility of danger to himself, had been talking to Cardonnel and was now actually prepared to have the impertinence to sacrifice him, Anstruther, as the cause of Pargiter's death. Even though he was, accidentally, the agent by whom Pargiter had died, that was no business of Ford's. In time he must be punished for that too. But would there be time? Cardonnel, the dull, boring Cardonnel, seemed to hover in front of him, a menacing figure of inexorable justice from whom there was no escape. All that night and the next he dreamed of Cardonnel.

At the other end of the line Ford put down the receiver, as he said to himself, 'with a gratifying feeling that his duty had been done'. Forgetting that he had done exactly what Cardonnel had told him not to do, that he had in fact betrayed the confidence reposed in him in a most scandalous way, he congratulated himself on his diplomacy.

Anstruther had sounded annoyed – naturally perhaps; the accusation that you were a thief was one that any gentleman might resent – but he would get over that, and in the meanwhile two very solid advantages would be gained. First, Anstruther was now fully on his guard as to why Cardonnel was asking all these inquisitive questions which must seem so very peculiar to him, and must surely now be able to dispel the amateur detective's hopes of catching him, and with that gone Cardonnel might abandon his idea of worrying about how Morrison died. And secondly, Anstruther, despite his protests, would keep away from the Club, so that the threats in the unpleasant letter he (Ford) had received could not be carried out.

With the doctor out of the way, and Cardonnel quieting down – though the difficulty of an absent Anstruther soothing an inquisitive Cardonnel did not occur to Ford – time would be gained, and, said Ford to himself, 'something will always turn up'. It might even be possible to give Hughes his summer holiday earlier or find him a job with another club? Perhaps it was, but Ford was very ignorant about finding jobs for other people. Indeed, how he kept his own was a mystery to himself, but not to himself alone.

As to the possibility of the threat, whatever it might be, being carried out elsewhere, Ford was completely indifferent. So long as this tiresome man would refrain from killing the members *inside* the Club, he was perfectly happy, at least unless copies of letters addressed to him should be found lying about. He wondered if he could induce Anstruther to destroy everything he had received? It would be much more prudent.

CHAPTER 26

ONCE MORE THE SHERRY

*

FOR a few seconds Anstruther stood outside the Whitehall Club and looked at it. From an architectural point of view, he was prepared to agree that the exterior was a success, though why light coloured stone should invariably be regarded as the proper material for a city where it was certain to get dirty in the shortest possible time, he never could guess. Still, the outside was all right, and the inside, if very undistinguished, was passable. If only there had been any ventilation! However, it was of no importance that evening. Even if the smaller library had reached a temperature of eighty, he would not have to stay there any length of time.

Hanging up his hat and coat, he made his way up to a billiard-room at the top of the house, so cunningly concealed among the bedrooms that many who had been members for years had no idea that such a room existed. As he had confidently expected, the room was deserted. There was no obstruction to putting the first step of his plan into operation. He rang the bell and immediately walked out again. No one could know that he had been in the room.

The next step required the assistance of fortune. He had to hope that the passage outside the service bar on the library floor would be empty for the necessary minute or less. Luck was with him. There was no one about. It was the work of far less than a minute to slip into the bar and out again. By the time that Hughes had returned down the back stairs, wondering why ghosts had taken to ringing the bell in the billiard-room, Anstruther was sitting in the small library. Five minutes later he rang the bell again and asked for a glass of sherry.

Once more fortune favoured him. Just as he was about to raise the glass to his lips, Ford, engaged in one of his aimless prowls round the club to see if 'everything was all right', came in and started violently on seeing the doctor. The presence of two other members absolutely prevented him from saying anything.

Even if it had not been a silence room, there was a certain
difficulty in opening a conversation which could be overheard,
with the remark that Anstruther had been advised not to enter
the club. It was open to the most slanderous misinterpretations.
Ford was reduced to scowling and shaking his head.

Neither shake nor scowl had any effect. To his slight surprise,
Ford saw that Anstruther was in a more genial mood than usual.
Instead of ignoring him completely as he had expected, the doctor
actually smiled and raised his glass and drank about a third of
it. For so reserved a man, it was an unusual gesture. Besides, it
was early in the evening to start drinking sherry. Ford began to
think that Hughes's allegation that Anstruther was too partial to
sherry, must be correct.

Suddenly, however, he saw that this particular glass offered
no temptations. With a wry face Anstruther put it down; then
with a puzzled expression he raised it again to his nose and
smelt it; then, hurriedly returning it to the small table by his
side, he put a handkerchief to his mouth, rushed past Ford and
fled from the room.

Recovering himself, Ford first picked up the sherry and smelt
it. He could detect nothing unusual in it. He would have liked
to have sipped it, but, after all, it was not his, and even if the
doctor did not appear to like it very much, he felt that he ought
not to touch it without his permission. He put it carefully in a
corner, and went to see if anything was really the matter. Somewhat belatedly he remembered that there had been a threat
against possibly Anstruther's life or more probably his comfort,
and that though he had warned him of Cardonnel's activities,
he had made no mention of that. He was relieved to find that
though the doctor was being violently sick, apparently nothing
worse was likely to occur.

Characteristically, at the first moment when Anstruther was
able to listen to him, he commented with relief on the fact that
he had not died. It might, had not the doctor been completely
aware of what was happening, have been rather an alarming
remark. How long he would have stood by, inactively uttering
platitudes, is uncertain, but after about the third trite remark,
he was suddenly interrupted by one of the other two members

who had been in the library, also overcome by sudden and irresistible nausea. It flashed through Ford's mind that, despite the inconvenience he was undergoing, Anstruther seemed sardonically amused to find a fellow sufferer. By now, however, the doctor had sufficiently recovered to be able to gasp out a few words.

'The sherry, you fool. The sherry.'

Somewhat late in the day it dawned on Ford's mind that there might be something wrong with the sherry. It might even be advisable to prevent any more of that particular bottle being served. He arrived just in time to prevent a third man from receiving an unexpected and powerful emetic. Telling Hughes to open a fresh bottle, he himself took the decanter and the remains of the two glasses to his office. He returned to find Anstruther consoling his fellow sufferer.

'Something wrong with that sherry. You'll take it away?'

Ford nodded.

'Mr Warrington here,' Anstruther continued, 'tells me that he fortunately only took the slightest sip.'

'Knew it was wrong at once. Wine had a sort of dull taste. Thought it was a dirty bottle at first. It used to happen years ago before the bottlers got new modern processes, but that sherry has only been in bottle a short while; shouldn't happen with it.'

'It must have been something worse than that, sir,' Anstruther suggested. He was pleased to see that the suggestion was both readily agreed to by Warrington and disturbing to Ford. 'A dirty bottle could hardly have so powerful an effect.'

Ford reluctantly agreed. And as a gesture, which, if futile, was well meant, he remarked:

'I can only offer you the club's most ample apologies.'

Warrington nodded. 'Been a member for forty-two years, and never been poisoned in the club before. Extraordinary thing.' (Apparently he meant that it was extraordinary that he had been poisoned now, not that he had never been poisoned before.) 'Most extraordinary. But the wine should not be served if there is any doubt about it.'

At the suggestion that it was in some way Hughes's fault,

Ford rushed to the defence. He pointed out that there was very little wrong with the smell – he had himself smelt it – and that he did not want to encourage the waiters to sample the wines for obvious reasons.

Fortunately Warrington was a good-humoured and just man. He saw the point and he also saw the opportunity to make a joke.

'I suppose, Mr Secretary, that you weren't trying to find out if there was any unauthorized sampling going on, and then forgot to remove the bottle! It would have been a pretty conclusive automatic test!'

In silence Anstruther listened to the conversation going on. He was not quite sure as to the exact chain of circumstances which would ensue; it would depend on the individual and on the amount drunk, but he thought that probably by now the effect had passed off. All the same he was none too certain. He felt fully justified in recommending Warrington to go straight home and go dinnerless to bed.

Warrington was rather annoying him. He was an accidental victim, it was true – he had imagined that the first action of any man would have been to see that the sherry decanter was instantly put aside, and he had not reckoned with the extreme slowness with which Ford's mind moved – still Warrington *was* a victim, and as such was behaving very badly. Not only was he not really angry, but he did not seem even to have undergone much pain. He felt a strong sense of grievance rising against Warrington. The man had no right to deprive him of his pleasure!

He was longing, too, to tell Ford what was wrong with the sherry. He felt that the use of perchloride of mercury was artistic. As he had slipped it into the decanter in Hughes's bar on his way down from the billiard-room, he had congratulated himself on using a substance which would dissolve rapidly in alcohol, which would not produce too strong a taste or smell, and which must bring back such very awkward recollections to Ford. For full artistic effect he would have liked to have served it in some way as vanilla by the agency of Benson, but in so imperfect a world it was not possible to have everything, and, failing Benson, Hughes was the next best agent.

For the moment, however, he contented himself with sending

Warrington off home. He gave him advice which sounded speciously good, but unfortunately as the contingency was not one which he had foreseen, he had not got ready at the tip of his tongue the remedy he would have liked to have proposed. Had he known of one, he would have suggested something which, though generally a suitable thing to prescribe, would in the case of perchloride of mercury poisoning actually irritate the symptoms and certainly cause the utmost inconvenience to anyone who took it. But there it was, something so seemingly right and so actually wrong was not to be thought of in a flash.

When Warrington departed, he turned his attention to Ford. He would have liked to have spent some time dexterously turning the thumb-screw, but unfortunately he did not really feel quite fit enough, even for that delicate pleasure. Besides, in the state of health he was in, he might miss the full savour.

He contented himself with suggestions that there was something after all, perhaps, in Warrington's complaint that Hughes should not have served the sherry, and then leaving that aside, went on to advise that the sherry be analysed. Finally he began to hint that Ford must be keeping something back from him. He refused to believe, he said, that the fact that it was he who was the first to suffer was a coincidence. Somehow or other that glass had been planted on him, and there must be some reason. Moreover, it seemed to him to be extremely suspicious that this should occur immediately after Ford had tried to keep him away from the club on an obviously frivolous pretext. He ended by indicating that he did not feel well enough to continue the subject that night, but that he did not intend to let it drop.

Left to himself, Ford remarked that troubles never came singly, by which apparently he meant first Warrington and then Anstruther. Next he sent down to the hall porter and obtained a list of all those who had been in the club immediately before Anstruther had been given that very doubtful glass of sherry. When it came, it proved to be a startling list to him. It was not very long, and it contained absolutely no one who had previously been connected in any way with any of the untoward incidents, as he euphemistically termed them. Ford found it absolutely baffling.

'The long arm of coincidence,' he murmured to himself. 'It does seem a singularly long arm.'

He looked again at the list of members he had just obtained and tried to remember something of each of them.

'A. J. Burke,' he read. Burke, that was a man who used to come in every day at lunch time, eat two sandwiches and retire to the library where he would throw himself into a chair with an air of complete despondency. He would then light a cigarette, heave a deep sigh and order a large liqueur brandy which he would swallow in a gulp. Finally throwing away the half-finished cigarette in a way which seemed to imply that the human race was damned, he would leave hurriedly and return about six to read the evening paper with unexpected eagerness.

Simonds, the next man on the list, had no fixed time at which he was in the Club. His only constant habit was to start *The Times* crossword puzzle in ink and leave it incomplete and mainly wrong, to the distraction of anyone else who tried to finish it. Moreover he usually had at least six reference books brought to him and left them all over the Club. A tiresome man, but irrelevant to the matter in hand.

The next name on the list was that of a country member who visited the Whitehall too seldom to be considered to have any habits; but both he and all the others on the list were united in one thing. They had no apparent connexion with his problem.

Meanwhile in the service bar outside the library Hughes too was thinking. On one point his mind was quite made up. If the members chose to kill each other, that was their business – but when it came to doping 'his' sherry, then it was quite another matter.

CHAPTER 27

ANALYSIS

*

THE mistake which Anstruther was making was in assuming that Ford's mind would work as logically as his own.

To the doctor the process of reasoning was so clear. Ford had been told that he must get rid of Hughes. He had been warned that if he did not, unpleasant consequences would happen to himself, Anstruther. Ford had rashly left him unwarned and those consequences had happened. That was a legitimate griev-ance that he had against Ford, and considering all that had happened, the secretary ought to think twice before he risked turning Anstruther into an enemy.

Besides there was Warrington. It was annoying that Warring-ton took it all so calmly – still he ought to make some sort of complaint, Anstruther felt, and what between that and the very well justified grievance that he could express in his own person and the influence that he could bring anonymously – well, even Ford ought to see that he must give way about Hughes.

Being the secretary of one club he might perhaps be able to arrange to find him a job at another and so soothe his conscience that way? That was Ford's business, but surely he must get rid of him somehow – and quickly. Perhaps it would help if he realized that the poison in the sherry was perchloride of mercury? The hint that the incidents were connected must then be obvious even to Ford.

But Ford was not so logical. He started from his fixed and immutable principle that those whom he had selected to work under him must be right. Therefore the fact that the sherry was poisoned, though unfortunate, must not be attributed to Hughes. Herein he happened to be perfectly right, even though his belief was founded on instinct rather than reasoning or knowledge. Though his sense of logic may not have coincided with Anstru-ther's, his sense of justice was a good deal higher and, tempting though it was to take the line of least resistance, Ford refused as yet to contemplate anything of the sort. To his mind now that

Hughes was under a slight and quite unjust cloud, it was all the more necessary to behave properly to him.

But that that should be Ford's line of thought never entered Anstruther's head. It was in a mood of tolerable confidence that he went up to Ford's office.

The room, he was glad to see, was in even more than its normal state of untidiness. Ford must be really upset! The sherry, however, was not visible. That was hardly surprising. If it had been, anyone else who came in might have made some facetious remark about it, and the laborious explanation might have given away too much.

Ford seemed genuinely glad to see him. He expressed his pleasure that Anstruther had apparently perfectly recovered from his indisposition. 'Warrington's perfectly well, too. I've just been speaking to him on the phone. I was going to ring you up as well, but I thought you might be busy.'

'So I ought to be, but I made time to come and see you. You must have that sherry analysed.'

A shadow seemed to cross Ford's face. 'Do you know, I think it would be best not.' Then, seeing the silent disapproval in the doctor's face, he went on: 'Once I take it to an analyst it means that there is an outsider who knows all about it. He may go and tell someone – you never can tell, and we cannot have all the facts coming out until we know who our man is.'

Anstruther started. 'But do you really think you are going to find out who it is?'

'Oh, yes, certain to find out some time. Much better that you and I – and Cardonnel' he added as an afterthought, 'should find out for ourselves. Once we get outsiders in, there's no knowing what might happen. Besides, there's the wine merchant. *He* won't like it if I have his sherry analysed, and there'll be another person to keep quiet.'

'But this is ridiculous. You and I have found out nothing so far. In fact you seem hardly to have tried.'

'Oh, yes, been doing a lot of work about it. I'm quite sure I shall find out, and very soon too.' Considering that he had no ideas in the world, Ford's airy confidence was amazingly optimistic.

'With the aid of Cardonnel,' Anstruther looked grave. 'Look here, how much have you been saying to Cardonnel? You appear to have forgotten that I told you to say nothing to anyone, and certainly not to Cardonnel. As I have told you before, you are taking Cardonnel too much into your confidence. He knows too much already. I do not trust that man, nor should you.'

The close-set eyes peered into Ford's face with an intense stare. Up to now by the superiority of his will power he had forced the secretary to do what he wanted. But now he appeared to be losing his grip. Some other influence must be obtruding. What was it? A sense of justice? Anstruther brushed the suggestion aside. Ford could not be so foolish! No, the more he thought of it, it must be Cardonnel, and the more he thought of Cardonnel, the more he came to the conclusion that he must take action. His thoughts were recalled by hearing Ford too speaking of the abominable Cardonnel, and with admiration too.

'Not trust Cardonnel? But he's a most reliable man – and very able too.'

With an unpleasant feeling that the last fact might be true, Anstruther determined to obtain more knowledge. 'How much have you told this man Cardonnell?' A pause. 'How much?' Still silence. 'How far have you betrayed my confidence?'

Ford wriggled. In actual fact he had betrayed Cardonnel far more than he had betrayed Anstruther. Indeed, he had only told Cardonnel so much as he had out of sheer necessity. Still, that did not save him from having a thoroughly guilty feeling. 'Well, I had to let him know about Benson's mistake.'

'Oh, you did, did you? And why?'

'Well, he was worrying about Morrison's death.' The sigh of relief which nearly escaped the doctor's lips would anyhow have been suppressed when Ford went on: 'And about Pargiter's.'

Anstruther leapt up. 'About Pargiter's?'

'Yes, but I think I headed him off that neatly.'

'You flatter yourself, I fear. Once more, if you have any decency, any loyalty, you will stop talking to Cardonnel, and if he worries you again, let me know. You're not fit to be trusted by yourself.'

'Well, really, is there any need to be offensive?'

'Seeing that you appear to be likely to get both of us hanged, it seems to me that there is.'

'Not *hanged*, surely?'

With a complete disregard for the probabilities of the law, Anstruther assured him that he had rendered himself so liable. At least it was true as to his own share in the matter. 'That being settled, to return to the analysis.'

Once more Ford refused, but this time in a more diffident way. 'You see, it's impossible. I'm awfully sorry, but you see it's impossible – now.'

'Now?'

'Yes. As a matter of fact,' brightly, 'I've just poured it away into the gutter.'

'The gutter?'

'Went up on to the roof and poured it into the gutter there.'

'With all that poison in it?'

'Oh, well, come.' Ford looked a little worried. 'It didn't kill you or Warrington, so I suppose that when it's even more diluted it won't do anyone else any harm. At least no real harm.' Even to himself his action seemed a little casual after the event.

With the advantage of knowing not only what the poison was but exactly how much there was, Anstruther had to admit to himself that the risk was slight. He could not make up his mind whether the fact made him glad or sorry.

'But what about Warrington? How are you going to explain it to him?'

'Oh, that's all right. I've done that.' Ford looked triumphantly happy. 'I told him a version of the Benson vanilla mixed bottle incident and, though I don't think he quite understands it all, he's a very good fellow and since he sees that it wouldn't do the club any good, he's promised me to keep quiet – too,' he added as an afterthought. 'Besides, he knows what a good servant Hughes is and though I have told him it wasn't Hughes's fault really, he thinks it might have been, and so, as a decent chap, I am sure we can rely on him.

'Rather a clever idea of mine,' Ford continued, 'pretending that it was the lotion stuff. From what I can make out, it would have had just the effect it did on you and Warrington.'

Anstruther considered the question. It was irritating that he was not going to make a fuss, but apparently Warrington was going to keep quiet, and it was quite certain that the sherry was no longer available to be analysed. That being so, perhaps he could get the effect he required in another way.

'The curious, and perhaps the awkward point is that I am almost sure that it *was* perchloride of mercury.'

Ford looked genuinely surprised. 'Surely not. Why should it be?'

'Well, partly because, as you have already said, the symptoms almost exactly coincide. And secondly because of what I think the motive was. There was something in that sherry. I suspect that it was put in with the deliberate object of poisoning me to force your hand. In other words, I suspect that you have been disobeying our friend's orders. I would equally suspect myself, only I happen to know that I have not. In fact I have received no orders recently, which in itself is suspicious, and from what I can see of our friend's character, the use of the poison which started the whole matter would be exactly what he would do.'

It occurred to Ford that there might be another reason why the doctor was so certain. 'And is perchloride of mercury one of the poisons you have recently been supplying to him?'

As this was a detail which Anstruther had not decided upon, he ignored it. It would not matter much if Ford did think he had. He countered with another direct question. 'Have you received any direct orders recently from this man?'

Ford's face took on a look of mulish obstinacy. 'I'm not going to sack Hughes,' he said sulkily.

'Oh, so that's it.' The going had been more difficult than he had expected, but at last he had brought him to the point. 'You prefer to sacrifice me or anyone else in the Club rather than Hughes?'

'Well, you and I are in it anyhow. Poor Hughes has got dragged in quite by accident. It was no business of his, and I really do not see why he should be made to suffer.'

'And wasn't I dragged in accidentally? At least you might call it deliberate, but in that case you did the dragging. Why should I suffer?'

The logic seemed inexorable to Ford, but in that case he had got to let down one of two innocent parties. And that was frightful. He tried to find a loophole somewhere.

'But – at any rate, you – you can look after yourself.'

'Especially last night.'

'And even supposing I did sack Hughes, the fellow would only want something else.'

It was as well that Ford did not see the smile that came into Anstruther's eyes. He had every intention of wanting plenty of other things! Lest Ford should notice, he went on talking.

'I suppose you *are* quite sure that it was not Hughes's fault all the time?'

'How could it be?'

'Well, no one could have doctored the bottle more easily than he could.' Anstruther pulled himself together. The word 'doctored' was careless. It was too near the truth!

'What! In order to force me to sack himself?'

'To keep suspicion from himself by a double bluff. Has it occurred to you that no one is better placed for knowing too much than Hughes? That he was there when both of those rather unregretted patients of mine died, and was in the best position to guess that something was wrong? If all this fellow wants is that Hughes should be sacked, I should do it at once.'

'Wouldn't that rather call his bluff – to put it mildly?'

'It would. But if it is Hughes, he is confidently relying on the fact that you won't. Still, I think you are probably right.

'I do not think that Hughes put that perchloride in himself. But someone did. Someone who was anxious to force you to get rid of him and who does not apparently care what discomfort he causes you or me or anyone else so long as that is done. Obviously because he thinks Hughes knows too much. Frankly I see no reason why Warrington or I or anyone else should go through a similar experience to last night for the sake of Hughes. It isn't fair on the members and it isn't fair on the Club. Your proper course of action is plain enough to me.'

Ford ran his hands despairingly through his hair.

'It may seem plain to you; and it *is* frightful to think that you and, I suppose, other people are in danger of I don't know what, but all the same I cannot bring myself to do it. I suppose I might manage to give Hughes his holiday a little earlier and see what happens while he is away.'

'A holiday – in January or February? My dear Ford!' Then more resolutely: 'It's no good, you'll have to do what you are told.'

A weary sigh was all the answer. The idea, almost the phrase, was becoming distressingly familiar. He was tired of the virtue of obedience. Again Anstruther pressed him, and this time Ford asked to be allowed to think it over, a request of which the doctor definitely disapproved. The last thing he wanted to give the unfortunate man a chance to do was to think. He might see so many other better courses! But it was impossible to insist any further without running the risk of awakening a suspicion in Ford's mind that there might be some other motive behind the pressure. Besides, even that was a weakening, and once Ford began to weaken, he had no doubt that he could once more control him.

As he went away rapidly towards Hyde Park on his neglected professional duties, Anstruther became more and more convinced that he would win his point fairly soon, provided that he could keep Ford away from any other influence.

But that was exactly the point. What certainty was there, even after all that he had said, that Ford would not go instantly and babble to Cardonnel? Once more Anstruther cursed that he was yoked in the business to a fool. His pace quickened as his mind grew clearer. It was impossible to alter Ford's nature, but might it not be possible to remove Cardonnel somehow? And might it not be necessary?

CHAPTER 28

THE FINAL RELIEF

*

NIGHT and day Cardonnel was never out of his mind.

By day as he went the rounds of his patients or saw them in his consulting room, he could think of nothing but the probability that by then everything had been found out. As he looked back on the events since Pargiter died, he could see dozens of signposts pointing to himself. He was constantly wanting to go back and try to cover up some detail that seemed to him glaringly obvious, and then remembering that the very act of so doing would point even more clearly to the fact that it was necessary for him to do so.

He was afraid to open a letter lest he should find in it a request for an explanation, or a warning from Ford. Every policeman who walked towards him he feared was coming to arrest him; every man who looked at him he imagined to be a detective watching his movements and ready to pounce on him.

It was strange that he should be haunted in his dreams solely by Cardonnel. It should have been Pargiter, but except as a man who had betrayed him by having indifferent health, Anstruther never gave a thought to Pargiter.

Not for a single instant did the idea of remorse even enter his head. But every night as he tossed feverishly from side to side, it was Cardonnel whom he pictured.

At first it had been the class of dream in which he had been walking along the street, happy and carefree, and on turning the corner he would suddenly see the neat little figure that he dreaded coming towards him, and he would turn to run and find that he could not move. There had been variations of that, including a peculiarly distressing one in which he took to flying and found Cardonnel's hands stretching up to grab his ankles. As he moved along, more and more figures, all resembling the lawyer, would appear, and if he went higher, their arms would become longer, and he would turn giddy and begin to fall.

Then his dreams would take a professional turn. He would be

going to his old hospital to witness an operation, though why he could never understand, and when he got there he would be told that after all it had been decided to use him as the patient. So as to give everybody as much experience as possible, the anaesthetist was to act as the surgeon, and the man who swept out the laboratory was to give the anaesthetic. At that he had protested that he had come to see the operation, not to be operated on, whereupon the Chairman of the Finance Committee, who seemed somehow unexpectedly to be in charge of everything, had said that in that case if he was so anxious to see everything, they would omit the anaesthetic, and before he knew where he was, he would find himself tied down, not even to the operating table, but to the chair in the library of the Club where Morrison and Pargiter had died. Hughes would be holding him down, and the dreaded face of Cardonnel would be peering into his, sharpening one of the club book-markers which he was going to use as the operating knife. From this dream he awoke with his mind at last made up. Anything would be better than the state of mind into which he was rapidly drifting.

In fairness to Anstruther it must be remembered that his suspicions were not all imaginary. In addition to the numerous occasions when some trivial and irrelevant incident was construed by the doctor's disordered brain into being some fresh manoeuvre to entrap him, there were several actual cases when Cardonnel was in fact watching him and was detected by Anstruther to be doing so. How was Anstruther to know that all that interested Cardonnel (or very nearly all) was the theft of the books? In the same way that if a part of the body is hurt it seems that the injured finger or foot is wanted for every action, so when one idea presses constantly on the brain, everything seems to be directed to that.

It would have been difficult to say at this time whether Anstruther was wholly sane or not. Certainly worry had driven him a little to drink, though perhaps not quite to the extent that Hughes considered that it had, even a little to drugs, but though the effect had been to cloud his brain to some extent, he had not entirely lost control of himself. It was just worry that was distracting him. A man who lives in a constant state of fear cannot be quite sane, cannot view with a proper sense of proportion even those events that relate to the subject of his fear.

But whatever else Anstruther was, he was not a coward. Here was a man, perhaps two men, who were dangerous to him. There was no question in his mind but that they must be faced up to and overcome. In his own quiet, reserved way he was an intensely proud man. He had successfully surmounted so far the difficulties connected with Pargiter's death; it never occurred to him that he could not get over the present ones, if he resolutely decided to do so.

It was true that so far he had failed to have Hughes removed; but that would happen in due course. In his opinion Ford was clearly hesitating. With Cardonnel out of the way he would hesitate no longer; he would do what he was told.

Cardonnel, then, must be removed.

It was symptomatic of what had been happening to Anstruther's character that when for the first time he contemplated a murder in cold blood, he found nothing so very strange in the idea. In a clear, calm, dispassionate way, totally different from his feelings of frenzy after he had accidentally killed Pargiter, he came to the conclusion that a mere temporary removal of the lawyer, a sea voyage of however great a length, was insufficient. In an equally unemotional and logical manner he set to work to plan the details. There must be none of the half-hearted measures in which he had been indulging, more to gratify his sense of humour than anything else, with the various salts of mercury.

Equally there must be no error.

In his new mood, with an object in life once more, Anstruther saw clearly that he must avoid the danger of repetition. Not only the perchloride, but the hyoscine, and indeed all other poisons must go. There must be some carefully prepared accident, carried out in such a manner that suspicion, even if it should glance in his direction, could never be turned to anything more definite. Already he had in his mind an idea as to where the accident should take place. It was more difficult to see how he could get Cardonnel to the point of danger.

The first thing was to go down to the big library, the cold library. It was not usually difficult to find it empty round about dinner time – and Anstruther desired to be alone. He had no wish that he should be seen very carefully inspecting a spot which was to be the scene of a tragedy soon afterwards.

Luck, however, was against him. One other member was using the library, and so, impeded from carrying out his primary object, Anstruther was forced to sit down and wait. He could at least use the time to plan some further detail of the subject about which he never stopped thinking.

But coherent thought was rendered difficult. The other member present seemed to have been suddenly smitten with a desire to extract small pieces of knowledge from books all of which were situated on the very highest and most inaccessible shelves. Having seized a long ladder, he was rushing about the room, planting it sometimes on the carpet, often on the polished boards to which in places the carpet did not reach, and barely looking to see whether the head of it was resting securely against a shelf or was merely poised against a row of books, he was charging tumul-tuously to the top to snatch one book, descend rapidly, read about half a paragraph, if so much, and then once more tear up the ladder, replace the book, and then repeat the process else-where.

Anstruther could not but admire the scrupulous manner in which he replaced each volume. If only Cardonnel would show an equal rashness! Somehow that lawyer must be induced to come to the library, somehow he must be induced to step out through that large window on to the balcony from which so extensive a view of London's chimney pots could be obtained – and then, well, the ancient railing round it was already so rusted that he thought it might need no preparation to ensure that at the first moment that any weight was put on it, it would give way; after that, it was a very long way to the pavement below and opposite was no vantage point from which the happenings on that balcony were likely to have been observed.

At last his fellow member ceased his Alpine feats and An-struther was able to slip out quietly through the window. To his annoyance the railing was in a better state of repair than he had expected. Still, a little deft, quick work, and it could soon be made sufficiently weak ... It was nervous work, though, and he hurried through it as fast as he could. He had no desire to stay there longer than was absolutely necessary, since the appearance of anyone in the room would be fatal to his whole project. If anyone did appear, at the very best, even if his presence was not discovered, he would have to wait until the room was empty again.

Fortune, however, was on his side. He was indeed disturbed once, and that disturbance was of a sufficiently alarming nature, but as good luck would have it, it was only temporary. As he was bending over the staple that fastened the whole structure to the wall, and wondering if that could be turned into an additional weakness, he suddenly heard a footstep in the room behind him. Cautiously peering through the curtains, he saw Hughes walk to the door and turn off the lights. On the whole this was excellent. He had not liked to turn them off himself for fear that the very absence of light should attract attention, but now no one could enter the room without his knowing it.

A few minutes later he was back in the library. So far as he could make out, no one had seen him from the time he stepped on to the balcony until he was once more in the hall. The first part of his arrangements for Cardonnel was complete.

Returning to his flat, he found a letter from Ford. So completely had he been absorbed in the consideration of Cardonnel, that it came almost as a shock to him to find the secretary discussing the question of Hughes. Even more remote did the other matter which the letter mentioned seem.

I have been turning over in my mind the conversation we had yesterday, wrote the secretary in his best style, and the more I think of it, the more I grieve that you should suspect me of not having been completely above-board with you. I thought that I had told you freely, really rather more freely than I should, of all that concerned you, and I thought that I had fallen into line with every suggestion you had made.

As to the matter of Hughes, I cannot agree with your, if I may so describe it, extremely ingenious theory, either that he put in the poison, or that it was put in deliberately, or even that it was poison at all. There is many a slip, as you know, betwixt the decanter and the glass, and this was one of them. But not Hughes's fault, I am sure, nor, as I have said, necessarily poison. Certainly, there is no real evidence as to perchloride of mercury being present, and surely there might be other, quite natural causes, which might have so regrettably upset you. Even in the best family wine merchants accidents will happen, you know. There has been nothing wrong with the rest of the wine, but strangely enough a similar thing has occurred only to-day at tea time, and as you were not in the club, it cannot have been intended to injure you. Nor was it directed against or controlled by Hughes, since the buttered toast, which is believed to have caused the trouble, was served in the smoking-room, not the library. I think it must be something in the atmosphere. Perhaps all this wet after all this drought, like the sore throats last summer.

Despite his weariness, Anstruther smiled sadly. His little joke, then, was beginning to work, but he was no longer able to be interested in it – not until after he had dealt with Cardonnel. Meanwhile he felt it would be easy to get Ford to change his mind as to Hughes. Even in this letter he was protesting too much.

The next paragraph, however, was really interesting. Had he not had his plans matured, it would have been alarming, but as it was he felt that it could easily be made to fit. In fact it made his task easier.

But my real object in writing to you concerns the other matter of which I spoke to you. I have had a letter from Cardonnel telling me that he has now completed his investigations. He thinks that he is able to prove his case. I very much doubt that, since there has been no recurrence of the trouble recently, but anyhow we shall see what he has to say very soon. He asks me to ask you to be so good as to meet him at the Club at the earliest date convenient to you. Would to-morrow evening be suitable? As to the meeting, any time will do. I thought, however, that I ought to tell you at once. Is there anything particular you would like me to know beforehand?

Anstruther put down the letter. He knew what to do now. Decision, and with it relief, had come at last.

CHAPTER 29

CARDONNEL'S REPORT

*

GLADWIN, and his friend the author, who some weeks ago had suggested that Cardonnel had better be appointed Club house detective, finished their lunch and started to go to the smoking-room.

'I always wonder,' remarked the author, 'whether that weighing machine is put just outside the coffee room as an awful warning to all those inclined to get stout, or a kind of "abandon hope all ye that enter here" message.'

'Or as an encouragement to the lean kine? Anyhow I wonder what I do weigh now.' Gladwin sat down on the machine and started to adjust the scale at the side, grunting with disapproval as the balance stayed obstinately in the air. He was sure he was lighter than that!

Meanwhile his companion idly picked up a book lying beside it. 'I always mean to stake a claim to a page in this and note down the answer every time I weigh myself, with appropriate comments.'

'Comments? I'm sure this machine is not adjusted properly. I've never been twelve stone before.'

'That's the lunch. Treacle pudding indeed! Most fattening. You had better put in like this man' – he pointed to the book – '"after a heavy meal". Amazing how people try to deceive themselves about their weight, and how self-revealing! Look at this: R.H.S. remarks – "14 stone 7, despite putting on winter underclothes". Really he might preserve a decent reticence.'

'And what, may I ask, do you weigh?' Gladwin surveyed the author's rather plump figure.

'I? I never weigh myself.'

'Do you call that not deceiving yourself?'

'Certainly. I merely suspect the worst. Come along and have coffee and don't put one toe on the ground to try to make yourself think you are a little lighter than you are.'

With a slight blush the K.C. walked downstairs. Somehow or

other he must get more exercise or he would die suddenly like
poor old Judge Skinner whose end a fortnight ago had upset him
badly. The pair of them joined Cardonnel and his chartered
accountant friend in their usual corner.

'This club' – too much lunch always made the accountant
pontifical – 'is going to the dogs. There was a short moment a
few months ago when I thought it was going to pull itself together.
But now it's sinking back into the old rut again.'

'What's your particular trouble now?'

'Well, the food for one thing. You never get a decent potato –'

'That's in the interest of slimming. I have just been watching
Gladwin weigh himself and he's over thirteen stone, only he
won't believe it.'

'Twelve, Henry, not thirteen.'

'Every night that I dine here,' the accountant went on, ignoring
the interruption, 'I am made to eat dory, halibut or brill. And
have you ever studied the sauces?'

'I have.' (This from Cardonnel.) 'There are exactly three, perhaps four. A brown substance of uncertain taste, called generally
"Sauce Robert", which disfigures cutlets and suchlike, or has
pepper added and arrives again under the name of "Sauce
Diable" with grilled chicken. That's one.'

'The second and most frequent,' went on Gladwin, 'is a yellow
abomination. I think it starts life as a mayonnaise. When it begins
to go sour it is put on the fish and called "Bonne Femme".'

'And when really unpleasant, is termed "Au Vin Blanc".'

'Thirdly we have a red one usually called "Tomato". I apologize to my readers for mentioning it.' Henry waved his hand
airily to an imaginary audience.

'In the interests of accuracy I must add mint,' concluded
Cardonnel, 'but that is all, absolutely all. Plenty of names, but
just those four colours. Personally, I want a blue sauce – with
purple spots.'

'What about oyster with very indifferent cod, and mustard
sauce with the all too rare herrings?' The accountant was trying
to be fair.

'Both variations of the yellow variety. In one case mustard is
added. In the other, nothing whatever, the flavour of the oyster

being supplied by the imagination of the diner. It's a sort of confidence trick.'

'What about "au gratin"?'

'I groan that you should mention such a thing, Henry! The yellow variation again, slightly impregnated with Canadian cheddar.'

'"Yet each man gets the cheese he craves, by each let this be known", as the poet did not say. One day I'm going to write a book about cheese in which you shall all get what you deserve.'

'Well, put me down for Double Gloucester when you do.'

'I am not quite sure whether you are worthy. But, look here, Cardonnel, you're on the Committee, can't you do something about it?'

'The ability of our worthy secretary and of Benson, our still more worthy chef, to put up a display of passive resistance is far superior to any little feat that Wellington accomplished with the lines of Torres Vedras. And, just between us four, what help should I get from Laming?'

'That's all very well, but you can't evade your responsibilities that way,' Henry began. He had suddenly remembered the mock appointment he had conferred on Cardonnel, and was about to ask him to report progress, when the chartered accountant, coming out of a reverie, interrupted him.

'But, going back to the sauce, there seems to be something wrong with the tea.'

Gladwin looked at him solemnly. 'A sad case. To think that he once had sufficient brains to understand a balance sheet (subject, of course, to the information and explanation being given to him), and now he thinks that you serve tea with some sort of sauce.'

'Well, something is being served with the tea.'

Henry sat up. 'I did hear a rumour of someone being upset yesterday – Munro I think it was.'

'And I see that Mr Justice Bird is indisposed to-day and can't sit. You know he always has tea and a muffin here.'

'There was a rumour, too, that Warrington and that little doctor man, Anstruther, were made thoroughly ill by some sherry the other day.'

'Oh, I know all about that.' Gladwin stirred his coffee. 'Warrington told me about it. He was frightfully ill, but he doesn't want to cause trouble about it because, as a decent fellow, he does not want to get the library floor waiter into trouble.'

Cardonnel seemed to be interested. 'What, Hughes? What's he been doing?'

'Oh, he made some muddle or other about a bottle of lotion supplied to him for a boil or something. Warrington says Ford's story was very incoherent and he could not understand it, but he gathered Ford wanted him to accept the apology and keep quiet. So, if that is good enough for him, it is for us, I suppose.'

'Very curious,' remarked Cardonnel, toying with a cigar-cutter. In his own mind he thought it more than curious. Frankly he did not believe that the same sort of accident could happen twice. It must then be Ford's invention. But even if he had invented it just to quieten Warrington down, what had Ford thought had really happened? And, for that matter, what was the truth? He decided it was a question which he must investigate further. Meanwhile he added aloud: 'But that was not tea. Tell me more about this tea business.'

'Personally, I think it's the butter, although I know I said tea originally.'

'Why?'

'Well, every case that I have heard of, and there have been quite a number who have been sick or upset, have had something toasted with butter for tea – buttered toast, or a muffin, or a crumpet, or tea-cake.'

'Toasted bun?'

The accountant thought for a moment. 'No, not that I have heard of.'

'Very odd. Look, Cardonnel, this is another case for you.'

'Another?' queried Gladwin.

'Yes, don't you remember that I appointed him Club house detective over the missing library books?'

'So you did, but we've never had your report, Cardonnel.'

'Well, I never accepted the job.' Cardonnel laughed. 'All the same, I did do it, just for fun. I was going to tell you soon about it. In fact I hoped I could let you know the *dénouement* to-morrow, or soon after, except perhaps the fellow's name. You see, I might only get my confession by promising to say no more about it.'

'Conniving at a felony, my learned friend?'

'Maybe. But anyhow, have you noticed that during the last fortnight the theft of books has stopped?'

'I hadn't noticed it, but has it?'

'You look at the list of "books missing" hanging over there above the shelf where they are kept. The last date that one went is over a fortnight ago, and Ford tells me there is nothing new to be put down. Of course I admit a fortnight is a short while, but I rather fancy, from something he let slip, that Ford gave the fellow a warning. Of course I told him to do nothing of the sort, but you know what Ford is. I have no doubt' – his voice took on a mocking, sing-song tone – 'he meant well.'

'Just like Ford. And I suppose that cramped your style?'

'A little, but anyhow I think I have fitted in the missing link now. I worked first of all on the times he was up and the events happening at the time. That gave me a lot of facts about him, although I got a bit astray because he used to live in one place and now does not. Then I went on to his tastes and his relations –'

'Relations?'

'Well, that was a bit involved, but I got it in the end. Then I must admit I got a valuable hint from Hughes, the library waiter you were mentioning just now. He very nearly caught the man red-handed.'

The memory of an incident shaped in Gladwin's mind. 'You do not mean green-handed, do you?'

'I do *not*, emphatically. That was an individual turn on the part of Ford – and not very helpful.'

'Pummy stone,' giggled Henry.

'Quite. Well, having got so far, I shadowed my man until I found that he did fit. I am afraid he saw through what I was trying to get at – perhaps Ford's warning was earlier than I imagined, I don't know – anyhow, he lied a good deal, but yesterday I got my final piece of evidence.'

'Which was?'

'I am afraid I can't tell you without letting you know too much. You see, I want to see what happens when I do talk to this fellow.

I have asked him as a matter of fact to meet me here as soon as possible, preferably this afternoon, and until we have had our little talk, perhaps I had better say no more.'

At that moment a page-boy came up to him with a note. He opened it and quickly read the few words, and then told the boy to tell the secretary that he would be with him almost at once. Quickly finishing his coffee, he rose to go. 'Our secretary,' he commented, 'seems agitated. This is barely a request to come to his office, it is almost an order, and there is not even a platitude or a misquoted proverb to palliate it. This sounds interesting. I wonder into what new trouble Ford has got himself!'

He walked deliberately to the door, leaving behind a slight feeling of mystery and unsatisfied curiosity, but a strong impression that he was a very shrewd man.

CHAPTER 30

A MATTER OF REPETITION

*

'I GATHER that what you want to say to me is fairly private – at least that's what Ford gave me to understand.'

The pretext was a thin one and Anstruther was surprised to see how easily Cardonnel allowed himself to be persuaded. Together they started to go up the stairs towards the silence library, Cardonnel falling into step without question and with unexpected docility. Arrived at the door of the cold library, he did seem for a moment to hesitate.

'In there? But we are not supposed to talk in there.'

'Oh, there's never anyone in there at this time of day. We're sure to have it all to ourselves.' Anstruther pushed the door open to be met with a rush of air of a temperature which though definitely lower than the rather stuffy atmosphere of the Club, was still not really cold.

As if struck with some premonition, Cardonnel shivered slightly. 'Rather chilly, won't it be, in there? It looks though as if you must be right about the room being empty. No member of *this* club would sit in such a draught! One would almost think that the room had been specially cleared for us.'

'I like it, you know. As a general rule I find this club a great deal too hot. It's quite a mild day to-day, really, believe me. You see that curtain there doesn't blow about in the very least.' He pointed to the folds of the heavy red material which hung from ceiling to floor beside the window through which the air was blowing, and with apparent indifference strode to the french window and out on to the balcony. 'Really, it's quite warm out, you know,' he added.

After a prolonged stare at the curtain, Cardonnel followed him and, giving one glance at the silhouette of the roofs opposite, looked down at the pavement so very far below and shuddered slightly. 'Certainly we are alone here,' he commented as cheerfully as he could, 'but, you know, looking down any height always makes me giddy.'

Anstruther nodded grimly. He hoped that fact was known to others. It might serve as a possible explanation! For the rest, he had fully intended to have no spectators – that was why he had opened the window – now that at last he was to have it out finally with this meddlesome fellow. But it was unwise to waste time. They always might be disturbed. He brought Cardonnel to the point. 'What was it that you wanted to discuss?'

'When I wrote to you it had been my intention to discuss the books –'

'The *books*?'

'Yes. Come, my dear fellow, you know that books have been vanishing from the Club and you also know that you borrowed *The Ways of Melanesia* for some considerable time. You practically admitted it to me the other night.'

With a glance at the railing, Anstruther granted the point. In the circumstances it really was of no importance. 'But what of it?' he went on. 'Wrong, I know, but I brought it back, and really, if you will pardon my saying so, it hardly seems of sufficient importance to worry about unduly.'

'If that were all –' Cardonnel broke off, while Anstruther waited anxiously to hear what the rest would be. If it were only a question of other books – an absurd mare's nest – how happy he would be! In that case what he contemplated would be unnecessary perhaps.

'But I am sure that you are aware,' went on the lawyer's precise voice, 'that many books have gone, and gone regularly. I have worked out a chart and from it I was able to ascertain a great deal as to the hobbies and circumstances in life of whoever is mainly responsible for their loss. A most interesting piece of work. I really should like to show you how it was built up.'

'But, excuse my interrupting you,' Anstruther fearful of an interruption, was beginning to find the delay trying to his nerves, 'how does this concern me?'

'I next studied your character and antecedents. There was *The Ways of Melanesia*, you see, and in many ways you fitted the part. But not,' Cardonnel shook his head sadly, 'not entirely.'

'And have you really summoned me merely to inform me that

you once suspected me of stealing books from the Club? I can assure you that I have not done so – even you apparently almost recognize that.' Anstruther drew himself up and stepped back from the railing. If that were all, his labours then were wasted. Cardonnel was rapidly shrinking in his eyes from the monstrous figure of his imagination to something almost insignificant and unimportant. The lawyer's next remark however dispelled this pleasing hope.

'No. That is not the only reason why I asked you to meet me in the Club, if not exactly here, this afternoon. In the first place I am not yet satisfied as to the books. I should have liked, if the circumstances as well as the locality had been more suitable, to have presented you with a little evidence, but, as it is, the whole subject has become a detail with which I need not worry you further. You see, in the course of investigating the question of the books, I have recently, quite recently, had my attention directed to some rather odd events.'

He looked his companion full in the face and went on. 'Doctor Anstruther, it seems to be dangerous to take tea in this club.'

He paused for a second time, and then added quietly but significantly: 'It seems to be even more dangerous to be a member of this club *and* to be one of your patients.'

Anstruther, conscious that his face was being carefully scrutinized, allowed no trace of emotion to be expressed by his thin lips or his half-veiled eyes. But though he remained calm, it was only by a violent effort. After all, then, the final settlement with Cardonnel was going to prove necessary! He was surprised to find that he was almost glad; glad, he supposed, that the suspense was over and that the time for action had arrived. To Cardonnel's amazement he actually answered with a smile.

'Dangerous to take tea?'

'Yes. You see I have had the contents of some of the little salt containers analysed. Some of them contained salt and salt alone. Others had calomel; a few perchloride of mercury – two powders which as you well know, are very difficult to distinguish from salt, at any rate when mixed together, but whose presence cannot be accidental; which must have been added deliberately by someone who, perhaps from a perverted sense of humour, enjoyed giving pain – someone with some knowledge of poisons and an easy method of obtaining them.'

'And what of it? There are many such people and both the drugs are common. Calomel of course is not even a poison.'

'Strange, Doctor Anstruther, that you should have been the first victim of a bottle of sherry into which perchloride had just been added, a poison whose use had previously been feared (though groundlessly) to have occurred, and stranger still that you should have so readily identified that poison.'

'Not at all. An intelligent and apparently accurate guess based on my professional knowledge.'

'By itself that might be so, but even the long arm of coincidence has its limitations. It cannot be extended indefinitely. It was strange that there should have been an attempt to lay the blame on the shoulders of the only quite independent witness – for Ford was far too involved to be called independent – who knew anything of the death of *both* your patients.'

'That is the second time you have mentioned the death of my patients. Morrison died of heart failure, Pargiter of a clot on the brain. A loss of professional income to me in both cases. Otherwise I have nothing to say.'

His thin-lipped mouth closed with a snap. There was still a chance that action would not be necessary. Unfortunately close to the truth though Cardonnel might be, it was clear that he had no proof at all so far as Anstruther could make out. A little bluff and – who knew? – perhaps he might drop the whole thing. It was time to take a strong line.

'Mr Cardonnel,' he started, 'since you are an older member and an older man than I, I have listened very patiently to a number of very wild accusations by you, ranging from the theft of books to professional incompetence – if that was the object of your last insinuations. I can now understand why you wished this conversation to take place without a witness. As a lawyer I need not suggest to you my obvious course of action had there been one. But I have listened for long enough.'

'Not quite, I think,' Cardonnel interrupted gently. 'I am not speaking entirely without proof. The chain of reasoning is long, almost as long as that which connected you with the books,

although I have had less time to work it out. But it is more conclusive. Indeed there are quite a number of points in it which I
think would in themselves induce you to believe that the matter
cannot thus lightly be dismissed. I will however mention just
one of them. There was just one point over which you gave yourself away rather badly.'

Anstruther moved back from the railing to the window, and
answered with a cold, almost contemptuous voice, but with his
brain acutely responsive, ready for immediate action: 'Well, I
am listening.'

'I have had the advantage of a long conversation with Ford in
which he at last told me everything that he knew – a breach of
confidence, no doubt, but that has not been confined, I gather,
to one side only. It appears that he told you much about my suspicions and activities and you warned him that he was taking me
too much into his confidence and that I knew too much already.'

'Well?'

'Ford happened without thinking to repeat the remark to me
verbatim. Apparently you impressed it on his memory in some
way or another. He seems to connect it with an intense stare.
Without, I think, quite realizing what he was doing, it came trip-
ping from his tongue automatically, like a lesson he had been
made to learn – even now I doubt if Ford has seen the point, but
he *is* prepared to swear to the actual words you used. You pre-
faced your remark by the words "As I have told you before".'

Cardonnel paused and moved a yard away from his companion
so that he stood with one hand on the railing. Then he added:

'So you had. But it was in a letter that you were not supposed
to have read, still less to have written.'

The words were hardly uttered when with a sudden spring
Anstruther jumped forward. If Ford had not seen the point, with
Cardonnel out of the way, there was still time! Exerting his whole
strength he pushed the lawyer violently against the railing on
which his accuser was apparently relying. If it were firm, Cardonnel would be safe enough, but he knew that it was not.

To his amazement and horror, however, the railing held. Instead of the wiry body of his adversary hurtling through space to
the hard pavement below, it was still present on the balcony.

Anstruther had just time to notice the look of intense relief that had spread over Cardonnel's white face, when he felt the collar of his coat firmly seized from behind. The reason why the curtain had not blown about at last became clear. All the while that he had been talking to Cardonnel, Hughes had been behind it, keeping it still.

CHAPTER 31

THE FINAL RETICENCE

*

'AND now, still with the object of avoiding any scandal in the
Club, which of course has been the motive influencing all our
actions, perhaps you will be so good as to promise me to walk
quite quietly to bedroom Number 4? You will observe that we are
still uninterrupted, but that is due not to luck, but to the fact
that Ford has been standing for some time outside the door to
prevent anyone from coming in. You may find that it adds to the
piquancy of the situation when I tell you that Ford has no idea
of what he is there for. I was afraid he would not let me carry out
my little experiment and so I relied entirely on Hughes. After all
he was the man who saw you tampering with the railing – and
had the sense to come to me as well as the secretary. Then we had
it repaired. But to go back, I want your promise to walk there
without taking any action of any kind, partly to save you from
the indignity of being forcibly pushed through the corridor and
partly to avoid the risk of anyone seeing us and asking awkward
questions.'

So long a speech gave Anstruther time to recover. The limp
form stiffened while still in Hughes's firm grip. His pride was
coming back to him. Whatever was coming to him, he would
meet it like a man and not a cry-baby. There was determination
in his voice as he answered: 'You have my promise. Leave go of
me.'

With the ingrained habit of obedience – after all he was unused
to laying violent hands on his members – Hughes relinquished his
hold and then, mistrusting Anstruther, would have jumped forward to regain it if Cardonnel had not motioned him to stop.
With a firm step Anstruther walked to the bedroom where previously he had helped to carry both Morrison and Pargiter. How
long ago all that seemed now!

He looked round the familiar room until, hearing a noise
behind him, he turned to see Ford shutting the door. With real
hate he glared at the secretary. 'You incompetent fool, you

babbling, disloyal, senseless idiot. I can bear being beaten by Cardonnel's brains – Hughes's too – but to find that one has been let down by a snivelling old woman like you, whose black silk petticoats one can hear rustling as you walk – ah! If only I had just a little hyoscine available now.'

'So it was hyoscine, was it?' Cardonnel broke in.

'Yes, if you must know, it was hyoscine – for Pargiter, and a mistake at that. As for Morrison, to the best of my knowledge and belief it *was* heart failure. You see,' he turned to Cardonnel, 'that is where the disadvantage comes of having to deal with a fool. It puts such a temptation in one's way. It was too easy to hoodwink and, as it were, blackmail Ford. Pooh, you, you fried curled whiting!'

'Stop it!' Cardonnel's voice cut in quickly. He had no desire to see Ford lose his temper, and if Hughes laughed he was afraid he might. 'Sit down everybody. I shall be rather glad to do so myself after the last half hour. Anstruther, sit on the bed; you there, Ford. Hughes, first of all get me some brandy. I'm not so young as I once was and I never had any head for heights.'

'I think a little would do me good too.' Anstruther calmly sat down where he was told.

It takes a good deal to shake a club servant out of the correctness of his attitude, but this was too much. 'Well, I'm damned,' Hughes burst out, 'of all the cool fish.' Suddenly he recovered himself. 'I beg your pardon, sir. You would prefer the '51 or the ordinary club brandy?'

'The '51 of course,' said Anstruther severely. 'This habit of trying to foist one off with inferior wines, spirits rather – it's too bad. On the whole, though, you know, I think he's right about one thing – *you* seem to be the "pretty cool fish." Supposing Hughes had not turned up in time? I should have had you over in a minute in any case, even if I had to accompany you myself.'

'I hate to suggest it, but isn't it you who are being a little slow now? I thought I had explained that it was no accident that Hughes was there. As a matter of fact,' he went on slowly, 'I suppose that you were more right in your desire to get rid of him than in anything else. He has for a long time suspected you and been trying to work out the details. That's why he spotted you so quickly about that book.'

'Do stop talking about books. For the hundredth time I tell you that it has got nothing to do with me.'

'I believe you, and yet it was the cause of – what has happened. You see, it was in considering the subject of the books that I first began to take an interest in you, and it was over the books that Hughes first began watching you – wasn't it?' he added as Hughes returned, 'and it was while watching you that he saw you arranging that the rail of the balcony was weak. He had the sense to go away and turn out the light as if he had not seen you.'

'So you knew everything! Well, I reiterate "Cool fish". I wonder you did not make the conversation a bit shorter.'

'I had to make sure. It was essential to catch you absolutely red-handed. But it was not very pleasant, even though I had the advantage of knowing that you were relying on the railing, which I knew had been repaired.' He shuddered slightly at the very thought of that nervous half hour.

'I see. Nevertheless,' Anstruther raised his glass, 'I drink to your courage.'

With an admiring glance, Cardonnel responded: 'And I to yours.'

'This is preposterous!' broke in Ford, speaking for the first time. 'You cannot go on behaving like this to the man who has tried to murder you within the last half hour and whom during the next hour you are going to hand over to the police.'

Slowly and deliberately Cardonnel replied: 'I am not so sure that I am going to do anything of the sort.'

'Eh?' The other three all started violently.

'As to what has happened, no one knows outside we four. Obviously we *can* carry on in the way you suggest, Ford. It may indeed be necessary. But who is going to benefit? You yourself will come out of it pretty badly, you know. You will have to admit that you connived at hushing up what you thought were two murders, though actually we are given to understand that there was only one.'

'One, thank you.'

'There are rather a number of things,' went on Cardonnel, acknowledging Anstruther's interruption by a slight, rather formal bow as if he were obliged for an interesting but unimportant correction on a point of detail, 'which you will have to explain to the Committee as well as the police. I do not envy you your position. You will, I think, escape prison, though undeservedly, but you are hardly likely to remain here as secretary.'

Lest Ford should express his belated desire to sacrifice himself on the altar of justice, he turned to the waiter. 'And you, Hughes? Are you anxious to have a scandal in the Club?'

'No, sir.' The answer was prompt and emphatic.

'Don't be too quick. If this comes out, a great deal of credit will very properly accrue to you. The Club as a whole should be very grateful to you, quite apart from the debt which I owe you myself.'

'What's the good, sir, of making a fuss? It won't do the Club any good, and what doesn't do the Club any good doesn't do me any good. Besides, sir, from what you told me when we talked this over after I told you about the railing, Mr Ford could have made things a lot easier for himself by getting rid of me, and if he didn't then, I don't suppose he will now. No, sir, I do what you two gentlemen tell me.'

'Thank you, Hughes. You are right about the Club too. That is what is influencing me mainly.' He paused and surveyed the figure on the bed.

Anstruther sat quite still with an almost maddening appearance of being entirely detached from the proceedings. Of the four present only Ford showed any signs of any nervous strain. Cardonnel was in command and knew his own intentions, Hughes was content to obey – that Ford could understand – but that anyone should be so resigned that he should view his ultimate fate in a spirit of scientific observation was an attitude far too cold-blooded for so simple and impulsive a nature as the secretary's.

Once more Cardonnel's voice went steadily on. 'So now we come to you, Anstruther. An appeal to loyalty or to sentiment would, I think, be regarded by you as an insult to your intelligence; but you have, I believe, your pride. You would rather leave behind a reasonable, I might say a respected, name. Besides, the legal process of a trial will be not only unpleasant, it will be extremely dull.'

Ford shook his head. How anybody could be bored at their own trial for murder, he could not understand. But, in any case, how was it to be avoided? Cardonnel's next words reassured him to some extent.

'Make no mistake. I am not suggesting that you simply disappear, still less that you get off scot-free. Very far from that. No.' For a while he stopped as if searching for a phrase and then unexpectedly ended: 'Do you happen to be acquainted with the new criminal law of Latvia?'

'Of Latvia?' For a while Anstruther remained impassive, then gradually comprehension and interest dawned on his face. For several minutes there was silence in the room. Hughes stood solidly with his back to the door. It was no part of his business to understand now. His active thinking in the matter was over; the rest he was quite content to leave in Cardonnel's hands; secretly he was rather glad that no decision apparently rested with Ford. The secretary was the only restless one of the three. He started to fidget and drum his fingers on the table, until a glance from Cardonnel, sitting quietly and sipping his brandy, restrained him. Try as he would, he could not understand it. How on earth were they to avoid calling in the police? All the same, Cardonnel was right; the consequences were going to be most unpleasant. The chair on which he was sitting creaked ominously.

Suddenly the tension was broken by Anstruther leaping to his feet. 'Very well, then,' he cried. 'I accept. To the laws of Latvia!' He drained his glass.

Cardonnel too jumped up. 'Excellent. When shall we – hear from you? To-morrow morning? Good.' He motioned Hughes out of the way and flung open the door. Before Ford could say a word, Anstruther was gone.

'But, but,' protested Ford feebly, 'he's gone.'

'So I am aware. It's all right, I tell you. The best possible solution.' Cardonnel sighed happily. 'Whatever I doubt in this

world, I do not doubt that that doctor will keep his word. A very
gallant man,' he ended slowly.

'But what are the laws of Latvia?'

'Oh, don't you know? Well, that I can explain to-morrow.'

CHAPTER 32

TWO LAST LETTERS

*

AFTER a restless night, Ford hurried down the next morning and rapidly looked through the letters addressed to him personally.

Nothing from Cardonnel. Nothing from Anstruther. What on earth was the plan that these two had concocted under his very eyes? The more he thought of it, the more he hoped that it was sound, above all that it was final. He had no wish to figure prominently in the publicity that would be occasioned by the trial of Anstruther; Cardonnel was certainly right when he said that it would do neither him nor the Club any good; but even more did he wish that the whole business might be over once and for all. He could not stand much more of it.

After vainly looking up 'Latvia' in the encyclopaedia, he went up to his office and tried to concentrate on his ordinary routine work, but he found it almost impossible. Everything that he touched served only to bring his mind back to the one absorbing trouble. There was for instance a long complaint that the window of the library had been left open with the result that the room was uninhabitable. Well, he knew how that had happened. In a sense it was his own fault that it had not been shut. But how to pacify the indignant member he had no idea.

He put it down, hoping that in some mysterious manner it would answer itself and found himself reading a letter quoting prices for sherry.

He never wished to hear the subject of sherry mentioned again. What between the great sherry controversy, the echoes of which had barely died down, and Anstruther's fancy tricks with the same wine, it had become a subject which filled him with the direst apprehensions.

His meditations however were soon interrupted by a knock on the door. No less a person than the hall porter arrived.

'The lady, sir, was very insistent that I should give you this note myself. She made me promise that no one else was to hand it to you. Moreover, sir, she left a large case in the hall with instructions that only you were to open it.'

He was just about to say that it must wait when he suddenly heard Cardonnel's voice: 'This intrigues me, Ford. Sorry if I overheard what the hall porter said. Most reprehensible, I know.'

'What –' Ford was about to ask whether any news had arrived concerning Anstruther, when he remembered that it would be wiser not to speak about the matter before a third person. The discretion was unusual. To get rid of the hall porter he told him to see that the case was brought to his office at once. Then he hurried back to Cardonnel.

But the lawyer was in an irritating mood. 'No, my news can wait. Let's hear what this further little mystery is.'

Reluctantly deciding that he would get nothing from Cardonnel until he had complied, Ford started to read:

Dear Sir,
    Since my dear father, the judge, died a fortnight ago, I have been occupied in the melancholy task of going through his papers prior to moving back to our old home in Nottingham.

'Nottingham!' interrupted Cardonnel.

Ford nodded and continued:

For the last few years my very dear father had been getting old and absent-minded, and unfortunately he had developed a habit of picking up things and then forgetting where they came from. He was, of course, as you well know, the soul of honour, and he could never have done such a thing intentionally, but the difficulty was that he so frequently did not know where the things had come from.

I must admit that in the case of the Club books which I have discovered hidden in the most curious places all over his sitting-room, which no one was ever allowed to tidy, he should have known, because of the markers, but I think the explanation can only be that he forgot that he had put them there.

I am therefore hastening to return all the volumes personally, and should I find any more, I shall pursue the same course. But I hope for the sake of his reputation, and even the worst of us prizes the reputation he or she may leave behind –

Cardonnel could not keep back an exclamation. Exactly the argument he had used to Anstruther!

– that you will find it possible to keep it quiet.

I am,

Yours faithfully,

MURIEL SKINNER.

A short silence ensued, broken at last by Ford complaining that the actual books were of little or no use to him. 'She makes no offer to repay what we have had to spend. How like a woman!'

'All the same I should write to her and comfort her. The judge was a very good fellow, really, and he was completely absent-minded. For the rest, you are getting quite used to "keeping it quiet", eh, Ford? For one thing, I hope you realize that this completely proves my theory as to Nottingham to be right. I am sure that if you looked into the rest of the Judge's habits, you would find they entirely bore out everything that I have deduced, though for myself I shall not worry to do so.'

Perhaps it was as well. As the days went uneventfully on, a legend grew up round the Club that Cardonnel had done the most wonderful piece of detective work with the result that, not only had the theft of books been stopped, but that many had been recovered. It was understood that the name of the member was carefully suppressed because he was dead.

Cardonnel, however, always avoided discussing it, being content with the certain knowledge that his reputation for sagacity was firmly established. Neither did he risk finding out more than he knew already about Skinner. Therein he was wise, since the Judge, as in his heart of hearts Cardonnel suspected, had never been to an Association football match in his life and did not know one musical composer from another. Wisely, however, as Ford would have said, he 'let sleeping dogs lie, considering that ignorance was bliss'.

Even at the moment that the letter from Judge Skinner's daughter was read, Cardonnel had a shrewd idea of how events would fall. He sat there letting his mind wander into the future, until his thoughts were brought back to the present by an exclamation from Ford.

'Anstruther?' he answered. 'Oh, yes, to set your mind at rest about that. I too have had a letter.' From his pocket he produced a typescript of a kind all too well known to Ford. 'May I read it? It begins:

'My dear Cardonnel,

'It may seem odd to you that I should so address you after all that has passed and still more after what has failed to pass between us, but somehow all the resentment that I felt towards you has vanished and I believe that you too are big enough to harbour no bitter memories.

'Whatever else may have happened, believe me, I respect your brains and your courage. I have also to thank you for offering, and offering so neatly, the way out of the difficulty. Fortunately I also had noticed, since everything connected with poison has recently had a type of fascination for me, the recent change in the laws of Latvia, so that your hint, though a little "precious" in form, if I may say so, was not wasted upon me.'

'Excuse my interrupting, but it still is on me.'

Cardonnel looked up impatiently at Ford. 'I thought you would have found out by now. In Latvia, let me explain, they have recently passed an act whereby any man condemned to death has the option to administer poison to himself. They were rather surprised when the first man chose to be hanged in the normal way.'

He stopped and then added quietly: 'Anstruther has chosen differently.'

Then, having seen that Ford had at last understood, he went on reading:

'You need not fear but that I shall keep my word. You will however, I am sure, excuse me if I so arrange things that it will appear that I have lost my life in the cause of medical science, as the result of the experiments I have recently been carrying out with hyoscine – one of which resulted, though this will not appear, so unfortunately for Pargiter. The evidence that this is so will be found neatly, but not too neatly, arranged in my consulting-room. I am sure that I can rely on you to assist me in giving the widest publicity to the fact, since as you rightly said, one does prefer to leave behind a good reputation. Though quite why one should worry about it so much, I do not know. Perhaps I am only anxious to provide myself with a last good laugh.

'Give what message you will to Ford. Read him this letter if you like. You will, I think, have no difficulty in persuading him to connive at yet another crime. He is getting quite accustomed to it by now. But this time advise him seriously that it would be better if he *really* kept it quiet.'

A CATALOGUE OF
SELECTED DOVER BOOKS
IN ALL FIELDS OF INTEREST

A CATALOGUE OF SELECTED DOVER BOOKS IN ALL FIELDS OF INTEREST

CELESTIAL OBJECTS FOR COMMON TELESCOPES, T. W. Webb. The most used book in amateur astronomy: inestimable aid for locating and identifying nearly 4,000 celestial objects. Edited, updated by Margaret W. Mayall. 77 illustrations. Total of 645pp. 5⅜ x 8½.
20917-2, 20918-0 Pa., Two-vol. set $10.00

HISTORICAL STUDIES IN THE LANGUAGE OF CHEMISTRY, M. P. Crosland. The important part language has played in the development of chemistry from the symbolism of alchemy to the adoption of systematic nomenclature in 1892. ". . . wholeheartedly recommended,"—Science. 15 illustrations. 416pp. of text. 5⅝ x 8¼. 63702-6 Pa. $7.50

BURNHAM'S CELESTIAL HANDBOOK, Robert Burnham, Jr. Thorough, readable guide to the stars beyond our solar system. Exhaustive treatment, fully illustrated. Breakdown is alphabetical by constellation: Andromeda to Cetus in Vol. 1; Chamaeleon to Orion in Vol. 2; and Pavo to Vulpecula in Vol. 3. Hundreds of illustrations. Total of about 2000pp. 6⅛ x 9¼.
23567-X, 23568-8, 23673-0 Pa., Three-vol. set $32.85

THEORY OF WING SECTIONS: INCLUDING A SUMMARY OF AIRFOIL DATA, Ira H. Abbott and A. E. von Doenhoff. Concise compilation of subatomic aerodynamic characteristics of modern NASA wing sections, plus description of theory. 350pp. of tables. 693pp. 5⅜ x 8½.
60586-8 Pa. $9.95

DE RE METALLICA, Georgius Agricola. Translated by Herbert C. Hoover and Lou H. Hoover. The famous Hoover translation of greatest treatise on technological chemistry, engineering, geology, mining of early modern times (1556). All 289 original woodcuts. 638pp. 6¾ x 11.
60006-8 Clothbd. $19.95

THE ORIGIN OF CONTINENTS AND OCEANS, Alfred Wegener. One of the most influential, most controversial books in science, the classic statement for continental drift. Full 1966 translation of Wegener's final (1929) version. 64 illustrations. 246pp. 5⅜ x 8½.(EBE)61708-4 Pa. $5.00

THE PRINCIPLES OF PSYCHOLOGY, William James. Famous long course complete, unabridged. Stream of thought, time perception, memory, experimental methods; great work decades ahead of its time. Still valid, useful; read in many classes. 94 figures. Total of 1391pp. 5⅜ x 8½.
20381-6, 20382-4 Pa., Two-vol. set $17.90

YUCATAN BEFORE AND AFTER THE CONQUEST, Diego de Landa. First English translation of basic book in Maya studies, the only significant account of Yucatan written in the early post-Conquest era. Translated by distinguished Maya scholar William Gates. Appendices, introduction, 4 maps and over 120 illustrations added by translator. 162pp. 5⅜ x 8½.
23622-6 Pa. $3.00

THE MALAY ARCHIPELAGO, Alfred R. Wallace. Spirited travel account by one of founders of modern biology. Touches on zoology, botany, ethnography, geography, and geology. 62 illustrations, maps. 515pp. 5⅜ x 8½.
20187-2 Pa. $6.95

THE DISCOVERY OF THE TOMB OF TUTANKHAMEN, Howard Carter, A. C. Mace. Accompany Carter in the thrill of discovery, as ruined passage suddenly reveals unique, untouched, fabulously rich tomb. Fascinating account, with 106 illustrations. New introduction by J. M. White. Total of 382pp. 5⅜ x 8½. (Available in U.S. only) 23500-9 Pa. $5.50

THE WORLD'S GREATEST SPEECHES, edited by Lewis Copeland and Lawrence W. Lamm. Vast collection of 278 speeches from Greeks up to present. Powerful and effective models; unique look at history. Revised to 1970. Indices. 842pp. 5⅜ x 8½.
20468-5 Pa. $9.95

THE 100 GREATEST ADVERTISEMENTS, Julian Watkins. The priceless ingredient; His master's voice; 99 44/100% pure; over 100 others. How they were written, their impact, etc. Remarkable record. 130 illustrations. 233pp. 7⅞ x 10 3/5.
20540-1 Pa. $6.95

CRUICKSHANK PRINTS FOR HAND COLORING, George Cruickshank. 18 illustrations, one side of a page, on fine-quality paper suitable for watercolors. Caricatures of people in society (c. 1820) full of trenchant wit. Very large format. 32pp. 11 x 16.
23684-6 Pa. $6.00

THIRTY-TWO COLOR POSTCARDS OF TWENTIETH-CENTURY AMERICAN ART, Whitney Museum of American Art. Reproduced in full color in postcard form are 31 art works and one shot of the museum. Calder, Hopper, Rauschenberg, others. Detachable. 16pp. 8¼ x 11.
23629-3 Pa. $3.50

MUSIC OF THE SPHERES: THE MATERIAL UNIVERSE FROM ATOM TO QUASAR SIMPLY EXPLAINED, Guy Murchie. Planets, stars, geology, atoms, radiation, relativity, quantum theory, light, antimatter, similar topics. 319 figures. 664pp. 5⅜ x 8½.
21809-0, 21810-4 Pa., Two-vol. set $11.00

EINSTEIN'S THEORY OF RELATIVITY, Max Born. Finest semi-technical account; covers Einstein, Lorentz, Minkowski, and others, with much detail, much explanation of ideas and math not readily available elsewhere on this level. For student, non-specialist. 376pp. 5⅜ x 8½.
60769-0 Pa. $5.00

THE SENSE OF BEAUTY, George Santayana. Masterfully written discussion of nature of beauty, materials of beauty, form, expression; art, literature, social sciences all involved. 168pp. 5⅜ x 8½.   20238-0 Pa. $3.50

ON THE IMPROVEMENT OF THE UNDERSTANDING, Benedict Spinoza. Also contains *Ethics, Correspondence,* all in excellent R. Elwes translation. Basic works on entry to philosophy, pantheism, exchange of ideas with great contemporaries. 402pp. 5⅜ x 8½.   20250-X Pa. $5.95

THE TRAGIC SENSE OF LIFE, Miguel de Unamuno. Acknowledged masterpiece of existential literature, one of most important books of 20th century. Introduction by Madariaga. 367pp. 5⅜ x 8½.
20257-7 Pa. $6.00

THE GUIDE FOR THE PERPLEXED, Moses Maimonides. Great classic of medieval Judaism attempts to reconcile revealed religion (Pentateuch, commentaries) with Aristotelian philosophy. Important historically, still relevant in problems. Unabridged Friedlander translation. Total of 473pp. 5⅜ x 8½.   20351-4 Pa. $6.95

THE I CHING (THE BOOK OF CHANGES), translated by James Legge. Complete translation of basic text plus appendices by Confucius, and Chinese commentary of most penetrating divination manual ever prepared. Indispensable to study of early Oriental civilizations, to modern inquiring reader. 448pp. 5⅜ x 8½.   21062-6 Pa. $6.00

THE EGYPTIAN BOOK OF THE DEAD, E. A. Wallis Budge. Complete reproduction of Ani's papyrus, finest ever found. Full hieroglyphic text, interlinear transliteration, word for word translation, smooth translation. Basic work, for Egyptology, for modern study of psychic matters. Total of 533pp. 6½ x 9¼. (USCO)   21866-X Pa. $8.50

THE GODS OF THE EGYPTIANS, E. A. Wallis Budge. Never excelled for richness, fullness: all gods, goddesses, demons, mythical figures of Ancient Egypt; their legends, rites, incarnations, variations, powers, etc. Many hieroglyphic texts cited. Over 225 illustrations, plus 6 color plates. Total of 988pp. 6⅛ x 9¼. (EBE)
22055-9, 22056-7 Pa., Two-vol. set $20.00

THE STANDARD BOOK OF QUILT MAKING AND COLLECTING, Marguerite Ickis. Full information, full-sized patterns for making 46 traditional quilts, also 150 other patterns. Quilted cloths, lame, satin quilts, etc. 483 illustrations. 273pp. 6⅞ x 9⅝.   20582-7 Pa. $5.95

CORAL GARDENS AND THEIR MAGIC, Bronsilaw Malinowski. Classic study of the methods of tilling the soil and of agricultural rites in the Trobriand Islands of Melanesia. Author is one of the most important figures in the field of modern social anthropology. 143 illustrations. Indexes. Total of 911pp. of text. 5⅝ x 8¼. (Available in U.S. only)
23597-1 Pa. $12.95

THE PHILOSOPHY OF HISTORY, Georg W. Hegel. Great classic of Western thought develops concept that history is not chance but a rational process, the evolution of freedom. 457pp. 5⅜ x 8½. 20112-0 Pa. $6.00

LANGUAGE, TRUTH AND LOGIC, Alfred J. Ayer. Famous, clear introduction to Vienna, Cambridge schools of Logical Positivism. Role of philosophy, elimination of metaphysics, nature of analysis, etc. 160pp. 5⅜ x 8½. (USCO) 20010-8 Pa. $2.50

A PREFACE TO LOGIC, Morris R. Cohen. Great City College teacher in renowned, easily followed exposition of formal logic, probability, values, logic and world order and similar topics; no previous background needed. 209pp. 5⅜ x 8½. 23517-3 Pa. $4.95

REASON AND NATURE, Morris R. Cohen. Brilliant analysis of reason and its multitudinous ramifications by charismatic teacher. Interdisciplinary, synthesizing work widely praised when it first appeared in 1931. Second (1953) edition. Indexes. 496pp. 5⅜ x 8½. 23633-1 Pa. $7.50

AN ESSAY CONCERNING HUMAN UNDERSTANDING, John Locke. The only complete edition of enormously important classic, with authoritative editorial material by A. C. Fraser. Total of 1176pp. 5⅜ x 8½. 20530-4, 20531-2 Pa., Two-vol. set $16.00

HANDBOOK OF MATHEMATICAL FUNCTIONS WITH FORMULAS, GRAPHS, AND MATHEMATICAL TABLES, edited by Milton Abramowitz and Irene A. Stegun. Vast compendium: 29 sets of tables, some to as high as 20 places. 1,046pp. 8 x 10½. 61272-4 Pa. $17.95

MATHEMATICS FOR THE PHYSICAL SCIENCES, Herbert S. Wilf. Highly acclaimed work offers clear presentations of vector spaces and matrices, orthogonal functions, roots of polynomial equations, conformal mapping, calculus of variations, etc. Knowledge of theory of functions of real and complex variables is assumed. Exercises and solutions. Index. 284pp. 5⅝ x 8¼. 63635-6 Pa. $5.00

THE PRINCIPLE OF RELATIVITY, Albert Einstein et al. Eleven most important original papers on special and general theories. Seven by Einstein, two by Lorentz, one each by Minkowski and Weyl. All translated, unabridged. 216pp. 5⅜ x 8½. 60081-5 Pa. $3.50

THERMODYNAMICS, Enrico Fermi. A classic of modern science. Clear, organized treatment of systems, first and second laws, entropy, thermodynamic potentials, gaseous reactions, dilute solutions, entropy constant. No math beyond calculus required. Problems. 160pp. 5⅜ x 8½. 60361-X Pa. $4.00

ELEMENTARY MECHANICS OF FLUIDS, Hunter Rouse. Classic undergraduate text widely considered to be far better than many later books. Ranges from fluid velocity and acceleration to role of compressibility in fluid motion. Numerous examples, questions, problems. 224 illustrations. 376pp. 5⅝ x 8¼. 63699-2 Pa. $7.00

THE AMERICAN SENATOR, Anthony Trollope. Little known, long un-available Trollope novel on a grand scale. Here are humorous comment on American vs. English culture, and stunning portrayal of a heroine/villainess. Superb evocation of Victorian village life. 561pp. 5⅜ x 8½.
23801-6 Pa. $7.95

WAS IT MURDER? James Hilton. The author of *Lost Horizon* and *Good-bye, Mr. Chips* wrote one detective novel (under a pen-name) which was quickly forgotten and virtually lost, even at the height of Hilton's fame. This edition brings it back—a finely crafted public school puzzle resplendent with Hilton's stylish atmosphere. A thoroughly English thriller by the creator of Shangri-la. 252pp. 5⅜ x 8. (Available in U.S. only)
23774-5 Pa. $3.00

CENTRAL PARK: A PHOTOGRAPHIC GUIDE, Victor Laredo and Henry Hope Reed. 121 superb photographs show dramatic views of Central Park: Bethesda Fountain, Cleopatra's Needle, Sheep Meadow, the Blockhouse, plus people engaged in many park activities: ice skating, bike riding, etc. Captions by former Curator of Central Park, Henry Hope Reed, provide historical view, changes, etc. Also photos of N.Y. landmarks on park's periphery. 96pp. 8½ x 11.
23750-8 Pa. $4.50

NANTUCKET IN THE NINETEENTH CENTURY, Clay Lancaster. 180 rare photographs, stereographs, maps, drawings and floor plans recreate unique American island society. Authentic scenes of shipwreck, light-houses, streets, homes are arranged in geographic sequence to provide walking-tour guide to old Nantucket existing today. Introduction, captions. 160pp. 8⅞ x 11¾.
23747-8 Pa. $7.95

STONE AND MAN: A PHOTOGRAPHIC EXPLORATION, Andreas Feininger. 106 photographs by *Life* photographer Feininger portray man's deep passion for stone through the ages. Stonehenge-like megaliths, forti-fied towns, sculpted marble and crumbling tenements show textures, beau-ties, fascination. 128pp. 9¼ x 10¾.
23756-7 Pa. $5.95

CIRCLES, A MATHEMATICAL VIEW, D. Pedoe. Fundamental aspects of college geometry, non-Euclidean geometry, and other branches of mathe-matics: representing circle by point. Poincare model, isoperimetric prop-erty, etc. Stimulating recreational reading. 66 figures. 96pp. 5⅝ x 8¼.
63698-4 Pa. $3.50

THE DISCOVERY OF NEPTUNE, Morton Grosser. Dramatic scientific history of the investigations leading up to the actual discovery of the eighth planet of our solar system. Lucid, well-researched book by well-known historian of science. 172pp. 5⅜ x 8½.
23726-5 Pa. $3.50

THE DEVIL'S DICTIONARY. Ambrose Bierce. Barbed, bitter, brilliant witticisms in the form of a dictionary. Best, most ferocious satire America has produced. 145pp. 5⅜ x 8½.
20487-1 Pa. $2.50

HISTORY OF BACTERIOLOGY, William Bulloch. The only comprehensive history of bacteriology from the beginnings through the 19th century. Special emphasis is given to biography-Leeuwenhoek, etc. Brief accounts of 350 bacteriologists form a separate section. No clearer, fuller study, suitable to scientists and general readers, has yet been written. 52 illustrations. 448pp. 5⅝ x 8¼.   23761-3 Pa. $6.50

THE COMPLETE NONSENSE OF EDWARD LEAR, Edward Lear. All nonsense limericks, zany alphabets, Owl and Pussycat, songs, nonsense botany, etc., illustrated by Lear. Total of 321pp. 5⅜ x 8½. (Available in U.S. only)   20167-8 Pa. $4.50

INGENIOUS MATHEMATICAL PROBLEMS AND METHODS, Louis A. Graham. Sophisticated material from Graham *Dial*, applied and pure; stresses solution methods. Logic, number theory, networks, inversions, etc. 237pp. 5⅜ x 8½.   20545-2 Pa. $4.50

BEST MATHEMATICAL PUZZLES OF SAM LOYD, edited by Martin Gardner. Bizarre, original, whimsical puzzles by America's greatest puzzler. From fabulously rare *Cyclopedia*, including famous 14-15 puzzles, the Horse of a Different Color, 115 more. Elementary math. 150 illustrations. 167pp. 5⅜ x 8½.   20498-7 Pa. $3.50

THE BASIS OF COMBINATION IN CHESS, J. du Mont. Easy-to-follow, instructive book on elements of combination play, with chapters on each piece and every powerful combination team—two knights, bishop and knight, rook and bishop, etc. 250 diagrams. 218pp. 5⅜ x 8½. (Available in U.S. only)   23644-7 Pa. $4.50

MODERN CHESS STRATEGY, Ludek Pachman. The use of the queen, the active king, exchanges, pawn play, the center, weak squares, etc. Section on rook alone worth price of the book. Stress on the moderns. Often considered the most important book on strategy. 314pp. 5⅜ x 8½.
20290-9 Pa. $5.00

LASKER'S MANUAL OF CHESS, Dr. Emanuel Lasker. Great world champion offers very thorough coverage of all aspects of chess. Combinations, position play, openings, end game, aesthetics of chess, philosophy of struggle, much more. Filled with analyzed games. 390pp. 5⅜ x 8½.
20640-8 Pa. $5.95

500 MASTER GAMES OF CHESS, S. Tartakower, J. du Mont. Vast collection of great chess games from 1798-1938, with much material nowhere else readily available. Fully annotated, arranged by opening for easier study. 664pp. 5⅜ x 8½.   23208-5 Pa. $8.50

A GUIDE TO CHESS ENDINGS, Dr. Max Euwe, David Hooper. One of the finest modern works on chess endings. Thorough analysis of the most frequently encountered endings by former world champion. 331 examples, each with diagram. 248pp. 5⅜ x 8½.   23332-4 Pa. $3.95

THE COMPLETE BOOK OF DOLL MAKING AND COLLECTING, Catherine Christopher. Instructions, patterns for dozens of dolls, from rag doll on up to elaborate, historically accurate figures. Mould faces, sew clothing, make doll houses, etc. Also collecting information. Many illustrations. 288pp. 6 x 9. 22066-4 Pa. $4.95

THE DAGUERREOTYPE IN AMERICA, Beaumont Newhall. Wonderful portraits, 1850's townscapes, landscapes; full text plus 104 photographs. The basic book. Enlarged 1976 edition. 272pp. 8¼ x 11¼. 23322-7 Pa. $7.95

CRAFTSMAN HOMES, Gustav Stickley. 296 architectural drawings, floor plans, and photographs illustrate 40 different kinds of "Mission-style" homes from *The Craftsman* (1901-16), voice of American style of simplicity and organic harmony. Thorough coverage of Craftsman idea in text and picture, now collector's item. 224pp. 8⅛ x 11. 23791-5 Pa. $6.50

PEWTER-WORKING: INSTRUCTIONS AND PROJECTS, Burl N. Osborn. & Gordon O. Wilber. Introduction to pewter-working for amateur craftsman. History and characteristics of pewter; tools, materials, step-by-step instructions. Photos, line drawings, diagrams. Total of 160pp. 7⅞ x 10¾. 23786-9 Pa. $3.50

THE GREAT CHICAGO FIRE, edited by David Lowe. 10 dramatic, eyewitness accounts of the 1871 disaster, including one of the aftermath and rebuilding, plus 70 contemporary photographs and illustrations of the ruins—courthouse, Palmer House, Great Central Depot, etc. Introduction by David Lowe. 87pp. 8¼ x 11. 23771-0 Pa. $4.00

SILHOUETTES: A PICTORIAL ARCHIVE OF VARIED ILLUSTRATIONS, edited by Carol Belanger Grafton. Over 600 silhouettes from the 18th to 20th centuries include profiles and full figures of men and women, children, birds and animals, groups and scenes, nature, ships, an alphabet. Dozens of uses for commercial artists and craftspeople. 144pp. 8⅜ x 11¼. 23781-8 Pa. $4.50

ANIMALS: 1,419 COPYRIGHT-FREE ILLUSTRATIONS OF MAMMALS, BIRDS, FISH, INSECTS, ETC., edited by Jim Harter. Clear wood engravings present, in extremely lifelike poses, over 1,000 species of animals. One of the most extensive copyright-free pictorial sourcebooks of its kind. Captions. Index. 284pp. 9 x 12. 23766-4 Pa. $8.95

INDIAN DESIGNS FROM ANCIENT ECUADOR, Frederick W. Shaffer. 282 original designs by pre-Columbian Indians of Ecuador (500-1500 A.D.). Designs include people, mammals, birds, reptiles, fish, plants, heads, geometric designs. Use as is or alter for advertising, textiles, leathercraft, etc. Introduction. 95pp. 8¾ x 11¼. 23764-8 Pa. $4.50

SZIGETI ON THE VIOLIN, Joseph Szigeti. Genial, loosely structured tour by premier violinist, featuring a pleasant mixture of reminiscenes, insights into great music and musicians, innumerable tips for practicing violinists. 385 musical passages. 256pp. 5⅝ x 8¼. 23763-X Pa. $4.00

TONE POEMS, SERIES II: TILL EULENSPIEGELS LUSTIGE STREICHE, ALSO SPRACH ZARATHUSTRA, AND EIN HELDEN-LEBEN, Richard Strauss. Three important orchestral works, including very popular *Till Eulenspiegel's Marry Pranks,* reproduced in full score from original editions. Study score. 315pp. 9⅜ x 12¼. (Available in U.S. only)
23755-9 Pa. $8.95

TONE POEMS, SERIES I: DON JUAN, TOD UND VERKLARUNG AND DON QUIXOTE, Richard Strauss. Three of the most often performed and recorded works in entire orchestral repertoire, reproduced in full score from original editions. Study score. 286pp. 9⅜ x 12¼. (Available in U.S. only)
23754-0 Pa. $8.95

11 LATE STRING QUARTETS, Franz Joseph Haydn. The form which Haydn defined and "brought to perfection." *(Grove's).* 11 string quartets in complete score, his last and his best. The first in a projected series of the complete Haydn string quartets. Reliable modern Eulenberg edition, otherwise difficult to obtain. 320pp. 8⅜ x 11¼. (Available in U.S. only)
23753-2 Pa. $8.95

FOURTH, FIFTH AND SIXTH SYMPHONIES IN FULL SCORE, Peter Ilyitch Tchaikovsky. Complete orchestral scores of Symphony No. 4 in F Minor, Op. 36; Symphony No. 5 in E Minor, Op. 64; Symphony No. 6 in B Minor, "Pathetique," Op. 74. Bretikopf & Hartel eds. Study score. 480pp. 9⅜ x 12¼.
23861-X Pa. $10.95

THE MARRIAGE OF FIGARO: COMPLETE SCORE, Wolfgang A. Mozart. Finest comic opera ever written. Full score, not to be confused with piano renderings. Peters edition. Study score. 448pp. 9⅜ x 12¼. (Available in U.S. only)
23751-6 Pa. $12.95

"IMAGE" ON THE ART AND EVOLUTION OF THE FILM, edited by Marshall Deutelbaum. Pioneering book brings together for first time 38 groundbreaking articles on early silent films from *Image* and 263 illustrations newly shot from rare prints in the collection of the International Museum of Photography. A landmark work. Index. 256pp. 8¼ x 11.
23777-X Pa. $8.95

AROUND-THE-WORLD COOKY BOOK, Lois Lintner Sumption and Marguerite Lintner Ashbrook. 373 cooky and frosting recipes from 28 countries (America, Austria, China, Russia, Italy, etc.) include Viennese kisses, rice wafers, London strips, lady fingers, hony, sugar spice, maple cookies, etc. Clear instructions. All tested. 38 drawings. 182pp. 5⅜ x 8.
23802-4 Pa. $2.75

THE ART NOUVEAU STYLE, edited by Roberta Waddell. 579 rare photographs, not available elsewhere, of works in jewelry, metalwork, glass, ceramics, textiles, architecture and furniture by 175 artists—Mucha, Seguy, Lalique, Tiffany, Gaudin, Hohlwein, Saarinen, and many others. 288pp. 8⅜ x 11¼.
23515-7 Pa. $8.95

CATALOGUE OF DOVER BOOKS

THE CURVES OF LIFE, Theodore A. Cook. Examination of shells, leaves, horns, human body, art, etc., in *"the* classic reference on how the golden ratio applies to spirals and helices in nature . . .. "—Martin Gardner. 426 illustrations. Total of 512pp. 5⅜ x 8½.   23701-X Pa. **$6.95**

AN ILLUSTRATED FLORA OF THE NORTHERN UNITED STATES AND CANADA, Nathaniel L. Britton, Addison Brown. Encyclopedic work covers 4666 species, ferns on up. Everything. Full botanical information, illustration for each. This earlier edition is preferred by many to more recent revisions. 1913 edition. Over 4000 illustrations, total of 2087pp. 6⅛ x 9¼.   22642-5, 22643-3, 22644-1 Pa., Three-vol. set **$28.50**

MANUAL OF THE GRASSES OF THE UNITED STATES, A. S. Hitch-cock, U.S. Dept. of Agriculture. The basic study of American grasses, both indigenous and escapes, cultivated and wild. Over 1400 species. Full descriptions, information. Over 1100 maps, illustrations. Total of 1051pp. 5⅜ x 8½.   22717-0, 22718-9 Pa., Two-vol. set **$17.00**

THE CACTACEAE,, Nathaniel L. Britton, John N. Rose. Exhaustive, definitive. Every cactus in the world. Full botanical descriptions. Thorough statement of nomenclatures, habitat, detailed finding keys. The one book needed by every cactus enthusiast. Over 1275 illustrations. Total of 1080pp. 8 x 10¼.   21191-6, 21192-4 Clothbd., Two-vol. set **$50.00**

AMERICAN MEDICINAL PLANTS, Charles F. Millspaugh. Full descriptions, 180 plants covered: history; physical description; methods of preparation with all chemical constituents extracted; all claimed curative or adverse effects. 180 full-page plates. Classification table. 804pp. 6½ x 9¼.
23034-1 Pa. **$13.95**

A MODERN HERBAL, Margaret Grieve. Much the fullest, most exact, most useful compilation of herbal material. Gigantic alphabetical encyclopedia, from aconite to zedoary, gives botanical information, medical properties, folklore, economic uses, and much else. Indispensable to serious reader. 161 illustrations. 888pp. 6½ x 9¼. (Available in U.S. only)
22798-7, 22799-5 Pa., Two-vol. set **$15.00**

THE HERBAL or GENERAL HISTORY OF PLANTS, John Gerard. The 1633 edition revised and enlarged by Thomas Johnson. Containing almost 2850 plant descriptions and 2705 superb illustrations, Gerard's *Herbal* is a monumental work, the book all modern English herbals are derived from, the one herbal every serious enthusiast should have in its entirety. Original editions are worth perhaps $750. 1678pp. 8½ x 12¼.
23147-X Clothbd. **$75.00**

MANUAL OF THE TREES OF NORTH AMERICA, Charles S. Sargent. The basic survey of every native tree and tree-like shrub, 717 species in all. Extremely full descriptions, information on habitat, growth, locales, economics, etc. Necessary to every serious tree lover. Over 100 finding keys. 783 illustrations. Total of 986pp. 5⅜ x 8½.
20277-1, 20278-X Pa., Two-vol. set **$12.00**

GREAT NEWS PHOTOS AND THE STORIES BEHIND THEM, John Faber. Dramatic volume of 140 great news photos, 1855 through 1976, and revealing stories behind them, with both historical and technical information. Hindenburg disaster, shooting of Oswald, nomination of Jimmy Carter, etc. 160pp. 8¼ x 11. 23667-6 Pa. $6.00

CRUICKSHANK'S PHOTOGRAPHS OF BIRDS OF AMERICA, Allan D. Cruickshank. Great ornithologist, photographer presents 177 closeups, groupings, panoramas, flightings, etc., of about 150 different birds. Expanded *Wings in the Wilderness.* Introduction by Helen G. Cruickshank. 191pp. 8¼ x 11. 23497-5 Pa. $7.95

AMERICAN WILDLIFE AND PLANTS, A. C. Martin, et al. Describes food habits of more than 1000 species of mammals, birds, fish. Special treatment of important food plants. Over 300 illustrations. 500pp. 5⅜ x 8½. 20793-5 Pa. $6.50

THE PEOPLE CALLED SHAKERS, Edward D. Andrews. Lifetime of research, definitive study of Shakers: origins, beliefs, practices, dances, social organization, furniture and crafts, impact on 19th-century USA, present heritage. Indispensable to student of American history, collector. 33 illustrations. 351pp. 5⅜ x 8½. 21081-2 Pa. $4.50

OLD NEW YORK IN EARLY PHOTOGRAPHS, Mary Black. New York City as it was in 1853-1901, through 196 wonderful photographs from N.-Y. Historical Society. Great Blizzard, Lincoln's funeral procession, great buildings. 228pp. 9 x 12. 22907-6 Pa. $8.95

MR. LINCOLN'S CAMERA MAN: MATHEW BRADY, Roy Meredith. Over 300 Brady photos reproduced directly from original negatives, photos. Jackson, Webster, Grant, Lee, Carnegie, Barnum; Lincoln; Battle Smoke, Death of Rebel Sniper, Atlanta Just After Capture. Lively commentary. 368pp. 8⅜ x 11¼. 23021-X Pa. $11.95

TRAVELS OF WILLIAM BARTRAM, William Bartram. From 1773-8, Bartram explored Northern Florida, Georgia, Carolinas, and reported on wild life, plants, Indians, early settlers. Basic account for period, entertaining reading. Edited by Mark Van Doren. 13 illustrations. 141pp. 5⅜ x 8½. 20013-2 Pa. $6.00

THE GENTLEMAN AND CABINET MAKER'S DIRECTOR, Thomas Chippendale. Full reprint, 1762 style book, most influential of all time; chairs, tables, sofas, mirrors, cabinets, etc. 200 plates, plus 24 photographs of surviving pieces. 249pp. 9⅞ x 12¾. 21601-2 Pa. $8.95

AMERICAN CARRIAGES, SLEIGHS, SULKIES AND CARTS, edited by Don H. Berkebile. 168 Victorian illustrations from catalogues, trade journals, fully captioned. Useful for artists. Author is Assoc. Curator, Div. of Transportation of Smithsonian Institution. 168pp. 8½ x 9½. 23328-6 Pa. $5.00

CATALOGUE OF DOVER BOOKS

SECOND PIATIGORSKY CUP, edited by Isaac Kashdan. One of the greatest tournament books ever produced in the English language. All 90 games of the 1966 tournament, annotated by players, most annotated by both players. Features Petrosian, Spassky, Fischer, Larsen, six others. 228pp. 5⅜ x 8½. 23572-6 Pa. $3.50

ENCYCLOPEDIA OF CARD TRICKS, revised and edited by Jean Hugard. How to perform over 600 card tricks, devised by the world's greatest magicians: impromptus, spelling tricks, key cards, using special packs, much, much more. Additional chapter on card technique. 66 illustrations. 402pp. 5⅜ x 8½. (Available in U.S. only) 21252-1 Pa. **$5.95**

MAGIC: STAGE ILLUSIONS, SPECIAL EFFECTS AND TRICK PHOTOGRAPHY, Albert A. Hopkins, Henry R. Evans. One of the great classics; fullest, most authorative explanation of vanishing lady, levitations, scores of other great stage effects. Also small magic, automata, stunts. 446 illustrations. 556pp. 5⅜ x 8½. 23344-8 Pa. $6.95

THE SECRETS OF HOUDINI, J. C. Cannell. Classic study of Houdini's incredible magic, exposing closely-kept professional secrets and revealing, in general terms, the whole art of stage magic. 67 illustrations. 279pp. 5⅜ x 8½. 22913-0 Pa. $4.00

HOFFMANN'S MODERN MAGIC, Professor Hoffmann. One of the best, and best-known, magicians' manuals of the past century. Hundreds of tricks from card tricks and simple sleight of hand to elaborate illusions involving construction of complicated machinery. 332 illustrations. 563pp. 5⅜ x 8½. 23623-4 Pa. $6.95

THOMAS NAST'S CHRISTMAS DRAWINGS, Thomas Nast. Almost all Christmas drawings by creator of image of Santa Claus as we know it, and one of America's foremost illustrators and political cartoonists. 66 illustrations. 3 illustrations in color on covers. 96pp. 8⅜ x 11¼. 23660-9 Pa. $3.50

FRENCH COUNTRY COOKING FOR AMERICANS, Louis Diat. 500 easy-to-make, authentic provincial recipes compiled by former head chef at New York's Fitz-Carlton Hotel: onion soup, lamb stew, potato pie, more. 309pp. 5⅜ x 8½. 23665-X Pa. $3.95

SAUCES, FRENCH AND FAMOUS, Louis Diat. Complete book gives over 200 specific recipes: bechamel, Bordelaise, hollandaise, Cumberland, apricot, etc. Author was one of this century's finest chefs, originator of vichyssoise and many other dishes. Index. 156pp. 5⅜ x 8. 23663-3 Pa. $2.75

TOLL HOUSE TRIED AND TRUE RECIPES, Ruth Graves Wakefield. Authentic recipes from the famous Mass. restaurant: popovers, veal and ham loaf, Toll House baked beans, chocolate cake crumb pudding, much more. Many helpful hints. Nearly 700 recipes. Index. 376pp. 5⅜ x 8½. 23560-2 Pa. $4.95

CATALOGUE OF DOVER BOOKS

ILLUSTRATED GUIDE TO SHAKER FURNITURE, Robert Meader. Director, Shaker Museum, Old Chatham, presents up-to-date coverage of all furniture and appurtenances, with much on local styles not available elsewhere. 235 photos. 146pp. 9 x 12.   22819-3 Pa. $6.95

COOKING WITH BEER, Carole Fahy. Beer has as superb an effect on food as wine, and at fraction of cost. Over 250 recipes for appetizers, soups, main dishes, desserts, breads, etc. Index. 144pp. 5⅜ x 8½. (Available in U.S. only)   23661-7 Pa. $3.00

STEWS AND RAGOUTS, Kay Shaw Nelson. This international cookbook offers wide range of 108 recipes perfect for everyday, special occasions, meals-in-themselves, main dishes. Economical, nutritious, easy-to-prepare: goulash, Irish stew, boeuf bourguignon, etc. Index. 134pp. 5⅜ x 8½.   23662-5 Pa. $3.95

DELICIOUS MAIN COURSE DISHES, Marian Tracy. Main courses are the most important part of any meal. These 200 nutritious, economical recipes from around the world make every meal a delight. "I . . . have found it so useful in my own household,"—*N.Y. Times.* Index. 219pp. 5⅜ x 8½.   23664-1 Pa. $3.95

FIVE ACRES AND INDEPENDENCE, Maurice G. Kains. Great back-to-the-land classic explains basics of self-sufficient farming: economics, plants, crops, animals, orchards, soils, land selection, host of other necessary things. Do not confuse with skimpy faddist literature; Kains was one of America's greatest agriculturalists. 95 illustrations. 397pp. 5⅜ x 8½.   20974-1 Pa. **$4.95**

A PRACTICAL GUIDE FOR THE BEGINNING FARMER, Herbert Jacobs. Basic, extremely useful first book for anyone thinking about moving to the country and starting a farm. Simpler than Kains, with greater emphasis on country living in general. 246pp. 5⅜ x 8½.   23675-7 Pa. $3.95

PAPERMAKING, Dard Hunter. Definitive book on the subject by the foremost authority in the field. Chapters dealing with every aspect of history of craft in every part of the world. Over 320 illustrations. 2nd, revised and enlarged (1947) edition. 672pp. 5⅜ x 8½.   23619-6 Pa. $8.95

THE ART DECO STYLE, edited by Theodore Menten. Furniture, jewelry, metalwork, ceramics, fabrics, lighting fixtures, interior decors, exteriors, graphics from pure French sources. Best sampling around. Over 400 photographs. 183pp. 8⅜ x 11¼.   22824-X Pa. $6.95

ACKERMANN'S COSTUME PLATES, Rudolph Ackermann. Selection of 96 plates from the *Repository of Arts,* best published source of costume for English fashion during the early 19th century. 12 plates also in color. Captions, glossary and introduction by editor Stella Blum. Total of 120pp. 8⅜ x 11¼.   23690-0 Pa. $5.00

THE ANATOMY OF THE HORSE, George Stubbs. Often considered the great masterpiece of animal anatomy. Full reproduction of 1766 edition, plus prospectus; original text and modernized text. 36 plates. Introduction by Eleanor Garvey. 121pp. 11 x 14¾. 23402-9 Pa. **$8.95**

BRIDGMAN'S LIFE DRAWING, George B. Bridgman. More than 500 illustrative drawings and text teach you to abstract the body into its major masses, use light and shade, proportion; as well as specific areas of anatomy, of which Bridgman is master. 192pp. 6½ x 9¼. (Available in U.S. only) 22710-3 Pa. **$4.50**

ART NOUVEAU DESIGNS IN COLOR, Alphonse Mucha, Maurice Verneuil, Georges Auriol. Full-color reproduction of *Combinaisons ornementales* (c. 1900) by Art Nouveau masters. Floral, animal, geometric, interlacings, swashes—borders, frames, spots—all incredibly beautiful. 60 plates, hundreds of designs. 9⅜ x 8-1/16. 22885-1 Pa. **$4.50**

FULL-COLOR FLORAL DESIGNS IN THE ART NOUVEAU STYLE, E. A. Seguy. 166 motifs, on 40 plates, from *Les fleurs et leurs applications decoratives* (1902): borders, circular designs, repeats, allovers, "spots." All in authentic Art Nouveau colors. 48pp. 9⅜ x 12¼. 23439-8 Pa. **$6.00**

A DIDEROT PICTORIAL ENCYCLOPEDIA OF TRADES AND IN-DUSTRY, edited by Charles C. Gillispie. 485 most interesting plates from the great French Encyclopedia of the 18th century show hundreds of working figures, artifacts, process, land and cityscapes; glassmaking, paper-making, metal extraction, construction, weaving, making furniture, clothing, wigs, dozens of other activities. Plates fully explained. 920pp. 9 x 12. 22284-5, 22285-3 Clothbd., Two-vol. set **$50.00**

HANDBOOK OF EARLY ADVERTISING ART, Clarence P. Hornung. Largest collection of copyright-free early and antique advertising art ever compiled. Over 6,000 illustrations, from Franklin's time to the 1890's for special effects, novelty. Valuable source, almost inexhaustible.
Pictorial Volume. Agriculture, the zodiac, animals, autos, birds, Christmas, fire engines, flowers, trees, musical instruments, ships, games and sports, much more. Arranged by subject matter and use. 237 plates. 288pp. 9 x 12. 20122-8 Clothbd. **$15.00**

Typographical Volume. Roman and Gothic faces ranging from 10 point to 300 point, "Barnum," German and Old English faces, script, logotypes, scrolls and flourishes, 1115 ornamental initials, 67 complete alphabets, more. 310 plates. 320pp. 9 x 12. 20123-6 Clothbd. $15.00

CALLIGRAPHY (CALLIGRAPHIA LATINA), J. G. Schwandner. High point of 18th-century ornamental calligraphy. Very ornate initials, scrolls, borders, cherubs, birds, lettered examples. 172pp. 9 x 13. 20475-8 Pa. **$7.95**

GEOMETRY, RELATIVITY AND THE FOURTH DIMENSION, Rudolf Rucker. Exposition of fourth dimension, means of visualization, concepts of relativity as Flatland characters continue adventures. Popular, easily followed yet accurate, profound. 141 illustrations. 133pp. 5⅜ x 8½.
23400-2 Pa. $2.75

THE ORIGIN OF LIFE, A. I. Oparin. Modern classic in biochemistry, the first rigorous examination of possible evolution of life from nitrocarbon compounds. Non-technical, easily followed. Total of 295pp. 5⅜ x 8½.
60213-3 Pa. $5.95

PLANETS, STARS AND GALAXIES, A. E. Fanning. Comprehensive introductory survey: the sun, solar system, stars, galaxies, universe, cosmology; quasars, radio stars, etc. 24pp. of photographs. 189pp. 5⅜ x 8½. (Available in U.S. only)
21680-2 Pa. $3.75

THE THIRTEEN BOOKS OF EUCLID'S ELEMENTS, translated with introduction and commentary by Sir Thomas L. Heath. Definitive edition. Textual and linguistic. notes, mathematical analysis, 2500 years of critical commentary. Do not confuse with abridged school editions. Total of 1414pp. 5⅜ x 8½.
60088-2, 60089-0, 60090-4 Pa., Three-vol. set $19.50

Prices subject to change without notice.

Available at your book dealer or write for free catalogue to Dept. GI, Dover Publications, Inc., 31 East 2nd St. Mineola., N.Y. 11501. Dover publishes more than 175 books each year on science, elementary and advanced mathematics, biology, music, art, literary history, social sciences and other areas.